First Publication November 2021
Indies United Publishing House, LLC

ISBN: 978-1-64456-333-5 [Hardcover]
ISBN: 978-1-64456-334-2 [paperback]
ISBN: 978-1-64456-335-9 [Mobi]
ISBN: 978-1-64456-336-6 [ePub]
ISBN: 978-1-64456-337-3 [Audiobook]

Library of Congress Control Number: 2021940968

INDIES UNITED PUBLISHING HOUSE, LLC
P.O. BOX 3071
QUINCY, IL 62305-3071
www.indiesunited.net

For Lee

"Logic will get you from A to Z. Imagination will get you everywhere." - Albert Einstein

To Diana
Lovely to see you
again.
thank you!!
♡ Lisa

NINETY-FIVE

LISA TOWLES

INDIES UNITED PUBLISHING HOUSE, LLC

PROLOGUE

"Ten dollars…each."

I reached for my wallet. Riley put up his palm. "We're guests of a member."

The bouncer eyerolled. "Who?"

"David Wade," Riley said.

"We're both students here. Asshole." I held out my ID.

"Wade's not here and I'm not going looking for him. Twenty dollars or leave."

I handed the guy two tens, then he stamped both our wrists. The entry doors opened with David Wade on the other side, hair styled like a teen magazine cover. Typical.

"Hope you didn't pay," he laughed. "You're my guests."

"Wade." I had a feeling I'd be doing that a lot this year. We followed him back to a booth by the pool tables.

"I've set up two meetings," Wade explained. "For each of you, and they'll be conducted separately."

"Why? Divide and conquer?" Riley asked.

"I shouldn't even be here," I said eyeing the door. "Riley's way more desirable to a fraternity. He graduated third in our high school

1

class." I was in the top thirty percent, if that.

"Dude, you are not leaving me here alone. This was your idea," Riley reminded me.

"Listen up. Sigma Chi's first, then Phi Gamma Delta." Wade with his frat salesman flair. Fine, I'd give them five minutes.

"What's your finder's fee?" Riley asked the most important question of the night.

A pitcher and three glasses appeared on the table. Funny how I never knew what I was drinking in this place. Just beer. Not IPA, Pilsner, Belgian. We were college students; we'd drink anything, right?

"You mean if you're selected? Less than forty-percent of frat recruits actually make it in." Wade lowered his head. "Even lower for enlistees."

I repeated Riley's valid question. "What do you get out of this? For some of these elitist Republican machines, the dues are like three hundred bucks a month."

"What?" Riley snapped his head toward me. "You're right. What are we doing here?"

"We're socializing, remember?" I said. "We just transferred two months ago. We hardly know anyone." I could barely remember NYU at this point. Chicago's a long way from home.

Wade smiled his smooth, snaky grin, enjoying the logic of my statement. He raised his glass. "Well, here's to new beginnings."

"Choke on it." Riley clocked Wade's glass. He glared at me while he guzzled the entire contents.

Wade refilled Riley's glass and disappeared with the empty pitcher. Now that the pool tables were filled, the noise had doubled, probably because we were getting drunker. Riley hated to drink. In fact, I was surprised he agreed to come in the first place. But it was on campus, just a short walk from Granville West, our home away from home.

"Hey." A new guy shoved into Wade's side of the empty booth. "Sigma Chi, how's it going? Which one of you is Zak?"

Riley and I pointed to each other. The guy had a peach fuzz crew cut. His face looked like it was scrubbed every thirty minutes.

"I can't imagine why you'd be even remotely interested in me," I admitted. "Riley's got a 4.0 GPA and a way better pedigree."

"Yeah, but you have lawyers in your family," Riley shouted in his bar voice. He leaned in and smiled in a way that revealed rising blood alcohol level. "More likely you'd be able to afford the fees."

The frat salesman shifted on the bench, sizing us up. He turned his head back toward the bar, probably looking for Wade, the eternal icebreaker.

"Fees are optional," he said in a bitchy tone.

I peeked one eye at the door, making sure we had a path of egress. Wade was naturally nowhere in sight.

How could Riley bring up my family like that? So crude and indifferent. He never could hold his liquor. I didn't mind paying to get in here, or even sitting through this ridiculous formality. It beat the monotony of hanging out in our dorm waiting for life to happen. But Wade had showed up at the door, vanished, and now I just felt played.

"Oh, I see," Riley broke in. "You only charge them to offset your legal fees resulting from discrimination, rape, and aggravated assault lawsuits? I get it. That must be really expensive. You know, hard to plan when all your Daddy's money's going to—"

"Riley," I clipped. "Shut it. Let's get out of here."

I scanned the interior. Pool tables, dart boards, wood paneled walls; I remembered reading that The Pub in the basement of University of Chicago's Ida Noyes' Hall had been run by descendants of the Medici's. The only thing missing in here was Sherlock Holmes. Raised voices caught my attention from the opposite corner, then the sound of a beer bottle breaking. Ah, the perfect diversion.

I yanked Riley's elbow and we headed for the entrance. Five seconds later, I looked back still plowing through the crowd.

"Where are they?" Riley asked.

I pulled open the door and we slipped out.

Two guys followed. One from Sigma Chi and another I didn't recognize. They were all the same to me.

"Walk faster," I said. "Follow the path, straight ahead." Sure, we needed to get away from these people, but the more important question nagging me was why we would be of interest in the first place. New to campus, barely social, not wealthy. What attributes would be of value to them?

"The Fountain of Time's up ahead," Riley said, speeding up. "Are they behind us?"

As I was about to answer him, two different guys cut through the evergreens to our left and blocked us.

"Hey guys," one of them said, palms up, toothy grin. "Look, Damen got us off to a bad start. Let's start over. I'm from Sigma Chi."

"And I'm from Phi Gamma," the other said. "Please, come with us so we can talk. That's all we want."

"We're not interested in you frat clowns, the world's fucked up enough already."

Riley drunk always cracked me up.

"We're all here because you think we might have the money to pay your dues so you can maintain your alcohol supply," he added.

The thugs squared off in front of us. Riley stepped back. When he crossed his arms, he lost his balance and fell back on the grass. Nice.

Phi Gamma dragged him off with an arm around his shoulders. Sigma Chi stayed with me, waiting. Watching. He sat on the grass and pulled out a flask. I kept my eyes on Riley, now twenty feet away.

"Liquid courage?" I crouched on the ground across from him, knowing at this point we'd need to listen to the pitch before they let us go. If.

Riley and Phi Gamma were no longer visible. Fine. I'd give this freak five minutes of my life, then I'd go find him. I had no fear of him at this point, just irritation. I watched the guy pour something into two little silver cups—one the lid of the shiny flask, the other from his pocket. What else had been in that pocket?

"Absinthe," the guy said with conspiratorial pride.

I raised an eyebrow. More impressive than Budweiser.

"With or without *thujone*?" I asked of the historical wormwood hallucinogenic constituent.

"You know your poisons," he replied. "Without." He handed me a cup and tapped it, then swigged his down in one gulp.

Where was Riley? What the fuck were we doing out here? I came to this school for a fresh start, as my mother put it, and somehow I didn't think this was what she, or even I, had in mind. Sigma Chi, my salesman, held out the shiny silver cup with a wet smirk on his lips. Was I about to end up in Mexico or as somebody's bitch in Danville Prison?

"Riley, you alright?" I shouted behind me.

No answer. Sigma Chi stared, wiggling the cup. At this point I was more annoyed than afraid. I wasn't happy at this place yet, at this University. Riley wasn't either. But I wasn't ready to throw it all in either. Had anyone ever died from absinthe? I grabbed the cup, swiveled it around a bit, smelled it, then chucked it back in my throat. Licorice, but more herby. Like sophisticated licorice. God help me.

NINETY-FIVE

CHAPTER ONE

Sunday morning, I had no idea what time. It was way too quiet in here. Wait. Where—

I snapped upright too fast, which made my head spin, my half-naked body clammy with sudden panic. Where were my clothes? Why didn't I remember taking them off? Calm down, Zak. Breathe. This wasn't my room. It was David Wade's down the hall. I recognized it from the Drake and Sia posters. What the fuck was I doing here? Possible scenario number one: I lost my key, couldn't get into my room and decided to sleep here. Ridiculous. I'd rather sleep on concrete. Then why was it so quiet? Was everybody out of the building already? Or were they all dead?

I lifted the sheet to see my bare legs. Just then the door opened. I covered myself like a prostitute caught in a congressman's hotel room. I looked to the doorway; everything got blurry.

"Good morning."

Fucking Wade, that toothy grin. Whatever happened last night was his fault. He didn't meet us when he said he would, so we had to pay admission unnecessarily. Why didn't I remember what happened next?

"What am I doing here?" My voice caught and my eyes filled up. My mother said I'd lost my ability to cry. I just think I never learned in the first place, or maybe never learned it was an acceptable thing to do.

Wade sat on the opposite bed sizing me up, fumbling with a cacophonous paper bag. "How do you feel?" he asked.

"How do you th—what the hell am I doing here?"

Wade tore open two sugar packets and poured them in a tall cup of hot liquid.

"I think I'm gonna throw up," I slapped my palm to my mouth.

"Calm down, this is just what you need, believe me. Drink it." He passed the cup over.

My hand trembled as I reached out. Naked, vision blurred, nauseous, disoriented. I started an imaginary list in case I ended up in the Emergency Room. Two sips of the warm, slightly sweet liquid calmed my stomach.

"I feel like I need a blood transfusion. What's wrong with my throat?"

"How's your head?"

I hated how Wade kept answering questions with questions. I hated how he was naturally athletic and good looking but didn't seem to care about either. Arrogant, full of himself, I didn't believe a word he said.

"I just answered that," I shot back with a loathing I never felt before now, certain he had all the answers I was looking for, yet more certain he'd never give them to me. I sipped more of what tasted like English Breakfast Tea. My stomach liked it, so I propped up the bed pillow. I leaned back and took three more sips. Head throbbing, my throat felt like broken glass. "Where are my clothes?"

Wade tossed my jeans and a shirt across from the other bed. I set the cup on the floor to pull them on, half listening to his story of a party, a bar, warring fraternities, how I apparently drank something intended for someone else. Great. Like he would have stopped me if he had the chance. I was standing now in the center of the room, clutching the cup of tea looking for my tennis shoes. I saw them inside the door. My heart pounded; I was dying to get out of there. But I needed to know how I got here. Even more disturbing was why I didn't remember. I started with basic questions:

"Today's Sunday October 11th. Confirm or deny?"

"Confirm." Wade smiled.

"Who brought me here?"

"I did."

"In a car? On a stretcher? What?"

"You walked. Barely." He seemed to enjoy the back and forth. I wondered how it would feel to punch the grin off his face.

"From where?"

"Fountain of Time."

"Who took off my clothes?"

"Not me." The look on his face confirmed that, during my period of lost time, I hadn't been violated, at least by him.

My brain struggled to remember Fountain of Time. "Hyde Park?" I asked. "I've never even been there."

"Well apparently you have," he corrected me.

Think like an investigator. "Who was supposed to drink what I drank? What was it?"

Wade settled back now on the other bed, leaning against the wall, still facing me. "Question one, I don't know." He paused.

"Question 2?" I pressed.

First, he stared, unblinking. Was this telepathy? It wasn't working. "Tamango," he said.

I only knew this drink from reputation, or at least until today that was true. "What's in it? I mean, is there…"

He read my thoughts. "No, nothing that would cause permanent damage."

I paced around David Wade's room and the floor was surprisingly clean, for a college dorm. "I need some answers," I said, torn between wanting to run out the door screaming and pounding every answer out of Wade's smug face.

He moved to his closet, rifling through a stack of books, all the while telling me about Tamango's frightening list of ingredients, only two of which were actually known to man. 85% grain alcohol mixed with Roselle leaves, in addition to a mysterious concoction of purportedly hallucinogenic African herbs.

"First of all, I was told it was absinthe. I feel like I've seen my entire body from the inside out. I seriously remember the color, the texture of my blood, my muscles, organs. Is this, like, normal?"

"Last night was a glimpse into what we're not really supposed to see," Wade explained.

What was he, a science professor now?

"If you want a real glimpse, you need a guide to show you around. Come back here tonight at midnight."

No wonder he was pimping for fraternities. "No thanks, oh master of the opium den. Throw your own life away if I care. I'm gonna try to clean up. I need to feel normal."

"Try all you want, but I will see you at midnight."

"I'll see you in hell."

CHAPTER TWO

"Mr. Skinner, the Dean will see you now."

A fortyish woman in a dark skirt, flat shoes and a stern face held open the heavy wooden door that just added to the pre-existing dread of being called in on a Sunday afternoon for an "academic review." Did they work seven days a week? Why did they care what my GPA was as long as my mother kept paying $46,000 a year?

"Hello." I approached a gigantic walnut desk attended to by Dean Agnus, who belonged in a Harry Potter movie. Thin, old, lanky-bordering-gaunt. I outstretch my hand, eyes wide, face frozen. He sat back, allowing my arm to just hang there for a spell, untouched. Seriously? Should I stay here like this, or would a magic machete materialize and chop it off at the wrist?

"Sit downnnn…Mr. Skinner."

Thank God because my legs still felt like jelly since this morning.

"Do you know why you're here, Mr. Skinner?"

A Brit, he looked to be around six foot four by the way his head and torso towered over his desk. Somehow, I felt glad to see him properly suited. The Dean of Engineering, including a silk, buttoned vest that hadn't been part of men's attire for about thirty years but added to his commanding presence. I was barely breathing, waiting for him to start his attack.

"Are you awake, Mr. Skinner?" He leaned forward onto his elbows, studying me.

"Uh, I haven't chosen which branch of engineering I want to major in, if that's what you mean, Sir. Or perhaps that I'm failing thermodynamics?" I didn't mean to sound like a smart ass. It just came out on its own.

"Right and right," he said with pointed head snaps on each word. "The first infraction is not significant in that you are a mere freshman. The second infraction is significant because you already took thermodynamics at..." He flipped through a file. "NYU. And failed."

"Yes," I replied, already resolved that saying yes repeatedly would get me out of here faster. I especially liked the way he used the word mere, making absolutely certain I understood how worthless freshmen were in his mind.

"But you got As in everything else," he argued, almost a whine. "So. What am I to make of this? Of you, Mr. Skinner?"

I so wanted him to stop addressing me with every question. "I've never missed a single thermodynamics class," I blurted, hurriedly filling the silence.

"Yes. I see that," he said, staring. "Yet you have not turned in a single homework assignment in that class, which to me shows compliance but lack of engagement. Tolerance but lack of interest." Shaking his head now.

I was unsure where he was going with it. "Does it matter that I'm getting As in all my other classes?"

"The problem, as I see it, is not your brain, Mr. Skinner, but your heart." He folded his hands, waiting for a reaction I didn't give. "Do you want to be in school?"

"Of course," I lied without thinking about it. I mean, what else would someone say to the fucking Dean of Engineering on a mandatory Sunday review meeting?

"Well, yes." He chuckled at his own joke. "I suppose no one's ever said no to that question, have they? How about this one: why do you want to be an engineer?"

He knew he had me, and he knew that I knew I'd been had. Shit.

"I like math and science, well…more than other things."

"Well, what's the problem then?" He raised his voice. "I look at your SAT scores." He shook his head disapprovingly. "They're, well… excellent!" He waved his arms now while he talked, enjoying the flair of judgment. "I look at your grades in calculus from NYU, your thermodynamics class notwithstanding. You have the makings of an exemplary student. So again, Mr. Skinner, I return to the question not of the brain but of the heart. Do you have some unique problem with this class, the professor perhaps, or do you just not want to be here?"

I felt sick, suddenly, as in about-to-vomit sick like when I first woke up in David Wade's bed. I leaned down and quickly put my head between my knees to settle myself. Just get through this godawful meeting. I can be in my own room, my own bed in twenty minutes.

Dean Agnus stood, looming over me, looking down with squinted eyes. "You haven't fainted, have you? No one's done that in years."

"Thermodynamics, sir," I moaned. "It's a room without a door. I'm memorizing the laws, I'm reading the material, but I'm still not finding a way in."

He walked around the desk. "I can't show you that door, Mr. Skinner. I mean, I can show you *that one*," he said, pointing. "But the door to which you speak will be unique to you, and I venture to say it's different for everyone. I don't know where it is."

He pulled me upright from the elbows, walking me out to the dark skirted lady, mumbling something.

"Go find your door, Mr. Skinner. Stop by the Wellness Center if you need medical help."

———•••———•

Aside from humiliation, my head felt sort of tampered with, like everything that should be there was accounted for, just in the wrong place. Bed, I kept saying to myself. I put one foot in front of the other down the paved walkway from the Admin building, past Student Services, the main campus quadrangles, and the tennis courts that nobody used. Getting close, I longed to lie down and rest in my rock-hard but familiar twin bed in my own room, my own scratchy sheets. The sky had darkened. It was now close to dinnertime, and I couldn't remember actually having eaten anything today. How could it be this late already? Had someone tampered with time, too?

Go find your door, Agnus said, making fun of my metaphor, then showing me the exit door to his office. Pompous fuck. I stepped through the main entrance of Granville West and down the bright corridor toward Kenwood, my home on campus. Climbing the stairs, I could see lace panties dangling from my doorknob. God, not now. I crouched low to place my ear near the door. Heavy breathing.

"Dammit Riley," I said louder than normal. Not consciously wanting to interrupt what I knew was a pleasurable experience for him, perhaps the first of its kind, like ever, I would have done anything right now for my empty room.

"Riley?" I said with my mouth in the doorjamb. Thumps and mumbling on the other side, I leaned my back against the wall in the narrow hallway to steady myself. Finally, the door clicked. Thank God.

"Hey."

Shit. It was Mellon's door next to us, not Riley. Melton Federman, a/k/a Mellon, was our straight-A study-maniac next-door neighbor, who lived alone in the biggest room on the floor. He was reported to never sleep. Not insomnia, just never needing sleep like an artificial life form. And there were rumors about that. I felt sure we'd eventually get around to tormenting him and testing that theory.

"Everything's cool, Mellon. I'm just trying to wake up Riley to let me in."

"Yeah, um. I saw who knocked on your door an hour ago," Mellon said. "I guarantee he's not sleeping."

The door creaked open two inches. I knelt low to put my face near the crack. "Is it her?" I whispered to my roommate and best friend, knowing he'd been pining away for a third-year business student he met in Debate Club. This must be her.

"Yes. Now please go away," he whispered back. I peered through the opening. A light showing from the desk behind cast him in silhouette. His hair stuck up straight and he tried not to smile. "You can come back later."

"Five minutes?" I joked.

"Don't be a dick. Give me an hour, I really want date number two."

"Okay, Casanova, work it." I backed away.

"Are you okay?" Riley asked. Those three little words somehow made me feel not quite so alone in this big, strange Chicago-world.

"Never better," I lied, mustering the last vestige of charity my heart could produce.

————————•————•••——•————•

My stomach growled, desperate for food and hydration. I turned toward the bathroom at the end of the hall. David Wade's door was ajar. I swear I was headed toward the bathroom, but I somehow ended up in the hallway right outside his room. What was it about this guy? Karma?

"Hey," he said, ever cheerful. Was he ever in a bad mood? "Everything okay?"

Yeah great, I thought. I'm flunking out of engineering school for the second time in my life.

Wade peered out of his doorway. Did he actually care whether I was okay or not?

"Apparently, according to Dean Agnus, I need to go find my door. Whatever that means." In the bathroom next to Wade's room, I pulled a paper cup from the wall dispenser and swigged three cups from the tap. Wasn't sudden thirst a sign of diabetes? Or was that pregnancy?

Wade snatched a hoodie off a hook in his room, grabbed his keys, then nodded. "Let's go."

CHAPTER THREE

Just when I thought things couldn't get any weirder, David Wade and I arrived at the home of someone called Jane. A neatly bearded man dressed in an off-white suit with manicured fingernails. Not painted, not even clear polish, but hands that were professionally worked over, with buffed fingernails. Unclear what I was specifically expecting, this wasn't what I pictured of David Wade's magic door. Jane's home could have modeled for Architectural Digest. Manicured lawn, pretentious lighting, everything drowned in white marble. A few steps ahead of me, David shook Jane's beautiful hand, leaning in to mumble something. I slid past him and moved around the space like a sullen teenager, assessing reliable wi-fi for my Lyft app should I need a quick getaway.

I stopped at the sight of a mortar and pestle on the kitchen counter. This brownish red, thick substance fouled the air with a putrescence of sulfur and chocolate. Gross.

"Ever heard of *yage?*" Jane, my tour guide, or maybe the owner of this mansion, dragged a stool from under the kitchen counter and sat.

Sure, I'd heard of it. A basic vocabulary of street drugs was as necessary to collegiate success as mastering the basics of sexual intercourse. A ceremonial DMT hallucinogen from South America made from like eight types of tree bark. I leaned my face down for a closer inspection of the bowl. My head recoiled.

Wade was nowhere in view now. Not sure why, this realization unglued me. Was I stranded without him, or trapped? No one had told me I couldn't leave. So why did I feel like that wasn't an option?

"Where's Wade?" I stood over seated-Jane, arms crossed, feet firm.

Jane stared, waiting, watching me like a rat in an invisible cage. I heard a story about Wade during our orientation week, which I had neither proven nor debunked, about how he alienated his wealthy parents by blowing every cent of his $20,000 high school graduation gift on a mission to feed the poor in Nicaragua. From this, I inferred that Wade could never be bewitched by something as mundane as ecstasy or LSD. Apparently, yage was the door he had in mind. God help me.

"What am I doing here? You seem to have been expecting me." I intended to keep asking questions until he answered one.

"Not what you expected?" he asked of the bowl and its putrid contents.

"When I think of *ayahuasca*, I imagine low lighting, candles, fraying tapestries, sitar."

Snide smile. He looked about forty, but with eyes that had seen more than one lifetime. I could have been blindfolded for all I remembered about the ride here. Wade had screeched his brand-new SUV down side streets. After about sixty seconds it didn't even look like Chicago anymore. We had to be about thirty minutes from campus.

• ——— •••• ——— •

I roved around the kitchen, memorizing the shape of the yard out the tall windows. Jane kept his eyes on me. "You have questions," he said. "There's plenty of time."

He got up, stepped down the two stairs into the sunken living room and perched on the edge of a white leather couch. I followed not wanting to sit opposite him but beside him would have been even more awkward. Would it be rude to ask him if he got his hands professionally manicured? Did his expensive suit help David Wade sell drugs to unsuspecting students, like me? I wanted to know who owned the house we were in, and who boiled the herbs for my *yage* concoction.

Question, okay. Sure. "So. I'm guessing you're my Guide or something?"

"I can be." He sat back and crossed his legs.

"So, Wade's my…what, Assistant Guide? Where did this concoction come from? What's the cost of it?"

"First ride's free," he said.

"Why do I feel like I might end up in a documentary, or the morgue?"

He pressed his sweating palms into his pants, then cleared his throat. "Ayahuasca is a mixture made by cooking down two powerful hallucinogenic herbs—an MAOI inhibitor and DMT. You mix the herbs with either water or vinegar and boil them down for four hours into a sort of tea, like this." He waved his hand over the bowl.

"Then I drink it and spend the next eight hours vomiting?"

"Shouldn't be eight." Slight grin. "Plus there are precautions you can take to prepare your body, mind, and spirit for the journey."

"But since I'm doing this now, those probably won't be possible for me. Right?"

Wade caught my eye in the foyer. Where did he come from? "We can delay if you like," he said. "Come back in a few days. There's no harm in…"

Guide Jane smiled for real that time, held up his palm to Wade, lit a candle on the coffee table, which I hadn't noticed before. He carried the bowl from the kitchen to the coffee table. It was covered in a protective yellow towel, probably in case the liquid sloshed around to prevent it from burning a hole in the floor. And I'd considered putting this in my body?

Wade lit sticks of incense that I also hadn't noticed before, and was waving around some kind of smudge stick, making circles of smoke. Jane sat close to me now on the white sofa. He reached over to grab both of my hands.

"Do you have a burning question you are hoping the yage will answer?"

"Besides what the fuck I'm doing here?"

"Yes, besides that."

Moving beyond the confines of how to pass thermodynamics, I had so many questions. Like why the world needed so many different kinds of engineers to keep it moving, why we were growing more accustomed to moving too fast but seeing nothing. I told myself I was here because I was curious. Was that the real reason?

"Are you happy right now?" Jane set the bowl on the table and sat back.

"No."

"Why not?"

"I'm nineteen. Is anybody happy at my age?"

"What do you need, Zak?"

Somehow, despite all the pretense, I really heard his question. *What do I need?* Almost like somebody else had asked it. Me, maybe?

"A way in," I mumbled.

Jane leaned forward. "In," he repeated.

I looked for Wade but he'd vanished again. What the fuck? My heart pounded and my face grew hot. These waves of rage kept roiling through me, but felt an odd calm in this beautiful, smelly house.

"I once read about how the scientific community believes that humans are only capable of seeing five percent of what's really there in the world. And the rest is considered dark energy or dark matter. I guess I'm curious to see more than just five percent. I'm looking for the other ninety-five, and the door that might lead me there." I could hardly believe I'd said it after hearing the words, appalled that I'd used Dean Agnus' stupid door metaphor again. But, in a strange way, it sort of fit.

Jane nodded. "Don't believe anything you see but believe everything you hear."

I raised a brow. "Okay."

"Are you ready for this?" he asked.

"No." I was as sure of that as anything. "But I'm here, and I don't believe in accidents."

CHAPTER FOUR

#Wtfwasithinking

The viscosity of the air felt spongy between my fingers. When I stood and walked, a resistance held me in one place. Jane, my Armani-clothed guide, wanted me to sit in one place for the next ten hours without moving from what he deemed "the circle," even though no visual circle existed. Like Wade, Jane sort of floated in and out of view. But now other, more interesting, visitors arrived to keep me company.

First, the Nausea Fairy. A young woman in a cobalt dress presented me a vomit bucket and said in an ethereal voice, "Release." And another time, "Let go." I didn't know where she came from but knew she didn't exist outside of my head. I felt Jane's warm palms on my back and sometimes shoulders, guiding me back to the circle in his sunken living room where I had ingested two or three spoonfuls of the magic tea.

Visitor 2: the air. It had not only texture but form. I could see it. Looking out into the sea of night behind Jane's mansion, luminescent pixels glowed and hovered—but only in my periphery. They followed me and my movements had entrails now—these swooshes of shiny pixilated air molecules that left a trail of where I've gone. I stood frozen on Jane's back terrace. The air cooled my hot skin. Every time my eyes felt swept away in the awe and beauty of everything around me, another wave of putrescence crawled up my intestines, choking its way out of my mouth into my best friend: Bucket. I was told that this primordial purge could last for five hours or more, depending on how much of the substance you ingested. Though it felt like it's been that long already, my watch showed thirty minutes. Time had slowed—not just inside my head but everywhere in the world. I was convinced of this as I moved my arms up and down to see the multicolored air surrounding me like wings. Even breathing, the air felt thicker in my body, pushing out against my insides. It took forever to fill my lungs.

I couldn't see Wade or Jane, but every time I ventured past the edge of the stone wall, I heard a stirring behind me, like they were huddled with a video camera behind the sofa, snickering. Good, let them. I wasn't ashamed of my vomit bucket and how I must look right now. I agreed willingly to take this uncertain journey, with the all too likely realization that I would not be the same Zak Skinner on the other side. Was that the point of this departure from normality? Did I like who I was? Did engineering school bring me happiness, or had it been intended to please my untouchable father?

The thought of my parents filled a hollow part of my chest with sudden sadness. But I couldn't cry right now because I might throw up again and not be able to stop. Was there such a thing as death by vomiting? Apparently, because my ayahuasca fairies had strategically placed glasses of water all over the backyard. I sat on the concrete wall now with a view of only the night sky. A colossal sea of stars reminded me of my mother. Tears slid down my cheeks without any gasps of sobbing. I knew what I'd lost, I knew what I was running from. Did everyone else know? Would they now?

Standing on the stone wall, I could see something, or someone, in the dark field ahead. I turned toward the house where my guides stood in the doorway doing their conspiratorial mumbling.

One of them said, "He's okay."

I took off at a breakneck turtle pace, one foot in slo-mo in front of the other. Once I got beyond the hundred feet of beautifully tiled slate on Jane's patio, I'd be at the edge of the field in, oh, an hour. Come on feet, move! But they were lead blocks, heavier than normal, floating through the thick coolness. When I inched closer, I could hear her, the Nausea Fairy's voice along with a tinkling of bells like a party of fairies preparing for a parade. In my state of heightened visual awareness, I was dying to get there, to see what they were trying to show me. Their parade, I felt certain, was specifically for me—a sort of psychology theater where each of the fairies acted out some aspect of my tormented personality to help me understand myself better. Wasn't that the point of hallucinogens, or was it escape? Half of me felt the lift of euphoria, the light of supreme awe. A dark shadow moved from my head down my body. I knew this shadow's name: fear. It was the door I'd do anything not to open.

The grass was ninety-seven shades of electric green. Why was it way taller than it looked from fifty feet away? I was crawling into a cornfield a mile high, completely buried in densely grown smooth blades. I felt it on my bare arms, I smelled peat moss, with an odd sort of manure from what must be horses or cows nearby. Wait, it was my vomit bucket. So gross. Keep walking, move closer to the party of field fairies who will guide the real essence of my journey. I stopped to inhale, holding the watery air in my lungs, trying hard not to throw up again. My head swayed from dizziness. Nowhere near the water glasses, I knew I was dangerously dehydrated. My dark panic returned. Where the hell were Jane and Wade? They just let me wander off into the woods unattended without water? What the fuck?

"Here," someone said, a female voice.

I moved forward a few more steps. I saw the edges of a blue dress and two bare feet with a toe ring. How exotic. I wondered what the rest of her looked like. Were you supposed to have sex on a yage trip? I remembered reading about avoiding sex for a month before and after a trip, which in my case would have been no problem. Until now.

I'd arrived in the field, though I had no idea where I was in proximity to where I started. The blue dress girl stood tall ahead of me. The fairies had attached themselves to her dress in various places— little sparks of flickering light, like they were sewing stars on the fabric with luminous thread. She was talking to them. They responded to her voice.

"Who are you?" I asked. Why did my voice echo?

"Sunita."

I noticed her brown skin and caramel eyes. She made a low sound and the fairies stopped moving to stare at me. Something hovered over her head. She pulled it down to her chest level and I saw it was a sacred chalice filled with sloshing green liquid. My stomach roiled.

"Please I beg you. Don't make me drink that."

"It will calm you," she said, reading my thoughts. "For each sip you drink, a sacred answer will come to you."

"Shouldn't I just pour it directly into my bucket since that's where it's gonna end up anyway?"

She held out the chalice while I decided. But I didn't need deliberation in this case. Unlike Wade or Jane, something about this girl and her silky voice and fairy dress felt safe.

The green liquid was cool; it carried a slight aroma of mint and tasted mercifully sweet. I took four swallows and handed the chalice back, awaiting my promise of four answers.

"You need to ask four questions first," she said. Her army of fairies arranged themselves in lines leading out along the edges of her long gown. Did they talk?

"When they need to." Sunita answered the question I had only asked in my mind. Wait. How could that be?

"There are no divisions here," she explained. There is no need to separate thoughts from speech. They, we, are all the same here."

"Where is here?"

She waved her hand, releasing more sparkly entrails.

"Can I write my four questions? I can arrange my thoughts better that way."

"If you like," she said, without moving her mouth.

I watched her face when she spoke to me through her mind. She was obviously some kind of extraordinary lifeform endowed with magical properties. Yet I was an ordinary college student. So why could I hear her? I explained I needed a journal and pen.

"Go get them; we will wait for you," she said with her mind.

I headed back inside with my turtle steps toward the house to attempt to explain the situation to my uncaring caretakers. Only Jane was inside.

"Sure," he said a little too easily. Made me wonder how many students like me he had subjected to his special tea. "I'll take you."

Where, though, would he be taking me to buy a journal and a pen in the middle of the night?

After packing me into his Porsche, Jane informed me of two

things: I can't take my vomit bucket with me, and I am no longer sick and don't need it. Great, problem solved. Let me just explain that to my cauldron of a stomach and I'm sure there'll be no disagreement. I had to close my eyes en route to keep my fragile brain from getting overloaded by the kaleidoscope of trailing images and exploding color all around me. Sure enough, there was a bookstore/coffeeshop open at 3:48 a.m., and oddly I no longer felt sick. Post-hypnotic suggestion? Could he also make me an A student?

"Want me to bring you one?" Jane asked, the dutiful guide.

No of course not. Notebooks are deeply personal things. The little indie bookstore on the edge of Clark Street in Chicago was full of students with laptops, coffee cups on every table. An all-night bookstore/cafe? Why didn't I know about this?

Jane took my elbow to guide me to the back of the store. A good thing, too, because I was still shaky on my feet from no food or water, unfamiliar drugs in my system, not to mention residual tamango from last night. I could imagine how my eyes looked. I was surprised people weren't pointing at the crazy guy lumbering through the store like a zombie.

"Here." Jane pointed to an entire wall of journals.

Ah, nirvana. In an instant I pulled down a blue, soft-covered book, the only one a full 8-1/2 x 11 size.

Jane stared.

"Size matters," I explained to someone who obviously knew nothing about personal introspection. I grabbed a pen out of a cup holder at the cash register labeled "$1.00/each" and set both on the counter. I reached around for my wallet, but my arms got tangled in the folds of my jacket. Lord, what a spectacle.

A twenty-dollar bill appeared on the counter. "Relax, I got it," Jane said with an odd, wide grin. The cute girl behind the counter explained his magnanimous gesture. I imagined the same twinkle in the cashier's eyes that I saw in Sunita's in the grassy green field minutes ago, in Jane's expansive back yard.

I stared at her for a moment too long and the mood felt awkward: Jane hovering behind me, the girl moving slowly.

"Receipt in the bag okay?" She put the journal and pen in a paper sleeve, with a twinkly glint from her eye again. What? I saw it, I know I saw it. The Sunita glint in the cashier's eyes. *Receipt in the bag okay...*I repeated it to myself on the ride back to Jane's house.

Receipt in the bag, receipt in the bag. What's going on? She said "okay" after asking as a question. Why should I care whether she put the receipt in the bag or handed it to me? Did anyone ever look at the receipt after they made an insignificant purchase? Sure, if you bought a washing machine, you might want to keep the receipt if it stopped working you could make them replace it. But why in the bag? Did that girl want to put my receipt in the bag specifically so I wouldn't see it? Was she trying to hide something on the receipt, hoping to conceal it in the bag?

* — • • • — •

Get a grip, Zak, you just bought a freaking notebook is all. Okay okay, breathe. I remembered to close my eyes on the way back to the house. It occurred to me that my Fairy Godmother and her team of under-fairies might not be waiting for me in the grassy field. That would mean I'd never get to ask my four questions. But then again, I drank the four sips of sweet, green liquid and Sunita said for every sip I'd get an answer. Did she mean it?

Maybe if I wrote the questions, she would give me the answers. Assuming I was right about her, I sat at the end of Jane's long dining table. The smooth, lined paper was easy to write on. Okay, four questions. Four. Getting nowhere, I paced for a while, drank a few sips of water, then felt woozy. I held the receipt in my hands without really reading it, more like looking through it, checking for a watermark, the front, the back, shape, dimensions, smell. I all but tasted it. Yes, the girl put the receipt in the bag because I didn't tell her otherwise.

I began writing: *Why do I feel like this receipt has some special meaning?*

I heard Sunita's familiar voice. As she spoke, her words appeared on the page of the notebook, written without a pen and just appearing like in Tom Riddle's diary in Harry Potter. I scanned the room looking for her, or Jane, or anyone. I was alone.

Numbers rule your life, Zak, she wrote.

I'd graduated to another stage of my ayahuasca journey. Hallefreakinglujah.

I recalled what Jane had said about seeing and hearing. Apparently Sunita lived in my notebook now and this was how she planned to talk to me. Could that be possible? Just go with, Zak.

Numbers rule my life. What does that mean? I lied to Dean Agnus and I actually hate math. That's why I'm failing engineering school. Again.

I said numbers, not math.

Again the writing appeared in the notebook, one word at a time like she, or someone, was actually writing it, but there was no hand, no girl, and no scratchy sound of the pen scribbling on the paper.

There's a whole layer of numbers that lives outside of computations, outside of physics. You hate math now. Soon you won't be afraid.

I never said I was afraid, I wrote, but knew immediately that was a lie. I was afraid, of so many things lately. Numbers were a reminder of how small my brain was, of what I didn't know and what I was afraid of learning. "You said *lives*," I wrote. "What does that mean? A layer of numbers that lives somewhere...lives where?"

For what felt like an eternity, there was nothing. Was she gone, had I offended my regal goddess? I had to know, or at least ask so I could understand these messages after I returned to, well, wherever I'd be returning to. A layer of numbers, I read the words again, then the Tom Riddle writing started again.

In patterns.

An invisible layer of secret numbers lives in patterns? I wrote.

Yes.

What kind of patterns, and where do I find them?

You don't, she wrote.

Let me guess. They will find me?

They already have.

Okay. If I understood this correctly, I could expect at some point in my near future to be chased by an invisible layer of numbers hidden in patterns. That made about as much sense as the walls in front of me that were undulating—white to gray, gray to white. Time to get back to the question at hand.

Is there some special meaning in this receipt? I set the receipt on the page of the notebook, thinking Sunita's eyes could read it if I laid it there, then feeling foolish from my assessment of her.

You already know the answer, she wrote back. *Now sleep.*

CHAPTER FIVE

At some point I'd collapsed on something called a Barcelona Couch, I learned from a woman named Paola. The skimpy cushion and spindly, metal legs surprised me with its comfort. Paola, crouched on the floor beside me, occasionally touched my forehead, each time checking my pulse. I was only half awake during her ministrations until she brought a tray of toast with black coffee. The aroma snapped open my eyelids. I'd always hated coffee. Somehow I knew that this too was about to change.

"Do you live here?" I grabbed the mug. Hot, acidic, bitter. Wonderful.

"That depends on your definition of live."

Please no more riddles. "Can you just answer the question?"

"I live here, yes." She was probably accustomed to bad morning-afters.

Her name and beautiful skin betrayed her as Peruvian or Bolivian, though her age could have been anywhere between thirty and fifty.

Short, thin, dark hair worn in a bun, she reminded me a little of my mother.

"Do you like my house?"

I gazed at the high ceilings. "So Jane, he is…"

"My nephew," she explained. "He lives here."

Did I believe her? No, of course not. They fed me bits of information like this that didn't fit, but I honestly had more important things on my mind. Like the receipt, my notebook, getting out of here.

"Where's my—"

"There." She pointed to the dining room. My notebook was still on the long table where I left it. I had no memory of walking to the couch. Did they carry me? Did I pass out?

She offered me sugar for the black coffee. The few bites of strawberries and toast felt good in my stomach. I asked for water but she made me eat first to help hold it down. Seemed opposite of common sense, but what did I know of entheogenics?

"I need to talk to Wade."

Paola stopped, sugar bowl in hand.

"David Wade. Tall, good looking fellow?" I pressed.

Of course she knew whom I was talking about, yet her face stared back with an uncertainty I couldn't pinpoint. Was she deciding how much to tell me? Had something happened to him? I really didn't care either way, other than catching a ride back to campus with him. When she left the room without answering my question, I glanced out the sliding glass doors, gazing at what couldn't possibly be: a vast, flat expanse. Flat as in undeveloped land without a single piece of vegetation growing on it.

No way.

I tore open the doors, standing barefoot on the flagstone terrace with my coffee cup, feeling oddly adult in this moment. My feet froze, October in Chicago, but I couldn't go back inside. Had I dreamed it all? How could that level of lush green detail have been manufactured by two teaspoons of yage?

"Paola!" I shouted into the house. My voice echoed. "Where's Jane?"

"He's not here," she replied, almost annoyed at the question.

I came back into the house. She held something low in her hands. A knife? Why would my mind naturally go there?

"I need to see Jane or Wade. It's urgent. I need a ride back to campus. Now."

"You should not go anywhere right now. Just sit. Eat. Rest. Soon I will bring you distilled water and you must drink it very—"

By then I had slipped on the shoes, sweater, and thin hoodie that someone had hung on hooks by the front door. My phone rang. I knew there was no way it still had battery charge, because it was at 3% when I checked last night. Did someone charge it for me then put it back in my pocket? Okay, micro-USB iPhone chargers were ubiquitous enough, sure. But who would care enough to do it? It continued ringing; Paola monitored me from behind the counter. I felt like I was on a movie set with a studio audience. Somewhere a Director was about to yell, "Cut. Take it from the top."

I pressed the green circle, afraid to answer. "Hello?"

"Zak Skinner, please." A stern, male voice I'd never heard before.

"This is Zak. Who's calling?"

"Campus Security." Pause. "We need you to come down here, Mr. Skinner"

"Down...where?"

"Campus Security, on Drexler."

"Why?"

"We have a few questions you need to answer."

CHAPTER SIX

The way I saw it, I had done absolutely nothing wrong. Okay yes, I took a hallucinogenic substance, so there was that. But I did it during off hours, on a weekend. I hadn't missed any classes, and I couldn't think of any campus-type of infractions that could put me on Security's watchlist. Had something happened to Riley? Or Wade? No, I didn't really care what happened to Wade, but if he'd disappeared, it happened because he took me to Jane's. So that meant I was at least indirectly responsible.

Twenty minutes and an Uber-ride later, I sat on a hard, black, wooden bench outside the glass doors of the main Campus Safety and Security Center. Not a bad looking building with modern décor, of course specifically designed to put students at ease during interrogations.

I flipped through my magic notebook, amazed at the sentences I hadn't written myself, which materialized before my eyes at Jane's dining table. So that was real? The writing was different but the ink color was the same. Was she using my pen at the time, or did she put some kind of spell on me where she wrote through me and I had no memory of this transference? I remembered an episode of *The Magicians* like this.

If Security was going to pin someone else's crime on me, what could I do about it? Sure, there were lawyers in my family. Once.

"Mr. Skinner?"

A military-like fellow with a crew cut and abnormally large neck told me to follow him and leave my belongings with a man at a desk who would return them before my release. I clutched the blue notebook tight to my chest, suspecting it would mold my future, or at least some part of it.

"That too," the officer demanded.

I set the journal on the counter and covered it carefully with my hoodie. I felt like crying. They asked to see my driver's license and student ID. Thank God I still had my wallet with me. At this point I wasn't even sure it was mine. We ended up—me and the crew cut fellow—across from each other at a rectangular, metal table in a cramped room with purposely, I was certain, dim lighting.

"What's this about?" I asked, careful to keep my voice calm.

The officer had a notebook in front of him with something written on the top page. I watched him flip the page and scribble something.

"When was the last time you saw David Wade?" he asked, without looking up.

"Last night," I said easily, without hesitation, and without a single micro-movement of my face. I knew he was watching me while pretending not to watch. I also suspected that the glass wall behind him had other Security personnel behind it, observing me while I spoke through an invisible speaker. Be cool, Zak. Listen, answer, don't react.

"Where?"

"His friend's house, on the south side of Hyde Park."

"Names?" the man asked.

"José is one, Paola is the other. Everyone calls José Jane. I don't know their last names."

No reaction.

"What time did you arrive last night?"

Shit. I had no fucking idea, and couldn't even really say, conclusively, that it had been last night because of the perception problem while on yage. So I guessed.

"Around nine p.m. I think."

With his head pointed at the notebook, his eyes darted up to glance at my body language and facial expressions, checking them into his algorithms of evaluation. I wasn't going for it. I was engineering my reactions so as to not appear outwardly hostile, nervous, uncertain, arrogant, or apathetic. I'd watched plenty of interrogation movies; I knew the drill. It was driving the man crazy. Good, my life had new purpose.

<hr />

New tactic—concern:

"Is David alright? Has something happened?" I asked, with a completely calm voice, expressed in low tones without any hint of emotion or change in body language. Only then did the actual realization sink in, that something very likely had happened to Wade, or else I wouldn't be there.

That also meant Jane or Paola had contacted the police. About me. Bastards.

"Let's start with my questions, Mr. Skinner. If there's time, I'll answer yours."

He was trying to rattle me, emotionally overpower me. It wasn't working.

"Alright, thank you," I said, dying laughing inside.

"What were you doing there at your friend's…José and Paul's…"

"Paola," I corrected. "She's from Peru."

His brow raised. "Pow-lah," he enunciated clearly. "Okay. And what were you doing there?"

"José, Paola's nephew, is a tutor. I'm failing thermodynamics and he was tutoring me on the movement of heat through air." My God, really? That lie flowed out of my mouth way too easily. I felt regret, for a half second, which quickly changed to jubilance.

The man blinked back, wrote something, then waited. So I kept talking.

"I'm an engineering student. I transferred here in August from NYU."

"Was Mr. Wade with you at the house the whole time?"

"No," I explained. "He just dropped me off and left at about ten," which I think was actually true.

"Do you know where he went after that?" he asked with an

urgency that made me wonder if Wade had done something terrible to someone. Theft? Murder even?

I shook my head slowly, thoughtfully. "José and Paola might know, but I haven't talked to them today." This time I squinted, showing the officer my visible concern for my good friend, David Wade, the poser, the arrogant un-guide, who could just as well be a vampire for all I really knew about him.

I must have done a good job sounding concerned, because they let me go after that. They never answered my question about what happened to Wade, or why they were looking for him.

At the front desk where I was about to pick up my blue notebook and hoodie, the old man was holding a white envelope with my name on it. "Someone left this here for you," he said, staring at it.

"Who?" I asked.

"I stepped away for a moment, came back and here it was on top of your stuff."

I grabbed the jacket, slid the notebook under my arm and opened the envelope, turning away from the security guard. It had a Post-It with the words, *Biology Lab* scribbled with an arrow facing left. Upon closer inspection, I discovered that the handwriting on the envelope and the *Biology Lab* note was the same as Sunita's handwriting in the Tom Riddle notebook. Jesus. She was real?

CHAPTER
SEVEN

I foolishly looked around as if I might see her crouched behind a car or a fence with the edges of her blue gown sticking out. I tore open the blue notebook as I exited Security.

Receipt in the bag okay? Was it still there? Had I really heard those words at the bookstore? I touched the edges of the receipt, considered snapping a photo of it with my phone. No. It would be easy enough for someone to hack into my iCloud account. I could make photocopies of it, sure. What if I was seen, though? Were they watching me? Who was they? I must be going insane. It was the only explanation.

I stood before the main security entrance. The arrow pointed to a clump of trees in front of a pagoda. I moved to the west side along the main street through campus. Walking around the back, I performed the same ritual. Nothing. That left the east side of the building, so by now Crew Cut Man would be watching me from between the blinds. I saw a campus sign but it was too far away to read.

I jogged through the trees toward the next building behind

Security. I could see the white lettering now: Biology Lab. I had no idea what I was doing, but following the Biology Lab note felt right. I used my receipt as a sort of divining rod, imagining her standing in the hallway, her long gown, caramel eyes, bare feet, speaking telepathically like we did together in the fairy field.

"Yes?" A purple-haired girl stared me down. "Do you need help?"

"Um, is this is the Biology Lab?"

"Yep."

Her eyes were impatient. Not even meeting my definition of attractive, she had this numbing effect on my speech. I could no longer use ayahuasca-inspired nausea as an excuse either. I held out the Biology Lab note to her.

She reluctantly pulled it out of my hand and looked up. "Oh, right. Down here." She led me down a long hallway to the left. I trailed Labrador-like and watched her turn right down another hallway, apparently still in the Biological Sciences building. She stopped, pushed a wall-mounted panel and a door labeled Infrared Spectroscopy opened. I had no idea what this meant but someone, somewhere, knew.

"Wait here if you like." The purple-haired escort pointed to an empty chair at a desk.

I climbed backwards onto the chair and rested my head on my forearms for a thirty-second nap. Self check-in: so far I'd had three bites of toast, the equivalent of a single strawberry and five sips of black coffee. The distilled water Paola promised never came, instead substituted by a Campus Security interrogation. I couldn't say what day it was, I hadn't been "home" in three days, I'd missed two full days of classes, was estranged from Riley, and David Wade had apparently vanished.

But now I was a suspect in his disappearance.

•———•••——•

Something guided me to open the blue notebook again. My fingers fumbled with the receipt. I knew obsessing meant I had no capacity to trust the authenticity of my drug-infused experience. I checked the front, the back, as if there was some hidden text I'd missed last night in my altered state. Out of the corner of my eye I saw a word in the Tom Riddle notebook page that definitely wasn't there before: *door*. I look down at a new sentence at the very bottom, same script, same ink color: *Bang five times on the wooden door.*

Was she following me now? Can she write in my notebook even if I don't have it open? How was that even possible? I'd read that DMT from ayahuasca only stayed in the body for twenty-hour hours. I look in both directions, scanning for danger. Paranoia crept in through my periphery. I looked down each side of the hallway.

"Mr. Skinner?" A different woman now, taller, older, heavier, out of breath, wearing a business suit and sneakers. "Sorry I'm late, you're here for the two o'clock tour?"

"Exactly," I said. What tour?

I followed her into a large office. The woman unlocked a door to a huge, glass-walled room and turned on the lights—low and blue.

She swept her hand right to left. "This is the infrared spectroscopy lab, in which I understand you have a keen interest from Dr. Stavros."

I nodded. I'd never heard the name Stavros.

"We're just delighted you've got some hours to spare this semester for volunteering. I've been looking for an intern forever. What hours do you have available?"

My mother loved watching retro TV shows, especially The X-Files and something called Quantum Leap, where a scientist floated around the time continuum from a botched experiment, constantly jumping into different worlds at different times in history. Had I just leaped?

Playing along, I said I was available Saturday afternoons and we continued this charade while I imagined Stavros, whoever he was, as a thin-lipped, crusty academic hunched in front of a blackboard covered with math notations. I tried to look interested in the history of the spectroscopy lab, but a wave of dizziness overtook me. I needed water like life or death right now.

"Oh my God, are you alright? Do you—need something to drink?"

I nodded. She disappeared, leaving me for a moment in silence to collect my thoughts. My eyes drifted around the room. There was a wall I hadn't noticed before—a narrow wooden panel positioned between all the glass.

Bang five times on the wooden door.

No handle, no trim, it didn't meet my definitions of a door. But with my chaperone gone, I had a quick chance. I considered opening the notebook for guidance but instead knocked on the smooth wood.

One, two, three. Shit, I heard the pounding of her rubber soles on the floor. She probably thought I was about to keel over. Probably true. She spotted me through the glass standing at the wall and ran toward me, water sloshing out of the cup, mouth formed in the shape of admonition. As I knocked a fourth time, the lab doors opened behind me. The wooden wall opened and slid into the doorway, called a pocket door I think.

And now facing me was a werewolf with horn-rimmed glasses.

CHAPTER EIGHT

"Geoffrey Stavros. How do you do?"

A smiling, dark haired man, about 6'2, 300 pounds welcomed me. Hair covered the man's cheeks. A scruffy beard, pointed incisors along with the horn-rimmed glasses just added to the overall comedy. He belonged in a B horror movie.

The man shook my hand with gusto, then pulled me toward him through the doorway. The wall/door automatically closed behind me. That poor seething woman with my cup of water.

"I've got him, Veronica. We're good," he shouted, then looked back at me. "Mr. Skinner I presume."

A Brit. "I...never told you my name."

The man moved to one of three white boards set up in the room just like I'd pictured. I was in another laboratory filled with what looks like high-powered imaging equipment. Long, flatbed scanners and closed laptops were attached to gigantic monitors. The spectroscopy lab next door had mostly tables with microscopes. I froze to appraise the situation.

"Do sit down," he said with an odd grin.

There were no chairs in the room. I still felt dizzy. I grabbed the edge of the table and sat, dangling my legs.

"Now tell me, what do you see?"

"Inside, outside," I replied quickly, first pointing to the other lab, then here.

He nodded. "They're both doing opposite things so that's not a bad guess." He pulled a stool from under one of the tables and plopped down.

"Sorry, but do we know each other?"

He looked at the ceiling. "Let's just say I'm not surprised to see you."

I have no idea what this means. "Any chance I could have some —"

"Yes, yes water. Sorry, coming right up." He filled a coffee mug with tap water from a sink in the back of the lab.

How could this man have been expecting me if my arrival was completely random? The woman in the hall knew where to take me after seeing a very non-specific note. Had she, like me, recognized the handwriting?

Paranoia, I decided right there, would be a very normal thing for me right now. Even so, I was taking direction from a self-writing journal and a blue-clad woman who may or may not really exist. My mind raced. I needed to calm down. I don't fear what I don't know. I fear what I don't trust, and right now I don't trust anyone. Great. Drink the water.

"Let's say we, um, know some of the same people."

Why was he choosing his words so carefully? Despite the hair, his friendliness put me at ease. But there were too many questions right now to relax. I had to keep up my guard, my mind sharp, and keep track of everything I saw.

"David Wade," I said to gauge his reaction. "Where is he? I've just been questioned by security."

Stavros shook his head. "Don't know him, but I do know your friend Jane."

I drank the water in small sips and my stomach felt like it had never experienced the substance. Cramping started low in my belly. I doubled over, pressing my warm palm into my lower abs.

"Are you alright? You don't look alright."

"So you're, like, some kind of Obi Wan Kenobi?"

He laughed out loud with his mouth wide and head angled up.

"Math guru?" I asked.

"I'm just an old R2 unit," he replied, getting the Star Wars reference. "Obi Wan's—" he pointed down the hall—"that way. We'll get there, don't worry. She's just as eager to meet you."

"She?"

He bent to pick up a piece of paper from the floor. I caught sight of the back of his head and a preposterous mound of hair, frayed in ninety directions, ink-black, and had obviously never been combed.

He eyed the blue journal under my arm. Did he know something? How could he possibly know, and who was down the hall? If this was Geoffrey Stavros, head of the Math Department, he was making time for me, so I needed to use that to my advantage. I pulled the receipt from the notebook and held it up.

"That looks like a store receipt," he said. "Cash or credit?"

Why would he care how I paid for something, and what an odd response from a complete stranger. Did that mean he wasn't a complete stranger?

"Why is that relevant?" I asked, not meaning to sound defensive.

He raised his bushy brows. "You tell me."

I thought about the trip to the bookstore. Jane had paid with a twenty-dollar bill. "If I'd paid with a credit card, that store would have my personal information available to them. Presumably."

"Presumably." He crossed his arms and stepped back like he was waiting for me to do something. What?

Receipt in the bag okay? I played the words back, remembering the scene, the store, the wall of journals, hipster jazz in the background. The girl behind the counter. I probably meant as much to her as one of the pens cupped by the cash register. What question burned in my mind right now more than any other? I glassed the laboratory with its array of equipment and a theory came to me.

"What could you hide in a store receipt?" I blurted. "And why?"

Slight smile. "Good. Keep going."

"My mind, I mean, when I bought this notebook..."

"Where and when?"

"Last night, some all-night bookstore. The cashier said something that my mind can't seem to let go of." I told him the phrase and his face remained blank. Did he think I was one of those crackpot conspiracy theorists lighting up Twitter in the middle of the night?

"I'm not sure I understand what you suspect is going on here."

"I think there's something in that receipt that I'm supposed to see."

"But that no one else can see? Is that what you're suggesting?"

Two second delay while I considered the question. "Yes."

"Define *in*." He took two steps closer.

"I can't. I mean, I don't know. Embedded maybe? I've thoroughly examined it on both sides and found nothing, no watermark." I shook my head. "Is there something here?" I looked around at the equipment. "Maybe in the lab that could..."

"You're thinking some kind of imaging equipment could show you something else in the receipt?"

"Yeah. Is that possible? I must sound crazy right now."

"Let me tell you where we are," the man said, motioning for me to get up. "That room you started in is the spectroscopy lab that uses infrared technology to detect hidden material, so to speak, essentially heat-trapped within other material. And this room," he made a voila motion. "The steganography lab uses different technologies to hide or encrypt messages inside other messages."

How had I not known about these things? "So I was right in a way," I suggested. "This room inserts hidden text, and that room pulls it out."

Stavros folded his arms, still standing, waiting for my next move.

"Okay, I can't explain myself very well right now, but my intuition is telling me that there's something in this receipt I can't see but that means something."

"I like how you said your intuition. Let me tell you what I do all day. I work with numbers, but not ordinary numbers. What do you know about number theory?" he asked.

"Um. Nothing?"

"It's the mathematics of patterns, essentially."

The word patterns triggered a bolt of lightning in my belly as I remembered the word patterns from Sunita in my magic notebook. Had she been the one to send me here on this wild goose chase?

"What that means is the properties of numbers and the study of the hidden messages in those patterns."

"All numbers?"

"Well number theory works with primarily positive integers, but the branch I deal with is transcendental numbers."

I blinked back, trying not to look as clueless as I felt.

"Transcendental number theory deals with imaginary or irrational numbers, like 'e' also called Euler's number, and also Phi. So with that in mind, I don't think it's an accident that you're relying on something esoteric like intuition to guide the next steps in your inquiry. Some aspects of math and science most definitely dictate the need for that kind of faith."

Faith. That word in the context of abstract mathematics seemed so strange. "What process are we talking about?" I asked.

He pointed at the receipt. "You received something totally innocuous, and your higher mind is attaching significance to it because, for you, there is some sort of meaning in some aspect of that object. So you've got a theory, but you haven't yet proved that theory. And numbers do that, sometimes, especially when you're dealing with characters like pi. The numbers can help you find things, reveal things, or relationships between things, that really shouldn't have any connection. Then it's up to me, to us scientists," he pointed back and forth, "to prove what we know in our hearts, or what our higher mind guides us toward. Theories are fine. Theories are great, they make up the foundations of mathematics. But it's the truth that comes from proven theories that helps us understand the natural world."

I listened, digesting it slowly.

"So your receipt could be some sort of key. You see, keys are related to my work as well right now. Number theory is used, currently, for encryption, being that number theory processes can be used to uncover patterns in data sets and data models."

"But I thought cryptography was the reverse of what I'm trying to do," I said. "You know what you need, and what you're lacking is the key to unlock that data set. What I have, according to what you described, could be a key but I have no idea what it's supposed to unlock. What the data set is."

"Well, let's have a look."

CHAPTER NINE

Stavros led us back to infrared spectroscopy and fed my receipt into what looked like a laser printer but was probably a forty-thousand-dollar machine. The text and numbers on the receipt displayed on a huge monitor, showing both sides of the receipt, but nothing other than what I had already seen. I stood back to observe, letting him do his thing.

"I'm not seeing anything interesting here. Let me try something else," he said.

We moved back to the secret lab behind the disappearing wooden door-wall and Stavros set my receipt on an imaging machine and pulled down a heavy cover that thunked, then clicked when he locked it in. He pressed a button in the middle. Part of the cover rose, leaving only a narrow arm hovering over the exact width of the receipt.

The receipt's text showed up on the far wall, displaying the front side, and something smudgy on the back.

"What is that?" I pointed.

Stavros hovered inches from the wall. He pulled up the arm and flipped the receipt over, then pressed another button and the new image projected on the wall, showing what I'd already seen as a faded version of the City Books address on Clark Street. He ran his fingers through his tangle of hair. I wondered if he'd ever get them out.

He snapped his fingers. "Let's try a holographic filter."

"Okay," I replied.

"It's a digital holographic microscope. You're gonna love this."

On one of the laptops, Stavros typed in a command, which sent a sort of humming scanner over the length of the receipt from top to bottom. It revealed nothing, so he lifted the arm again and flipped the receipt back onto its front side, again applying the filter and rescanned.

"What the—"

I gasped at a series of numbers arranged vertically down the center of the back of the receipt. These had not been visible in any other view. My heart thudded in my chest. Hidden numbers. Had my theory been right?

"What is that?"

"You've heard the bar code conspiracy theories, right?"

I shook my head. This guy was blowing my mind.

"Barcodes work with light and darkness. The scanner shines a laser, reflecting light back off the barcode into a photoelectric cell. The white areas of the barcode, stripes as we call them, reflect the most light, black will absorb the light. Anyway, the scanner moves over the barcode and that cell generates a series of pulses corresponding to the black and white stripes. So black and white would mean on and off. The electronic circuit in the scanner converts this pattern to binary code. Following me so far?"

"Sort of." I nodded.

"So there are lots of types of barcode scanners. Embedding people's personal data, like bank account numbers and social security numbers in seemingly innocuous bar codes of everyday products, like granola or coffee, wouldn't be difficult to do."

It seemed ridiculous. I shook my head. "Why would someone do that?"

"You're hiding illegal information beneath legal information. What's more, it's not just legal but it's what most people would deem completely worthless, to the point that no one reads it." He stared at the numbers on the wall.

"So you're saying these numbers are not an accident? That someone put them there?"

Another finger snap. "Very good, that's right. Some purposeful technology had to apply this number on this receipt."

"Why though? Most people won't ever look at a receipt," I said. "What would be the purpose?"

Wait a minute. Was I back on my ayahuasca journey, or maybe another round of it had released into my system? The paranoia returned. My arms and chest felt tight. Was Jane watching me from hidden ceiling monitors or cameras on the wall? I felt nauseous and wondered if the bucket lady would appear if I summoned her with the force of my will.

I drank a few more sips of the water while Stavros wrote the series of numbers on the top left of his white board—nine in total:

231 17 5 97 44 498 3 71 264

"Are they prime?" I asked, half surprised at the semi-intelligent question I was able to contribute.

"17, 5, 97, 3, and 71 are," he replied, mid-thought.

"But what?"

"Nine."

"Okay. Is that significant?"

"Well, history's replete with all kinds of lore, mythology, and symbolism surrounding the number nine, but this is the quantity nine, not the numeral itself."

"Is there a pattern?"

His eyes and forehead rose with amusement. "Maybe. That's the whole fun, right?"

Fun for him, maybe. "Sure," I went along.

"Leave this with me. I've got some colleagues who live and breathe this stuff every day. I'm sure they'd love to take a look at it. Let's exchange numbers," he grabbed his phone. "I'll be back in touch tomorrow-ish," he said with his tipped sideways. "Sound okay?" he asked, showing a full rack of yellowed, crooked teeth on the top and bottom.

"I need to leave my receipt with you?" I asked, like a child having to part with his teddy bear. What was wrong with me?

Stavros raised the lid on the machine to pull out the original receipt and handed it back to me. Whew.

CHAPTER TEN

All I really wanted now was to see Riley, plop down in my own bed in my own room, and maybe order in a pizza. I had a long walk back to Granville West, which was perfect because I needed time to think. I texted Riley while I walked, hoping he was still speaking to me.

Dude, you there?

Thank GOD I was seriously ready to call 911 and file a missing person's report. Where the FUCK have you been

Is my bed available or did you violate that too?

Omg you suck so bad

FU

Like where the f are you? Was your phone dead or did someone break both your legs or something?

Sort of

I thought you blamed me for getting laid for the first time ever

Did you get that second date yet?

Sposed to be tomorrow

Right on. I'm on my way back now
From where
Tell ya when I get there
Roger that
Order a pizza
OK

Shit. Tuesday night study group was underway in Granville Commons. That meant freaking forty-seven students sitting around debating, arguing over which position to take in today's political science problem. Engineering students were exempt, thank God. I would have done anything for an invisibility spell as I pulled open the clunky glass doors. Not surprisingly, every head turned to stare at the frazzled, unkempt, neurotic version of myself, a version I'd hoped would disappear by morning.

I used the secret knock we'd been using since childhood—knock-knock, knock-knock—in case he was getting dressed or something. It seemed unnecessarily polite, especially for college students, but codes were part of our history. Riley and I transferred here together from NYU; we'd been friends since the third grade. Ahhh, my own room.

"Dude…" Riley outstretched his arms at the sight of me.

I grabbed him and hugged him properly, which I realized I hadn't done in a long time. Not that I thought guys shouldn't hug each other but, I don't know, we sort of didn't need to do that because we spent so much time together anyway.

"You look horrible. What the hell happened to you?"

"I smell bad too, I need a shower."

I removed my jacket, replaced every single article of clothing with clean clothes, which felt transformative, and poured water from the filtered water pitcher Riley always kept on the mini-fridge. I ran through the past 2.5 days for him:

- Tamango cocktail followed by David Wade rescue and invocation
- Dean Agnus interrogation, the "door"
- Lace panties on the doorknob
- David Wade, Jane
- Jane, yage, fairies, the receipt
- Sunita
- Security

• Stavros

"My God, this is all my fault. If I'd let you in that night, I'm *sure* you wouldn't have met up with fucking Wade again. I'll never forgive myself."

"Come on, it's not like my life is over. It was an adventure. And I needed an adventure. All I want now is normalcy. My bed, my room..."

There was a knock at the door—pizza. I pulled cash out of my wallet but Riley got there first.

"Have you seen Wade tonight, or earlier today?" I asked.

Riley looked at the carpet. "Nobody's seen him since last night and he didn't check in. I was already questioned by the Resident Assistant, the Resident Master, and Security."

I didn't even know we had a Resident Master.

"They were all looking for you, too."

"I told them you usually study at the library during the week till about eleven."

That was sort of true, sometimes, mostly. Crap. Now I'd put Riley at risk, and what the hell happened to Wade?

"We've got to find Jane, and Paola," I said. I went through an explanation about Paola.

"Now?" Riley asked, bless his heart, in his flannel sleep pants and alphabetized book collection, color-coded closet, the guy who went to bed by nine o'clock every night of his life. I demanded details of his date while we grabbed the pizza box.

"You ordered onion and pepperoni?" I asked, dismayed, since we'd been eating untopped, naked, unadulterated plain cheese pizza since childhood. It was tradition.

Riley looked confused. "Hell no. Someone else on the floor must've ordered one." He stepped into the hallway, sniffed the air, and knocked on the door next to ours.

"Mellon, you in there?" he shouted with three bangs. "I think they got our pizzas mixed up." He knocked again and I heard it at the same time Riley did, the unmistakable sound of vomiting, thank God in the bathroom with the door closed. Amazing how hunger instantly evaporated. "Mellon, you okay in there?"

"What do you think?" Mellon's tortured voice echoed from the bathroom. Poor guy.

"Guess we're eating onion and pepperoni tonight," Riley said returning to our room.

"No thanks, I'm not hungry."

Riley returned to his spot on the floor with an impish grin, it seemed, happy to return to more important matters than pizza. "So... you remember her. Right?"

"Of course. Mari. So who asked who out?" I was only sort of listening.

Riley did that half-smile on the left side of his face. The look of love.

"What, she just came over?"

He nodded.

"Like...for that?"

"Well, so it seems. She didn't call or text first, and..."

He let his voice trail off. I allowed it because there were some things even best friends didn't tell each other, maybe because we didn't need to or because of some loyalties that were bigger than friendship. I was okay with that. From Riley, I could tolerate almost anything, especially now. He was the only one I could trust.

CHAPTER ELEVEN

Wednesday. End of October in what most people called the windy city and what I called the forever winter city. Even in summer, because we arrived here in August, it felt cold to me. Riley and I both had back-to-back nine and ten o'clock classes. For him, Advanced Algebra and Calculus, typical core classes for a math major. For me, Engineering Fundamentals and my apple pie elective: Economics, which I secretly loved yet barely understood. Didn't hurt that the professor was about thirty, unmarried, and more than just mildly desirable (more like adorable). But I also loved the subject. We hadn't even started talking about money yet. So far it was about decision-making, human behavior, and how people spend their energy.

We'd planned to meet in front of the Fine Arts building after our ten o'clocks, and from there call an Uber to try to find our way back to Jane and Paola's house to ask about Wade. The whole walk from the Engineering School to the art building involved chastising myself for my lie of omission—to Riley no less—and possibly the single most important feature of my adventure: the notebook.

I wasn't even sure Riley saw me take it out from where I'd hidden it—in my back between layers of my shirt and sweater, to slip it behind my desk. I could've done a much better job with the hiding place. Why didn't I just tell him? Because hearing it out loud would make me feel even more insane than I already felt. A self-writing notebook inspired by the whims of a fairy goddess brought on by entheogenics. I hadn't checked it since leaving Stavros' lab and I was afraid to. My God, who wouldn't be?

I caught sight of him fifty yards ahead with a ginormous book bag hovering up near his head like he was backpacking through Patagonia. I couldn't tell him about it. I'd show him as soon as we got back to the room later. Right now we had more important things to track down.

"Hey."

"Hey. Did you book it or do you want me to?" I asked of the Uber.

"We're booked," he looked down at his phone. "Eight minutes."

"Cool. On-campus or..."

"Relax, I can follow directions."

I'd told him earlier that we should book an on-campus Uber to find another student, like us, who might know about the all-night café slash bookstore.

"How was Dr. Evil?" I asked of his calculus professor.

"Man he was salty today. Trawling the aisles, thirsty for blood, handing out shame for what we didn't know. That treatment should be a federal offense."

"What happened?"

"He called on me and asked for a dissertation on a part of Chapter Seven I hadn't read."

I stopped walking. "You hadn't done the reading? You're a reading machine. You read in the shower. You read in your sleep and your comprehension's ridiculous."

I swear he was about to cry.

"What's the matter with you?" I demanded.

"Well what do you think? No I didn't fucking read for God's sake. I thought you, like, quit school or were kidnapped or dead or something."

OMG. I hated myself.

"When I said I was about to call the police, that wasn't a joke."

"I am so sorry," I said and completely meant it. I didn't like what I saw right now on Riley's face. Fear.

CHAPTER TWELVE

My phone buzzed with a text from Dr. Geoffrey Stavros.

I've got something, when can you be here?

This afternoon maybe how late can I come?

Late as you want. Listen, don't bring IT with you, matter of fact be a good idea to get rid of it. I've got it copied here anyway. You read me?

Got it

"Who was that?" Riley asked.

"Stavros."

"Friends in high places."

"He found something and wants to see me."

"Great," Riley said, watching my face. "Not great? What's the problem?"

"He told me to get rid of the receipt." I sort of said it under my breath, even though we were surrounded by noise: voices, cars, and bikes.

"Where is it?"

"In the room."

Riley shook his head. "I don't understand. Why?"

━ ● ◦ ● ━

A blue Honda pulled up to the curb, parked, and the driver slid down the passenger window and leaned toward us. "Uber for…Riley?"

"How's it going?" Riley touched the rear door handle, while a suited man yanked open the driver's side door, shoved the driver into the passenger seat and climbed in the car. Where the hell did he come from?

I threw Riley a panicked look and he backed away from the car. I was right behind him. Another car had parked directly behind the Uber, out of which a second and third nearly identical suited men emerged. Suit one was still in the driver's side of our Uber. Two and three loomed over Riley and me. Riley had the car on one side of him and a thug on the other, me positioned awkwardly between all of them, surrounded.

"Riley," I said. "Run!"

I bent low and sort of swiveled my head and shoulders in a U-shape. From there I managed to back away from the throng of men at the Honda and slip between the two cars, where I grabbed Riley by the elbow and ran straight ahead in the direction of the other thug car parked in the middle of the road.

"What the fuck…" he shouted as we ran side-by-side back toward the entrance to the Arts and Sciences building.

"I don't know, but…" The image of another thug, same kind of guy, same suit, stopped my train of thought. He and another guy stood in our path with something pointing from each of their jackets.

"Back to the car," one of them said in a monotone to me, then looked at Riley. "Blue Honda, move it."

Meaty hands rotated my body back toward the Uber and my captor jammed something hard into my spine, though I wasn't experienced enough in crime evasion to know for certain whether it was a gun or a Coke bottle. Riley, obedient as ever, was ahead three steps and we both knew, unspeakably, that we were getting in that Honda and there was nothing we could do about it now. We were far outnumbered, and whoever wanted us was willing to resource five operatives to bring us wherever we were going.

Riley was in the middle of the back seat, me on the right and our babysitter on the left rear side, with another one in the front along with a silver-haired driver, all three of them in expensive suits. Not your typical law enforcement or G-man suits. These men were something different. Intelligence probably—which led me back to the inevitable question of what they could possibly want with us. Riley and I didn't dare look at each other or communicate, and the car was moving so fast it was all we could do to just lean into each other every five seconds. The questions swarming in my head made me nauseous. Where were we going, and why were we forced into this car? My gut knew it had something to do with Jane and maybe even the receipt, which brought more credence to my theory. I have a receipt that might be important. More people know about it now, and we'd just been kidnapped. Our captors, the suits, were not average Joes, not pizza delivery guys. They acted like the thugs we watched in movies—trained criminals. Were they also trained killers? I knew this road—I think it was on David Wade's route to Jane's last night. We were headed to Jane's, which was an interesting twist, I thought, sort of saving us the trouble of trying to find it ourselves.

Ten minutes later, Riley and I were dumped on Jane's same white leather sofa on which I'd slept the previous night, with my dutiful attendant, Paola, sitting opposite us now, sobbing.

"I'm sorry," she lip-synched every time our captors looked or walked away. I had no idea what she meant. Was Jane dead? Had she killed him? Had she ratted me out to her handlers? Supposedly Jane was her nephew, though I'm sure that was one of many stories they told. Our captors stood at attention, one at each door front and back, hands at their sides and constantly rotating their gaze from outside to us to each other. What were they waiting for?

"Am I allowed a question or a phone call or something?" I asked and right away felt Riley's anxiety at my having spoken.

"What do you want to know?" one of them replied. They all looked alike and were probably clones.

"Where's Jane?"

One traded glances with the other man, but no answer.

"Is there any chance you could just kill us now rather than later? I mean, why procrastinate the inevitable?" I asked.

"What is wrong with you?" Riley said beside me loud enough for our captors to hear.

"Listen to your friend, Mr. Skinner. It won't be long now."

Paola wrung her hands and wiped her palms on her long skirt, her bare feet on the floor groping for shoes. A car door slammed shut out front and the back door guy moved to the front and opened the door. *Jane.*

He was dressed, now, like the other men—dark, expensive-looking suit with shiny shoes and a tight knot in his tie, unlike last night having worn a white silk shirt, loose pants and huaraches. Apparently that was *Shaman Jane* and today's version was Hitman Jane. It was hard to keep up. Paola sobbed at the sight of Jane.

"Calm down, everyone's fine. No one's gonna get hurt, Ima."

Ima?

"They don't know anything, they're just kids," she pleaded, still sobbing.

"Maybe," Jane said. He sat directly opposite me but spoke to Riley. "I'm José. I'm not gonna hurt you."

"Nice to meet you," Riley said and I turned to him.

"See, it wouldn't be Jane that hurt us, it would be—"

One of the suits raised his palm. "I suggest you stop talking, Mr. Skinner."

"Where's Wade?" I demanded. I went on to explain that I'd been questioned by Security, and so had Riley.

"When was this?" Jane asked Riley.

"Last night, they came around asking when I'd last seen him," Riley answered in a timid voice. Well, pretty much his only voice, other than the time we almost got run over by a train.

Jane's arms were crossed now and he was pacing slowly in thick-soled shoes over the marble floor, making some kind of a decision. Kill us or let us live? Or was it just logistics of where to dump our bodies? I knew Riley was on the verge of a panic attack right now and, for me, it just felt like theater.

"You have something we need, Zak."

Riley shot me a look and turned his head, which obviously signified to our captors that we did have something. Good job.

I looked down at my backpack. "Did you want to take a look at my Elements of Thermodynamics book, or perhaps one of Riley's calculus assignments? I have a wallet with my driver's license. Oh, and about twenty-seven dollars, did you want that too? Chop off my fingers first, maybe?"

I probably should have been freaking out at that point, but fatigue and malnourishment activated my frustration with the whole charade. Sure, I took a yage trip but now I was ready to get back to reality. Now these buffoons were in my way.

Riley looked down and touched his eyes. I knew he was losing all hope. But these men weren't gonna kill either one of us. I knew what they wanted, what they said they needed. But it wasn't on me. Until they could get their hands on it, we were safe. The only thing I didn't yet understand...was why.

CHAPTER THIRTEEN

Twenty-four hours, we were told, and we had to deliver what they knew I knew they wanted. The receipt. I just still couldn't figure out why it would mean anything to any of them, since I could barely explain what it meant to me.

Two city bus rides and an hour later, we arrived back on campus, without having spoken the entire trip.

"I'm sorry, okay?" I said as we headed down the path toward Granville.

"I doubt it," Riley replied.

"Really?"

"I'm just curious," he said, still walking. "If they'd had their guns out and pointed at us, would you have still egged them on like that? I mean, you do remember, right, that they had guns pointed at us to get us into the car. Guns. Do you remember that? Yes or no."

"We didn't actually see the guns. Probably a good assumption that they had them, sure."

"I can't think of anything else to say, Zak. That was close, way too close for me. Obviously not for you though. You're having some kind of identity crisis, which is causing you to, I don't know, seek out unnecessary risks."

"Is that so?"

"Look back on your drug history throughout your life, and then in the past week."

Damn, that stung. "Okay, you're right, about that anyway."

"So you're not having a crisis? This is normal for you?"

"No, I am definitely having a crisis, I'm not disputing that. Something...happened to me the other night."

Riley scoffed. "Yes, I heard all about it."

"But it's not what you think. When that woman put my receipt in the bag with my journal, her question opened something up for me. Okay yes, the ayahuasca had prepared my mind for being easily influenced, I admit. But I can think of a million more realistic triggers than that."

I heard his steps on the concrete walkway.

"Whether it was Jane, or the drug itself," I went on, "something about that receipt, or the numbers hidden in it, wants to be seen right now, and I feel like I have been chosen for this path, such as it is."

Riley stopped walking and faced me, just around the corner from our building. "You said journal—I thought you went to that bookstore to buy something to drink."

Shit.

———— • • • ————

There was a mini-courtyard outside Granville West with chairs set up in twos. I motioned for him to sit so I could explain what I should've explained already. He listened without talking at first, one of his best qualities.

"You've seen the notebook since you've come down from your... whatever it was?"

I nodded.

"All the writing was the same?" he asked.

This time I shook my head.

"It was gone?" Riley asked raising his voice.

"No."

"I don't understand..."

"There was more. More writing. It happened in the biology lab while I was waiting for Stavros."

"Jesus. No wonder you didn't tell me. You've clearly lost your mind."

"Thanks, that's comforting."

"Sorry."

"I think some part of me was trying to protect you," I said. "Maybe anticipating that what happened to us today would happen."

"We need to find the notebook and the receipt."

"I know I know," I interrupted, "I have an idea."

●——●•••●——●

The whole way up the stairs I prayed that our room hadn't been ransacked or burned down or something and that my new, highly valuable commodities were still reasonably intact. When we got to the room I made a "silence" motion to Riley, locked the door behind us and closed the blinds. I sat on the floor as an extra precaution.

"What are you doing?" he asked.

"Listen, we've got to assume from here on in that we're being watched all the time. That means we can't bring the notebook or the receipt back to this room again after tonight."

"But what—

"Our room's probably been bugged."

"Great. That's great. Should we get an apartment off campus or something? How about the Witness fucking Protection Program?"

"I think we can stay here, just not with Ashley and Megan."

I paused to see if he got it.

He stared. "Did I miss something?"

I waited, eyes wide. Finally he smiled and nodded slowly. "Okay. Ashley and Megan. Nice. Good, solid names. Which is which?"

"Ashley's the notebook," I whispered.

"Got it."

"And when we leave here, I'll take Ashley with me and you go with Megan, and then we'll all meet up in the Student Union where you can give Megan back to me."

"What are you gonna do with them?"

"I'll show you. Meet me in one of those photography booths in the Stu U basement. You know the ones with heavy black curtains?"

He nodded. "How long?"

59

I pulled out my desk an inch and heard a thud on the carpeted floor. I crawled under it and felt a clamminess in my palms as I touched it the notebook. I wanted to forget that night, not remember it. I slipped it down the back of my jeans a few inches over my shirt but under my sweater, then zipped the jacket over all of it. I looked down at the receipt and handed it to Riley.

"Hello, Megan," he said, and studied it with curiosity.

"Looks innocuous enough, huh?"

"Mmm hmmm."

"Think again," I mumbled.

———• ——— •••— •

I locked the door behind me and realized I hadn't opened the notebook to read the last page. When we approach the student union, I motioned for Riley to exit the back door. I exited the front, walked around the School of Engineering and then the literary center to get to the Stu U. Riley should be getting there a few minutes after me, so I stopped on the main floor of the Stu U and stood at the postal counter, bought a small, padded envelope and enough stamps to cover it.

"Can I borrow your pen for a few minutes?" I asked guy at the desk and took the pen, the envelope, stamps, and the notebook with me down two floors and slipped behind the heavy curtain of the 2nd photography booth. I sat on the hard, wooden bench and texted Riley.

You good?

Almost there

Booth 2

"By the way, this is booth four." Riley pulled out the receipt and sat beside me, watching. "No way. You're gonna mail it to yourself? That's brilliant."

"I can do that every day if I want, and just keep mailing it from different parts of campus. Are you ready to give Megan back now?"

He handed me the receipt. I took a long look at the back side where the string of vertical numbers had appeared in Stavros' lab and could hardly believe what was illuminated in red on the wall. I opened the notebook to the page last written on and held it out so we could both read it.

"I'm sorry I kept this from you," I said, ceremoniously.

"It's alright," Riley replied. "It's one in a long line of recent transgressions." He paused to reading the notebook text. "Okay, so you're being chased by secret numbers that live in patterns. That's provocative but I have no idea what it means."

"Look here." I pointed to the last line.

"Bang on a wooden door. Where was that?" he asked.

The floor vibrated under my feet.

"Did you hear that, or feel something?" I whispered.

He shook his head. I slowly peeled back one millimeter of the black curtain. There was no one in the corridor. One giggly throng of girls in a booth three down from us was all." *So what was the vibration?*

"Anyway, not where but when," I clarified. "At Stavros' lab…the next day."

"You just opened the book and saw another line written on it? Could've been done by anybody if the book was unattended."

I shook my head. "Could be, yeah, but the night I bought it, I *watched* the writing appear while I sat at Jane's dining table."

"Like Tom Riddle's diary," Riley mumbled and ran his finger over the magic script. I peeked out into the corridor again, still clear.

"Z-Z-Zak." Riley pointed down at the notebook page, his hand was shaking.

A line of text appeared on the bottom: *You're being watched even now. Use your mail trick, then leave it in your mailbox. Do not pick it up, they're watching you. I'll tell you when it's safe.*

I had to acknowledge. *Got it,* I wrote with the pen from the mail counter, which I'd borrowed to self-address the padded envelope.

I'll send you another notebook.

Like this one? I wrote.

Yes.

What did I see today at Stavros' lab? I wrote.

Nothing happened, no text. Then an answer was written on the same page. *A key.*

To what?

There's no time. Go now. I'll be watching.

Who are you???

A friend.

Riley and I staggered out of the photo booth, shaky on our feet. I climbed the staircase to the main floor, peered out first (as I was getting accustomed to doing lately) and headed to the postal services desk. I put the envelope on the counter.

"Is that enough postage?" I asked.

He weighed the package, then dropped it onto a conveyor belt where it disappeared into an opening on the left. My magic notebook was gone. I felt like crying.

CHAPTER FOURTEEN

I was desperate for three things right now: get back to a normal schedule, avoid giving the Janes, what they so desperately wanted and, more than anything, understand what I'd stumbled onto, and why I had been chosen.

To answer that last question, I needed Stavros. My gut was telling me to stay away, at least for now. He had to be in on it, whatever 'it' was. How else would the suits have known where to find Riley and me to force us into their car? I thought about my options while entering my Statics class.

I opted for a seat in the back row where the lights were dimmest. Lately, I rarely talked to any of my classmates, and my hermit tendencies were bleeding through my feigned extroverted exterior more than ever. My teacher, I didn't even know his name, wouldn't call on me today (or any day), because I'd deduced during the first class that he was excited by student engagement. I was disengaged, so he had nothing to give me, which, by all accounts, was suitable to my needs. I wanted to look like a regular, second-year college student unsure of his future and even less sure of anything else. I wanted this normalcy to be my guise for the people who were slumped down surveilling me in cramped cars wearing uncomfortable clothing taking orders from unreasonable madmen. I wanted them to see that I didn't fear them, and because of this fact I was taking away some of their power. Okay, yes, as Riley was constantly pointing out, they had guns pointed at us, real ones. I couldn't dispute the danger of guns but felt far more afraid of the danger of human intentions.

Another question: why would The Janes want my notebook? Because someone saw me put the receipt in between its pages, or was there another reason? If anyone looked at it, it looked like just normal writing, and there was no way of repudiating that claim for something else. Normal handwriting, like you'd normally find in a journal. Sure, okay, at one point it looked like a conversation between two people because of the handwriting, but it could have been two students in a library passing the journal back and forth. There was nothing obvious about the book's design to account for its magical properties. What about the rest of the journals on that wall in the coffee shop? Were they all imbued with magic, or just one, and somehow I had chosen that one? It seemed unlikely, but so did everything else.

What about the receipt? Why would The Janes want it? If somehow the nine red numbers that Stavros' equipment detected triggered something, then it was certainly possible that someone else knew about those numbers, that maybe they existed elsewhere, and that some hapless soul like me could accidentally stumble upon them.

But then again, I hadn't stumbled upon anything. Had I?

They were purposely concealed, hidden from any outward or obvious view. It took high-powered imaging equipment to reveal them and even that was temporary. They were only visible under the magnetic resonance equipment in Stavros' lab. Right now, for example, it was a normal looking receipt with its secret intact. But I still couldn't get my head around the question of why. If the yage made me suspicious of everything, why did my vulnerable mind cling to the question from the cashier? If there was something about the series of nine numbers, had I triggered this whole insane chain of events? It all seemed too fantastic to be anything other than random. But then why did I feel targeted?

So, just thinking now, if The Janes were somehow informed that someone detected the secret numbers, their system obviously had some kind of tracking because they knew where to find me. If they did want the receipt, was it so they could test it out themselves, or did they just want me to prevent showing it to somebody else? If I did, how could I reveal the secret numbers without Stavros' lab? None of it made any sense.

My statics professor was operating in a lecture-style class today, droning on about static equilibrium. I saw several people texting, one person playing Pokémon Go, and four people napping in the back row.

I went through different possibilities about the code to try to untangle the chaos. How many other receipts could have either that same code or a different nine-digit code as part of the same overall schema? I could calculate, well maybe not me but someone could, the probability that there were other receipts embedded with this same code. But I knew I couldn't contact Stavros right now to run it through his equipment even if I had another receipt. What I needed was Stavros' codebreaking team.

CHAPTER FIFTEEN

"Operative Riley, your report?" I said into the phone.

"You know we're on an unsecured line, Sir."

"Umm…"

"Why are *you* the commanding officer?" he asked.

It was a fake protest. "Fair question. I suppose because the secret code came to me. Not you."

He paused, and I heard his steps in the background through the phone. "True enough," Riley said. "Where are you now?"

"Two minutes from Outpost A," I replied in full tradecraft mode, meaning the men's room on the second floor of the Fine Arts building.

"That you?" I asked exactly three minutes later through the closed bathroom stall. The door creaked open. Riley knocked back twice like we agreed, settling into the next stall.

Without speaking, we went through a ritual of switching coats, folding and shoving them under the walls of the stall between us.

"I got it." I pulled a retro short jacket under the bathroom stall.

"Dude…" He struggled to drag my coat out into his stall. "Like, what is this thing?"

"What?"

"Come on. Did you rob a Buffalo Exchange or something? This is a freaking Perestroika trench coat; you could fit three of me in here. What is this, boiled wool? It's horrible. It must weigh fifty pounds."

"Put the fucking coat on and shut up," I barked. "The idea is that we don't look like ourselves. How about me wearing a stupid Members Only jacket. I'm gonna look like 1985. Give me your backpack," I said. I pretended to be annoyed but felt secretly glad for his company right now, and relieved that I'd finally told him everything.

"Can't we toss these over the walls of the stall?" Riley the germophobe, of course objected to the germs on a bathroom floor.

"You're such an old lady. Fine, chuck it over."

It was heavy with the weight of his math textbooks. I was sure my backpack wasn't nearly as heavy, symbolic I suppose. Riley always was smarter than me, and he appreciated the necessity for studying, a killer combination that would, no doubt, land him a CEO job or a Nobel prize. If we lived through this mess.

"Forgot to tell you," he said. "Remember Mellon getting sick the other night?"

"Yeah, how is he?" I asked.

"Food poisoning. Been in the infirmary for two days."

"What? The poor guy. I'm glad we didn't eat that pizza."

"That's cold, man."

"No, I'm just saying, you know."

"What?"

I didn't tell him what I was thinking, about the possibility that Mellon's pizza had very likely been meant for us and that our room might be bugged.

We stood there on the tiled floor of the men's room in our odd jackets fumbling with the long range, two-way radios I'd rigged with a handheld speaker mic. The idea was to have the radio hooked on your belt loop with the speaker mic plugged in and then threaded up through the sleeve of your jacket and coming out the top, essentially allowing you to just walk and then press a button on your belt and start talking, or listen. Mine was easy to hook up, but Riley with that huge trench coat… I couldn't help but laugh.

He rolled his eyes. "You try wearing this thing."

I gave him a minute and zipped my own ridiculous jacket, then finished it off with the Chicago Cubs baseball cap I'd stolen from the Granville laundry room.

"Ready?"

"Let's do it."

⸺ • • • ⸺ •

Per our plan, Riley exited the second-floor men's room first and I trailed him by about one minute. We walked like this, fifty feet apart, to Outpost B, the cafeteria. My right eye twitched as a man in a dark suit moved past the art storage building. I might be paranoid but his eyes seemed to be following us.

"Dude, you hear me?" I whispered into the speaker.

"I read you. You're behind me still, right?"

"Yeah, and so is one of our friends from the other day."

"Janes? Do they recognize us?"

I watched for a second, slowing my pace and sort of half-turned my head underneath my baseball cap, and the man's face was pointed at someone in front of him, not us.

"I think we're okay actually, but we should move to step two."

Silence.

"Did you forget already?" I'd raised my voice, then remembered we were in stealth mode.

I heard a long sigh. "Dude, we're bunglers," he replied. "We're college students, not spies. What do you want from me?"

"Don't worry about it. Step two is when we veer off onto separate paths."

"Okay, fine. What's the range on our radios?" he asked.

Great question. "Thirty-six miles."

Riley's magical math mind worked for thirty seconds while I kept to the path. "Okay, the whole campus is about 217 acres," he said, "which translates into roughly .33 square miles. So if we separate when we get to Mitchell Tower in about a quarter mile, we could walk in opposite directions and make a giant figure eight. You go to the right and essentially walk around the entire medical center, then head back here. It's all the same road. I'll do the same thing from the left side going around the sports arena."

I pretended to not be impressed. "Time?"

"At our current speed, I estimate about thirty-two minutes," he said.

"You're a machine, do you know that?"

"Oh, *now* you appreciate me?"

"Yes."

"Glad to be of service then. See you soon," he said as we approached the tower. Riley took the left road.

I went right, and this way if someone was tailing us, they wouldn't see us wearing what we usually wear, we wouldn't be together, and we'd be walking on a completely different road than we usually use to get to our classes. And this plan allowed us to go out to look for *them*.

Unfortunately, our plan hadn't accounted for a wildcard.

CHAPTER SIXTEEN

Wade.

It had barely been a week, now, since my magical mystery tour of planet ayahuasca and that meant exactly six days since I'd last seen our floor-mate, David Wade.

It went like this:

Riley on the path leading left from the tower, me on the opposite path heading towards the Medical School. The wide, paved campus walkway was filled with students, faculty bicyclists, (illegal) skateboarders, (illegal) golf carts stolen from the nearby course used in September during frat hazing, a few official Security-type vehicles. Today, sprinting in the opposite direction was, I was certain, a thinner, scruffier David Wade running for his life, or so it seemed.

"Hey, can you hear me?" I whispered. "Riley."

"Here."

"Keep a lookout for someone headed your way," I said.

"Who?"

"You'll recognize him. Well, maybe."

"Okay. Are they walking and wearing…"

I turned 180 degrees and walked, now ran, to meet him hoping we could stop Wade to get some answers.

"I'm on my way to you," I said, almost shouting and out of breath.

"What…why…and who is…."

"Stop."

"Why? What are you doing?"

"Stop…" I was panting and running, "Wade, when you see him. Stand in his path, trip him, shove someone into him if you have to."

"Wade's coming? Okay, okay, I'm on it."

I signed off so I could concentrate and remember what Wade had been wearing. Oddly I think he was wearing shorts and dressed like a long-distance runner, like in a tank top. I hadn't realized he was a runner, like a real runner. And I didn't believe it for a minute. He seemed way too lazy and entitled to have the discipline of an athlete. No way. It had to be a cover.

"Do you see him yet?" I said into the speaker.

"Got him, he's coming around the corner now. Well, it's a runner…are you sure that's him?"

"It's him. Stop him, can you—

"Excuse me," Riley was shouting, "you appear to be…"

Something crackled, followed by a dragging sound with more rustling. That freaking trench coat. Riley could easily suffocate Wade and probably himself in that thing.

I was almost there now, having been running nonstop for over three minutes, farther than I would have imagined I could go, and I saw what looked like a pile of blankets in the middle of the walkway, people circling around. I yanked Riley up from the coat collar and pulled him off the pile, leaving Wade bleeding on the ground.

"Hey, sorry to ambush you like that, but can we talk to you?" I asked, with unusual politeness. I stood tall with my shoes inches from his face on the ground.

"Watch out." Wade jerked upward and shoved his left shoulder into my calf and climbed to stand, looked behind us, then took off again.

I gave Riley the Go! look. He wriggled out of the trench and left it on the ground. Now I wished I was in better shape.

LISA TOWLES

CHAPTER SEVENTEEN

One of the suited Janes had twisted his ankle and limped behind us a few beats, allowing me to catch up with Riley. In front of him, Wade sprinted. I went into my runner's stride assuming perfect form, reminding myself not to breathe too deeply. Seeing Riley behind him, Wade ran faster. I stayed closer to Suited Jane still hobbling behind me with his suit jacket flapping open, heavy soles clomping like horse hooves on the ground. He could keel over any minute. Hopefully. Headed around the other side of campus, I knew what Wade was doing. Of course, it was Saturday. Football cheerleading tryouts, which had been happening the last two Saturdays. That meant throngs of scantily clad, jumping females with pompoms, lots of distraction, lots of activity to keep him from view. Love it.

Two runners ahead, Wade darted through the middle of a basket toss maneuver, all heads on him now. Riley, the practiced logician, ran around the whole mess and had almost caught up with Wade on the other side. How could he run so long without stopping? Or maybe there was something wrong with my own lungs. I felt like they were gonna crack open so I stopped and leaned down to breathe, of course allowing Suited Jane to catch up with me but I didn't care at this point. Now that I knew Wade was being chased by them too, I wanted him to get away. Riley was close behind. Meanwhile, my day was about to be ruined again as something hard shoved against my mid-back.

"Let me guess," I said.

"Move," the Jane said and thrust me forward with his other hand. Here I was on the open walkway, a Jane behind me like my Siamese twin, looking nearly identical to all the others: tall, blocky like retired wrestlers but dressed in t-shirts and suits, like nightclub bouncers, with short crew cuts. We were walking now, both out of breath. A side-glance showed that Riley and Wade had disappeared behind a building. Before they did, they had been running in sync, side by side. I saw them.

Allies?

"So just curious," I said, leaning my head back behind me, "you wanted me the whole time or just consented to take me instead of Wade because I was the slow, out-of-shape one?"

"You were already informed, by Jose, that you had twenty-four hours to deliver the object to us. I'm the collection agency."

Jose was Jane, I reminded myself. "Well, I hate to break this to you but I don't have it."

"Tell that to Jose when we see him."

"Sure I'd be happy to, and should I also tell him that the person who stole it is the one you just let get away?" I tried hard not to smile.

My ploy didn't work at first because this Jane dragged me back up to our dorm room and plopped me on Riley's bed while he searched the place, dumping piles of clothes on the floor, turning over crates. What kind of a spy did he think I was, anyway?

He picked up his cell phone and dialed. "Yeah, yeah, not here, it's not here, he says Wade took it. Right."

"Let's go." He pulled me into the stairwell by the collar, then smiled when Mandy Pierce from across the hall came out and lumbered downstairs with a basket of laundry.

"Hey Zak," she said in her raspy, lilting voice and sprang down the stairs in pink sweatpants.

I had sort of fallen in love with Mandy the first time I saw her, knowing full well that the Mandys of the world never went for intellectual brooding types like me. Still, her friendliness was a tiny bright speck in my heart on an otherwise dark day and I loved her for those pink sweatpants. At the landing, she looked up, not at Jane but at me this time and only me, looking at my face, seeming to understand that I might be in danger, yet careful not to look at Jane even for a second to let on that she knew or noticed something. That look told me that she was not just book smart but clever, wily, street-smart, and she might be someone I could trust if I ever needed someone other than Riley, down the road. Maybe not too far down either.

⁕ ━━ • • • ━━ •

By now I was handcuffed, doubled over in the backseat of the black SUV, same as earlier this week, with someone else in the front interrogating me.

"No, I don't know where the journal is or the item I kept in the journal—no, same answer. It was stolen by Wade," I maintained.

They weren't buying the story. I not only didn't care about that but I also didn't care that I'd essentially thrown Wade under the bus. I knew they'd been watching us, so they might suspect that I mailed the notebook to myself to keep it from being taken. So stories about Wade or anyone else stealing it was just a diversion from the obvious truth.

Here I was in the backseat, hands cuffed behind me, and Jane #2 standing guard outside the car awaiting further instructions from his superior. All the windows were rolled up, only single students walking silently past us in both directions, but I heard voices. From where?

Right, the radios! I'd almost forgotten that mine was still on my belt with the volume turned almost all the way down. Riley must have kept it on after ditching the trench and rethreaded the speaker through the sleeve on his sweater. Smart. Keeping my head aimed straight ahead, I kept my eyes on my captor outside the car. I pulled my left shoulder forward to bring my hands to the side, fumbling with the radio's volume button to turn it a half-inch in one direction, hoping it was the right one. The conversation was mid-sentence. Their voices sounded almost identical. I kept my head leaned forward but my eyes peeled toward my chaperone in front of me.

...*pretty good shape.*

Thanks, track team in high school. How about you? You're not even out of breath.

Hehe...good lungs. I guess.

You know we never actually met, I've just seen you around the floor. I'm Pat Riley.

You don't seem like a Pat.

Patrick.

Don't seem like that either.

So like what are you running from?

My, you know, employers, benefactors, johns, whatever.

John? They pimp you out? To who, and for what?

(Long pause here, the sound of a motorcycle in the background.)

Zak told you what happened the other night?

Yeah.

That.

Um..what?

(another pause)

I'm running because I owe them something. Or more like someone.

Owe who?

You know, the fat guys in suits. The same ones that're after Zak.

What do they want from you?

(another pause)

Okay. am I maybe asking the wrong questions?

I owe them...another Zak, and I was thinking it might be you. I'm sorry.

What? I don't understand. I thought...Zak told me he went with you to this guy's house, Jose or something, and Jose gave him ayahuasca and stayed with him all night and supervised his, ya know, trip, and he was horribly sick and it was a terrible experience, yada yada. Was there some other part of it Zak didn't tell me?

(pause)

You know what he...got...right?

Yeah, this stupid journal, a cash receipt from a bookstore and a whole lotta trouble ever since.

That's the scam.

I don't— Wait—

That's what they do, these people. They find college freshmen, sophomores maybe, but usually freshman who are totally overwhelmed with school and need to blow off steam. They give them this magical hallucinogenic experience...you know... a span of like eight or ten hours when they're like super suggestible, impressionable, you're like a freakin' sponge in that state, you'll believe any fucking thing anyone tells you, and everything has like monumental meaning. You see conspiracies everywhere.

Okay, okay—but you're saying they really do exist? I mean, is that what

they're doing, like they do this to lots of people?
(pause)
Yeah.
They did it to you?
Yeah.
Did what exactly?
(Sigh) They made me break into a gas station convenience store, and they have it on video. I could lose my academic honors, I'm on the soccer and basketball teams. I have a lot to lose I guess.
Whoa.
Yeah.
So what do they want from you? Why are you running?
I have to bring them someone, another, well…victim, every week. I gave them Zak and that didn't go as planned.
What do you mean? He's okay, isn't he? I mean no long-term damage, right?
He found something that night, something he shouldn't have (Wade was whispering now), he sort of, (another pause) stumbled onto another scam, but it's not theirs, and now they need to either shut it down or explain away their exposure.
Exposure? I don't understand. Who's exposed, and explain it to who?
I'm sorry, I can't say anymore right now. You'd better take off. I know they're watching me, they're watching all of us and they've probably guessed that I'd pegged you as next.
Jesus. There's no fucking way.
There's a way you can prevent it.
Yeah, fucking give them someone else! I've never so much as smoked a cigarette in my life. I know I'd never come back from something like that. Zak's much stronger than I am, I'm fragile by comparison, just ask him he'll tell you.
You can work for them.
Or I can report them.
(laugh) To who? What would you say? Do you have any proof?
No. What about Zak's code?
Have you seen it? Like the actual numbers?
Well, yeah, he showed it to me but they weren't on there.
What do you mean?
The numbers weren't visible on the back of the receipt. Zak only saw them because that professor ran it through some imaging equipment and the numbers became visible. I never saw them, only Zak did.
He knows what they are?
Um…he knows…

NINETY-FIVE

Has he memorized them, the numbers?! (Wade's yelling)

I-I-I don't know if he has or not. Probably, or knowing him he wrote them down somewhere. Why does that matter? Anyone with an infrared thermography detector could get them to display again.

What does Zak think they are?

Some kinda code. What do you think they are?

Leverage.

CHAPTER EIGHTEEN

Jesus, it smelled like damp swim trunks in here and my heart was pounding so hard I swore my captor could hear it outside the SUV. Lucky for me, the windows were tinted, because while Riley was taking Wade's confession, I used the Cross pen in my pocket to release the locking mechanism on my handcuffs. Now I was just waiting for my personal Jane to step away from the car so I could escape. While he had his back toward me texting someone, I pre-opened the rear passenger door so it would just push open when I was ready.

Another bit of luck: the SUV was elevated, so I could essentially just roll out and dodge past an oncoming car in the opposite direction and head for the nest of trees surrounding us, provided I didn't become roadkill in the process. My Jane had taken three inadvertent steps toward the other thick of trees. Was it far enough? Would he hear the door, or my footsteps? Another car drove, slowed, then drove off, the pattern of which caused my Jane to turn, glance at me still in the backseat, then turn back to his text message.

Now! I said to myself, pushed open the rear door with the tip of my sneaker, slid out, set (not clicked) the door closed, and waited, praying he wouldn't see the empty back seat and hoping for another, here it was, car to drive past. Thank God! I managed to slip to the other side of the road before the car drove past, using the time of its passing to make my way to the edge of the tree line. Now, by the time my Jane saw the empty back seat, I'd be already running toward the other side of the tower and the east side of campus. I decided not to call Riley for fear of Jane hearing my voice and tracking me. I tried to text while I was running, my ears peeled for sounds coming from behind me.

Dude, you there?

Did you hear all that? I had a feeling

Aggornstrove

Come again

Sorry running yes where can we meet off campus

I ran twelve steps before Riley responded.

Koi pond Osaka Gardens, in Jackson Park

Uber?

Uber, see ya when I get there

I booked a campus Uber, which meant they were supposed to be trawling around waiting for calls. It took twenty minutes and was nearly dusk by the time I got there. The Osaka Japanese Tea Gardens offered a perfectly concealed spot near the koi pond under a canopy of Japanese maple trees. On another day, in another context, it might be beautiful. Like postcard-worthy. Today, though, nothing more than security.

I sat under one of the maples watching the sun's glow on the still water change from golden to dark orange, brooding about my decision for the yage trip, appalled by what I'd heard through the radios. Thinking back to our arrival here, wide-eyed from NYU, a fresh start, an academic do-over, I could barely recognize my life now, and I sure as hell couldn't go back to our dorm room. I recognized the flat slap of Riley's Converse sneakers on the walkway.

"Hey," he said, and sat beside me on the ground, seeming, as always, to sense my mood.

I could honestly not think of a thing to say right now. The sky was finishing its last bites of daytime, the sun sinking behind the horizon as the color went gray.

"We could go to the police?" Riley said, as a question, and then thought better of it.

"No matter how fantastic the story, no matter how much proof we have, they would only listen up until the point of 'ayahuasca' and then lump us in a category with meth dealers."

"Yep," he affirmed, "with one correction—we have no proof. That wasn't a phone call; they were two-way radios. Untraceable."

"Right. What about Wade?" I asked.

Riley jerked his head. "Wade?? Jesus! What about me? He said I'm next! God knows what they'll do to me when I'm under the influence of whatever they plan to give me..."

"You're not taking any yage trip, Riley. You leave that to me."

The way he looked at me with watery blue eyes reminded me of him as a kid, the one who liked hearing about other people's adventures but never hungered for any of his own.

"They're looking for drug victims I guess, I'm still trying to understand it."

"What's something you don't have very much of?" I asked him.

"Everything?" he said. "I don't have a car, I don't have— Oh, I get it." Riley stopped himself. "Money."

"Right. If they promise college freshmen money to, say, buy a car while they're high, maybe they don't realize that they have to even pay it back or when it needs to be paid back. Under the influence of something like yage, they could even get students to sign documents, like a waiver or a contract—who knows. If the victims don't have the money to pay it back, they pay it back in, what, favors? And when that realization sets in, that's where their magic begins, their currency."

"What?"

"Fear," I said.

"So they're like, what, the mob, like loan sharks? Racketeering and shit?"

I nodded. "They're engineering a sort of student debt machine. We all owe them stuff, and are paying back with each other. I feel sick."

Riley rose and started pacing, with his arms folded into his sleeves. "But what did you find?"

"I don't know. I mean—"

"But *they* know," Riley added. "Not just the receipt or whatever number you found, but the notebook. They seem to know about that too." He sat down again. "Who are they?" he asked, moving an inch closer to me and looking back behind us. "They operate like the mob, but seem more organized, more efficient. Government? Military?"

I just shrugged and felt nauseous, suddenly, by the fear that my life as I'd known it so far…was over. "So what they want with us is…"

"The contents of your mailbox. The question…is why."

"So far I only know one person who could answer that question."

CHAPTER NINETEEN

I barely slept, not because Riley was up typing notes to himself on his phone all night and didn't turn off his volume. Click click click click. We didn't talk about the notebook or debrief yesterday's escapades at all. We'd both retreated into our tiny versions of solitude in a 10x14 room, moving around the room like cohabitating ghosts. I had enough on my mind to fill three lifetimes so I welcomed the silent space. My alarm went off seven a.m. and I dragged my tired bones out of bed. After going over the day's logistical details with Riley I hauled myself across campus.

Stavros shook my hand like an old-world professor, donning an expensive jacket that looked a size too long and way too wide. Definitely thrift store.

"I've got ten with me," I said in response to his prompt via text.

"Random, right?" he asked, with knotted brows.

"Yep, let's see." I took out ten cash receipts and fanned them like a deck of cards. "Student bookstore, cafeteria, Starbucks, Barnes and

Noble, oh, and I printed an Amazon receipt from an online—"

"Nope." Palm up. "Must be a regular cash register receipt."

"Right." I handed over the pile.

"Are they all yours?" he asked.

"No, I got three from Riley, who went off campus for a concert two weekends ago."

"That's fine, for now. Let's separate out the cash receipts, like your original, and the debit or credit ones."

I puckered my lips. "I think there's only one other that's cash."

"No problem." He laid them all out in a row on the thermography detector. I stood back as he made some calculations in his computer, set some preferences for how the text would display, and deployed the white screen on the wall. Then he pressed a green start button on the imaging machine and waited, arms crossed, both of us staring at the wall.

Riley was waiting for me in the men's room down the hall with a change of clothes and a different baseball cap. I'd instructed him not to come out or talk to anybody until I did the secret knock. The scanner turned on and moved over the surface, emitting a low frequency hum while it read the contents of each receipt.

A number, no, a series of numbers, displayed in bright red on the wall. But what interested me the most was that it was only *one* set of numbers out of ten receipts. Why?

"These are the credit/debit receipts?" I asked.

"No. It's all of them."

"What—do you mean?"

"Don't you get it?" he asked in a lower volume.

I didn't. "Why is there only one set of numbers on the wall?"

"No, no, no, you're looking at it the wrong way," he said. "This is terribly interesting, not just interesting but fascinating, astounding what you have somehow uncovered. You've *now* got more than just a one-off, more than a single anomaly." He stepped back.

"Well, we've got ourselves a data set."

•——••••——•

I called Riley out of the men's room and we just sort of sat back and watched. I introduced them and Stavros brought out his team of pre-geeks, a few years younger than us, high school maybe. They argued at the white board drawing circles, writing fractions, erasing things, yelling, pointing, and this went on for an hour, resulting in what we were now looking at: a white board filled with gibberish.

"Is it time for breakfast now?" Riley asked me.

"Sorry." Stavros looked sheepish, glaring at his young students. "You see, we've—"

"You're statisticians, right?" I asked.

Eight bleary eyes glared at me.

"Aren't you?" I pressed. "Sure, you might look like high school kids but I'd bet my life all of you have done work already for the NSA and have already been accepted at MIT."

Fingers pointed to the one in the middle. "He has," the other two said in unison.

"And you two stay up every night disproving Euclid's Infinitude of Primes theorem," the one in the middle said to the other two.

"I did prove it. It's not infinite," the middle guy replied.

"So…you guys are calculating the probability that if a set of 9 numbers appears on one receipt, and then now a second receipt, how many other receipts have a similar number," I suggested in my most intelligible voice.

"Right," one of them replied. "It's nearly impossible to know with any degree of certainty how many receipts exist in the world. I mean, even if we exclude global commerce and consider just within Chicago, that would still depend on too many variables."

They pulled a wheeled whiteboard away from the wall and had already written the two sets of nine numbers on them, and one of Stavros' minions stared at the data set while the other two worked on an in-progress proof, arguing about someone named Riemann.

Stavros, the translator, turned to Riley and me. "Infinite series theorems are only applicable if you're summing the numbers in the series, and we can't say whether the numbers are conditionally convergent or could be arranged in permutations…because so far we can't prove that it's an infinite series."

I had no idea what this meant, and I knew Riley was only thinking about food at this point.

"For now, it's just a series," one of them replied.

"No…two series," another corrected.

I'd written down the numbers, which reminded me of the notebook sitting in my mail slot. Had enough time elapsed for me to retrieve it yet, or do it safely?

We took several breaks while the theory development was in progress. We went to two classes each, ate in the cafeteria separately, constantly looking behind us en route, changing into different clothes every two hours. The whole thing felt ridiculous and nerve wracking, and I wasn't paying attention to anything other than getting back to the safety of Stavros' lab.

We met back there at 4 p.m. It was already getting dark. Riley and I knew we couldn't go back to our dorm. I looked up at Stavros looming over his young students and saw his compassion for them, his affection for their efforts. His presence felt so comforting tonight, I didn't want to leave. I wanted his genius team to leave so I could tell him our story, tell him how I felt fear every day now. Instead, I went into the men's room to change clothes again, not bothering to hide it from anyone. I came out wearing different pants, a football shirt, and a baseball cap. I half hoped one of the geniuses would ask me about my attire so I could hear the answer out loud.

In the hallway on my way back to the lab, I skidded to stop myself from colliding with a girl who had materialized out of thin air. I peered out from the men's room door and saw half of her face behind a wall. Mandy Pierce, the one person around whom I actually cared how I looked. "Hey," I said. "How're you doing?"

She narrowed her hazel eyes, hair in a ponytail today. She looked good, though I could tell she hadn't tried to look good today. She didn't need to try.

"I'm wondering the same thing about you."

She stressed the 'you' as if she could tell I wasn't quite myself, and God knows I wasn't, but I'd barely said more than ten words to her since arriving on campus. Even so, it was as if both of us sensed that our fates had some sort of divine entanglement, some larger plan that we would know each other better, deeper than just passing greetings on the stairs. Was this the door that would lead to that other place? Was she looking at me that way now? I couldn't tell, but I was too afraid to move or do or say anything, so I just waited, standing in my football shirt.

"You know, some people know what you're doing right now," she said quietly.

"You mean the math lecture I've just come from? It's not a secret,"

I said, typically protecting myself with the sarcasm pivot. She was unfazed by this attempt. Three steps closer to me and I could smell her shampoo. Give me strength.

"And other people know where you're going."

"Really? Well, could you tell me? Because I have no fucking idea about anything right now."

Tight-lipped, face grave, Mandy Pierce merely shook her head left and right, as if to say no I can't tell you anything at all but watch your sorry ass.

———————

"Is that you in there?" Stavros bent down to have a look under my cap. "It's not Halloween yet...what are you doing?"

"Staying alive," I mumbled and headed toward the door, checking back for Riley who was talking to Stavros' protégés.

Stavros met me at the door and grabbed my elbow. "You know, I only just now realized that...you look terrible. Have you eaten anything today?"

"Barely," I admitted.

"You guys live here on campus, right?"

"We did until today," Riley chimed in behind me. "Now we're sort of...is there a word for it?"

"We're fine, we'll check back with you tomorrow," I said, "and text me if you come up with—"

Stavros slid in front of the door blocking us. "Wait. I think you guys are coming home with me."

CHAPTER TWENTY

"You see, Carla's a genius," Stavros explained of his double Ph.D. girlfriend, who had skipped the fifth grade and went to MIT at sixteen, as we drove in his car out of the Applied Sciences parking lot. I didn't really hear anything after that due to a singular distracting thought. Riley was in the front passenger seat, Stavros driving, with me in the back behind Stavros. The configuration of passengers wasn't as important as the fact that this was the same car I'd been handcuffed in four hours ago.

WTF?

My heart pounded so loud in my chest I was sure Stavros could hear it. Now, I could spend the next week applying all the basic elements of logical reasoning to the situation, not to mention the most obvious facts, like:

    1. Stavros wasn't out of breath when I saw him.

    2. Stavros wasn't even remotely the same build as my Jane-captor, or the latest one…any of them come to think of it, not

to mention his hair.

3. There were no visible or obvious commonalities between Jane's house and Stavros' lab.

But none of those facts were as compelling as the nearly asphyxiating odor of damp swim trunks. The seat felt the same under my butt, the same nondescript black SUV. How could this be?

I pretended to listen to Stavros talking about his genius software developer girlfriend who had just invented a clone of the SMART notebook that wri—

"What the…Jesus! Riley? I—oh my God—"

We were hit, driver's side. We spun around three, maybe four times, said my roiling stomach, and stopped in a violent screech and thud. But I had this sensation of waiting for something. Stavros' car was smashed and pushed onto the shoulder of the frontage road near the Cumberland Street exit ramp off Interstate 90. I heard a car rushing up to us, I reached around to unplug my seatbelt with one hand and, with the other, reached forward to grab Riley's arm.

"What happened?" Riley shouted.

I looked left. The car coming up to us…wasn't stopping. Was it the same car coming to impale us again? "See if Stavros is breathing, and put the emergency brake on," I said.

"Dude, your seatbelt…"

But before I could put it on again I'd braced myself by holding onto the bottom part of the backseat, staring out to my left. Oddly, a third car collided with the assailant vehicle before it could hit us again. I had to be watching a movie or something. The demolition car screeched alongside us pushing us even farther into the shoulder, bouncing the rubber tires up and then down again, by then the first car screeched off down an adjacent dirt road and the Samaritan car tailing it. I felt sick.

"We need to get out of here. Zak, can you hear me?"

I think my forehead hit the back of Stavros' seat and everything looked cloudy. "See if Stavros is okay," I said.

"He's hurt." Riley climbed over the gear shift to investigate.

"Grab his phone, see if you find Carla's number."

I heard whispering up front, Stavros was mumbling something, and I heard him calling someone. Riley grabbed the phone from him.

Amazing how quiet the world became outside of the urban hubs. Side of the road, late at night in a broken-down car and injured was an interesting feeling. Normally cars brought a cocoon of safety, until you've been hit and the left side's completely caved in. After about fifteen minutes, a white car, looked like a Prius, parked directly in front of us. A woman got out. I tried to open my door but the collision had crimped the metal around the door opener, so I crawled out the right side and worked on getting Riley out. Carla, I assumed—I could barely see her—was tall like Stavros, whispering something in his ear.

"She called 911," Riley explained.

"Are you okay?" I asked.

"Who the fuck was that? They hit us twice, well, tried anyway."

"I want to know who prevented the second collision," I said, "and where all of them are now. There's not a car in sight."

I walked around to the driver's side and stood behind Carla. "Is Stavros okay?" I asked.

She turned quickly and glared at me.

"I'm Zak," I explained, like that would explain anything to her.

But she listened and stepped back, folded her arms and looked at me to assess the situation. "Do you know who hit you? Was it random, do you think?" she asked, her eyes filling up again.

No I didn't think it was random. I was sure none of us did. But before I could answer I saw red lights—no siren thank goodness—and a single EMT white van pulled up. A medic jumped out of the passenger seat. Riley, bless his heart, walked around the front of the car and introduced himself to the med tech, then to Carla, and explained the situation.

You know how the rest usually goes—they ask the family member to step aside, then perform a light-speed assessment of the criticality of injuries, and within about ten seconds another tech was wheeling a stretcher down the street to the car. It took two men almost fifteen minutes to maneuver's Stavros' large and now damaged body out of the car and onto the mobile bed, Carla trailing close behind. Wait, I thought.

"Carla?" I said plaintively to a woman I barely knew. She snapped her head back and glared suspiciously at me again. Why did it look as if she blamed me?

"You should let Riley go to the hospital with Stavros, I'll take you home."

"No. Why?"

"I know you don't even know me, but this collision was no

accident."

The EMTs stopped and exchanged glances in a silent deliberation. I was sure I'd end up at the police department tonight.

"If I'm right, for some reason, someone's intent was to cause Stavros harm. You could be in danger too. Let Riley go, he'll stay with him." I looked at Riley who nodded back to both of us. "He's been my best friend since the third grade, I trust him with my life."

And somehow, that last statement pulled this woman, Carla, out of her fear zone and she saw me now, and Riley, for the first time.

"Call me when you get there," she said to Stavros, who only nodded at this point, oxygen mask over his mouth and a silver blanket covering his chest. He was in shock. So was I. But the lights from another car were now getting closer.

CHAPTER
TWENTY-ONE

So, we left Stavros' broken-down vehicle on the frontage road. Riley rode in the back of the ambulance, and I rode in the passenger seat of Carla's white Prius. She sort of looked like him, like a prettier, refined version of him, but still tall with dark hair pulled back and Basque-features. I loved the freckles on the top of her nose. They made her look a little less serious.

"The EMTs said he's gonna be fine," I said, yet not sure of anything right now.

"He told me about you," she said. "Zak Skinner. He said you know things."

"Really?" I laughed sheepishly, playing the part of a clueless college student. In just five or six turns, we were rolling down an unusually wide, tree-lined street with two-story brownstones on each side. She did an effortless parallel park job, then stood outside for a few awkward moments. No doubt she was looking for the man she loved, and bewildered to only find me. I followed her up the front stairs, which were grand and wide with sturdy handrails. Not that I expected a flimsy apartment, but this was beyond a home; more of an estate. A Persian rug in the foyer covered a beautiful floor, a stained-glass lamp on a marble side table, chandelier above our heads. On a professor's salary. Sure.

Carla shrugged out of her white coat and let it fall on the back of a kitchen chair, where she folded forward with her head on the table. I went deeper into the room, found two glasses, and filled them with water. Blankets and water for treating shock, I remembered from last year's CPR training. I sat in another chair diagonally across from her, just staring off, wondering. Had someone just tried to kill us tonight, kill me, or kill Stavros? Carla would be asking that question, if not with her words then with her eyes.

She kept getting up, moving into different rooms, returning with things like plates and glasses, this time with two small snifters half filled with what looked like cognac or brandy.

"I made soup tonight too." She smiled for the first time, showing perfectly straight, white teeth. "Let's start with this first."

She swigged it down in one long gulp. I hated brandy. I also hated coffee but loved it the other day. I took a polite sip. Then another. It burned my throat. I liked the burn. "Guess I needed that."

She avoided my eyes like she somehow blamed me for the car wreck. I had logical reason to assume Stavros was complicit in Janes' crimes against me over the past three weeks. He lived in a mansion, and anyone could reasonably conclude that he was now connected to one of the Jane-mobiles. Now that car would go to an impound lot where it would await insurance company judgment of its market-worthlessness, probably to be sold to salvage. I had to find that car in case it contained some evidence of what I've found, and the object of Jane's search.

I mentioned the house to break the awkward tension. How long have you lived here, did one of you live here first, have you done any renovations, that sort of thing. She replied with a few dismissive yes/no's while moving around the kitchen.

"This was my grandfather's house," she said. "He was born in this house. I feel him everywhere."

While I'd prepared a "none of this is my fault" speech ready on my tongue, I couldn't say it, I guess because I didn't believe it. I did feel responsible, for Stavros and whatever snowball I had inadvertently launched toward hell.

The doorbell chimed. Carla's panicked face told me that Stavros getting run off the road might not have been an uncommon occurrence for them. She looked at me like I might have been expecting someone.

"Want me to answer it?"

"I'll get it," she said but the door opened itself. Several sets of footsteps pummeled the foyer. It was Stavros' young wizards from Applied Sciences.

"Yo dude, we need you." One of them gestured for me to follow. I looked back cautiously at Carla, who had a semi-smile on her lips.

"You know these guys?" I asked.

"They do that. Show up, run down the basement stairs, arguing over math problems all night. Sometimes Stavros comes upstairs to bed. More times not." Her hand moved to cover her eyes.

"He will again soon," I said.

The three geniuses stood in a semi-circle in the dark living room.

"Is this, like, a séance?" I asked. "Don't you need salt and sticks and white chalk?"

Not amused. They traded glances and finally one of them, a different one this time, spoke up. "We think we know what your code is. But we can't talk here."

CHAPTER TWENTY-TWO

Carla must have been used to these guys because she didn't bat an eye when they stomped in and whisked me down their creepy basement stairs. I waited on the bottom step in pitch darkness. "Um…" I said to break the silence.

Someone giggled.

"Do it."

"Hurry up, show him."

"Um…" I started again, "maybe I should go back…"

Just then the walls lit up one by one, first in a light gray flicker brightening gradually to a dim medium blue hue, they were beautiful in their orderly succession, starting at the left, then in the middle, and up the other side in a rectangular room that looked like the size of my parents' whole house. We were surrounded by a perimeter of low, blue lights with stainless steel cabinets. Between them were what looked like electronic white boards, the kind you can save as a JPEG before erasing the content. Not exactly your typical basement. What the hell did they do down here?

"This is Stavros' office?" I asked, not afraid to show I was impressed.

"He lets us work down here whenever we want." One of them flicked on a brighter overhead light and revealed a set of three whiteboards filled with mathematical notations. They were at attention facing me, all three. I couldn't help but feel intimidated.

"I don't even know your names," I said.

"You never asked."

Touché.

"I'm Carson," said the shortest, and the least friendly, guy.

"Chris." The one on the other end pointed to his chest. "And he's Dugger," Chris gestured to the tall guy in the middle. All wearing Coke-bottle glasses, Chris and Dugger had a sort of friendliness, almost happiness behind grim expressions. Carson, the short one, looked wary.

I wondered about Riley at the hospital. The one named Chris distracted me and moved to a whiteboard. I squinted to make it out.

SCLICLRUHOBHFPRNVHELI

"What is that? I asked.

"Dugger has an idea." Chris looked at Dugger, waiting for the go-ahead.

Dugger nodded.

"He thinks it's a Reece Cipher," Chris said.

Carson shook his head.

"Is that…bad?" Clearly I didn't belong here. Everything I knew about cryptography could fit in the palm of my hand.

"No. It just hasn't been used in like a hundred years."

"Why not?" I asked Carson.

"People died," Chris said. "The cipher worked but it was too dangerous, back then anyway."

I lowered myself in an office chair and realized my body hadn't been ready for my marathon run earlier. My butt and thighs ached. "So you think now someone is using it to imprint unreadable codes on store receipts?"

"Not unreadable," Dugger corrected me. "I can read them. But the result isn't an answer. It's another question. Get the poster," Dugger said to Chris, who moved to another computer.

I could tell no one gave orders to Carson and couldn't help feel interested in their group dynamics, jealous of their self-direction and ambition.

They tacked up a poster of the Periodic Table of Elements. Dugger stood beside it, the other two seated, and he used a laser to point to a square in the top left.

"Each square describes four features of a specific chemical element. For example, Titanium's atomic symbol is Ti, its atomic number is 22, and the atomic mass listed below, 47.9."

"Okay, how does that relate to my two receipt codes?" I asked.

"I think the letters correspond to atomic symbols." Dugger smiled and waited.

Was Stavros dying in this moment? Where was Riley, and why was there no ventilation in this basement?

"Frederick Reece was a chemist and a mariner," Dugger said. "A Merchant Marine, to be precise. Around 1916 after World War I broke out in Europe, Reece was on a navy transport ship in the North Sea and discovered where an enemy ship would be docking and wanted to inform his superior officer so they'd be waiting for it when it docked. But his message had to be encrypted in a code that the enemy (and there were many at that time) wouldn't be able to decipher. Being a chemist, Reece thought of hiding his message inside the periodic table to encode his message, knowing that he'd had many conversations about chemistry with his superior officer, told him about Dmitri Mendeleev who discovered the periodic table, and how they'd laughed about how useless his chemistry knowledge was at sea."

"Dude, how do you remember all that like off the top of your head?" Chris asked, incredulous.

"He has a photographic memory," Carson explained.

Dugger gave a 'whatever' fling of his wrist. "So, Reece sent a message that said something like this."

Dear Sir,
SCLICLRUHO, BHFPRNVHELI.
D. Mendeleev

"His captain, who was stationed on another ship at the time, apparently understood that the reference to Mendeleev was telling him to run the code through the periodic table. So, he took the first two letters, SC, and cross-referenced it with Scandium. The atomic number of Scandium is twenty-two. Next, Li—Lithium, atomic number three.

See where I'm going with this?"

I nodded. "So, you ended up with a series of numbers…"

"Two sets, yes, both nine digits each." Dugger gave us a minute.

"Dude, we already know what it is, we spent all afternoon in here with you," Carson said.

"Okay sorry," Dugger replied, looking at me. "What would you think a set of nine numbers might represent?"

"Phone number, social security number, lots of things."

"Keep going…"

"Jury participant code," I said, instantly causing raised eyebrows.

"Really?" they asked in unison.

"My dad's a judge," I explained, feeling a slight pain in the center of my chest as I said it.

"Why does everything have to be a quiz?" Carson complained. "Just tell him."

"Location," I blurted, thinking. "He's trying to tell his captain where an enemy ship will be, so they could presumably…bomb them I guess? So, do the numbers correspond to GPS coordinates? Longitude and latitude for that location?"

Three faces stared back with admiration. I'd apparently just been inducted into their little club of geekdom. Scary.

"Well done," Carson said in earnest that time.

"So, the Reece Cipher can be used to pull GPS coordinates through the periodic table to come up with corresponding letters, which together spell gibberish but that's the point I guess."

"Right."

"So then the letters are used to send a coded message leading the recipient to the Periodic Table to decode the numbers?"

Dugger nodded.

"So, I have two receipts that—"

"You have four actually," Dugger said, quietly.

There was one of those pregnant pauses then, with all of us actively participating in the act of not talking, observing some sort of new truth that was taking form right before us, something we all acknowledged.

"We took the other dud receipts and ran them through a plasmatic grating filter," Dugger explained, "and came up with two more, different codes but the same format, same number of letters, so we have to assume it's using the same cipher."

"No one's run it through the key though yet…" Carson said. "We were waiting for you."

"Do it," I answered, somehow feeling like the first two were flukes but now with four, two full sets of coordinates, it was more real than before. Maybe too real.

* ———— • • • ————— •

Chris opened a MacBook on the main desk area, which was set up as an island workspace that went all down the center of the room. Dugger was building two sets of coordinates from both sets of codes and wrote them on a clean corner of the whiteboard:

42.246218

-70.903333

The second set:

42.151633

-71.129883

Dugger returned to teaching mode. "Coordinates indicate the distance of a point from known references, like a big grid system. For latitude, that known reference is the equator, and longitude uses the prime meridian. Each coordinate is broken down into three parts—degrees, minutes, and seconds, the latter two corresponding to distance, not time."

He went on to explain what I already knew, while I considered where these receipts were leading me, how this related to David Wade and the Janes.

What the hell happened to Riley? I texted him for the second time while Dugger was on the calculations.

"Latitude degrees are 69 miles, longitude 42 miles."

Dude, did you make it there?

Affirmative

Stavros?

Bruised rib fracture to L elbow, should be released tonight maybe tomorrow

Jesus

There's more

What?

Jane

There?

One of them, and he seems to be standing guard

I thought about this a minute, listened to a bit more from Dugger and wondered why they were guarding Stavros and from whom.

Dugger had gone back now to the periodic table poster to run the two sets of coordinates through them. I was nodding my head doing my listening impression while he projected a superimposed image of a map of Chicago over a blank whiteboard next to it. I could see two red dots.

"They're *here?*" I asked in disbelief of the sets of coordinates.

"Where'd you think they would be?" Chris asked.

"I don't know. I guess, maybe, another country, the middle of the ocean or something? I mean why go through the trouble of imprinting a cipher on store receipts if it's leading to your fucking backyard?"

"Depends on what's *in* the backyard," Chris replied.

"It might not be our backyard," Carson said.

"Where are they?" I asked.

"West Elmwood and Pilsen," Dugger said. "Pretty rough neighborhoods, but—"

"Pilsen's not bad," Chris argued. "Reminds me of The Mission in San Francisco. Amazing food, amazing street murals…"

"You mean graffiti," Dugger countered.

"We disagree on that subject," Chris explained.

"All subjects," Carson added. "Look, I'm just saying that these coordinates are likely a door and the beginning of something, not the end."

Door. That word again. I moved closer to the wall map. "Do we have exact addresses?"

Chris pointed. "Yep. And I know someone who lives in Pilsen."

"I thought you weren't allowed to leave your mother's house," Dugger joked.

"We rented our downstairs apartment to this videographer from Pilsen. He moved out a month ago to go back to his old place. He took me there and showed me his recording equipment and video studio."

"What else did he show you?" Dugger smirked. "And whereabouts in Pilsen?"

Chris squinted at the map. "Right around— "Whoa. Mike's studio's a block from there."

All of us stared at the map now.

"I need to go," I said. "Stavros has a bruised rib and a broken elbow, and—"

"Shit, no tennis this week," Dugger said.

Carson shook his head. "That's all you can say about that?"

"I need to tell Carla he's alright, and go and meet them there. What are you guys gonna do?"

"Go check out the 'hood."

CHAPTER
TWENTY-THREE

It was dark, I was driving a strange woman's car, I didn't know where I was going and the best part—Carla was still crying. What's worse is that I couldn't even apply my superhero comforting skills that I learned from my mother because I was driving. Hugging, listening, eye contact, speaking softly. I'd been trained by a pro in this special art and was therefore singled out among all my peers. I was almost yelling now because her car motor was loud.

"He'll be fine, he's getting great care," I managed to say while she sobbed, shaking.

I asked Riley via text if it was safe to bring her upstairs, but there was no response. Carla was getting out of the car and I so wished for daylight right now. Too many shadows, too much uncertainty about Janes lurking behind cars and buildings. I tried Riley again.

Dude??!!

Still nothing.

"Follow close behind me, okay?" I said it like a command. Carla stared back with red eyes. "If someone wanted to harm Stavros tonight, I'll help you find out why but we need to keep you safe in the meantime."

"It's about his equation," her voice quaked.

"What are you talking about?"

"That's why you guys were hit. That's what they want."

I shook my head. "Who's they? What equation?"

We were now out in the open, accessible to anyone.

"Someone's been following Stavros for weeks," she whispered. "A black van with tinted windows. He knows about it but hasn't told anyone but me."

"Why? Did someone make contact or approach him?"

"Not in person," she said. "But they will. They want what he knows."

"What's this equation?"

"Stavros thinks whoever's following him thinks it's a script that could unlock the launch codes of a certain classification of missiles."

I took a second to process this unexpected information, still peering left and right every second. Launch codes. "Stavros was developing th—"

"Of course not. He's been approached by the DoD, DOE, the State Department. He wants no part of any government operation because he knows whatever work he does will end up weaponized. He's come up with an equation related to transcendental numbers and e. "

She searched my eyes and seemed to conclude I had no idea what she was talking about.

So, she added, "Euler's number, e, is probably the most famous irrational number. It lives somewhere between 2 and 3. But Stavros thinks of it as a sort of portal, like pi," she paused. "Stavros thinks it's some kind of door. He's basically spent his career so far trying to extrapolate where those doors lead, and in the case of e, he thinks he's found something. Shortly after he did, people started, well…watching him."

"Launch codes," I mumbled. "Why would Stavros' door have anything to do with—"

My phone buzzed. Text from Riley, finally.

All good here, c'mon up, 3rd floor recovery

"Let's go, we'll talk on the way." I touched Carla's elbow.

But there was no more talking. Carla was now consumed with

getting to Stavros' room, which I focused on trying not to get shot, maimed, or attacked on the way.

Riley's shape stood outside a room at the end of the hall on the left. I led the way with Carla two steps behind me, scanning the corridor in both directions.

"Hi." Riley nodded soberly to Carla and widened the door to let her through.

I looked back down the hall and stopped at a pair of unmistakable hazel eyes. Mandy Pierce glared from three rooms down, same side of the hall, just like in the Arts and Sciences building. She summoned me with a flip of her fingers. My first instinct was to see if Riley saw her too. Of course he knew her; she was the only hot girl living in our floor. I walked backwards toward her, my eyes still on the door to Stavros' room. *Why don't I trust her?* Then I turned toward her, not sure if she was a mirage. She emerged into the corridor in slim jeans, short boots, with an oversized red sweater obviously intending to conceal her figure. It wasn't working.

"Hey," I managed, peering into the empty room and empty bed behind her. Shame on me for thinking it. "What are you doing here?"

Mandy handed me a slim paper bag with something flat inside. *A book.* My God, I'd nearly forgotten by now the *yage* trip and Sunita and the magic notebook that...Lord, was it still in my mail slot? It all felt like a lifetime ago by now. The notebook-fairy warned that she'd get me another one. Was this it? Was Mandy Pierce...*her?*

"I'm told you'll know what to do with this." She smiled, like with her eyes and not her mouth, trying to reassure me. "No, I don't know what it is."

I loved the feel of her voice, the vibration. She didn't have any detectable accent, but there was something...I don't know, I can't explain it. I took the book, stuffed it in the back waist of my jeans under my jacket and by the time I got back to Stavros' room, Mandy was gone. I pushed the door open two inches, Riley at attention at the window, Carla draped over Stavros, who was trying to smile but looked uncomfortable.

My phone buzzed a new text. It was Dugger. *Call me back at this number*

I stepped into the hall and dialed Dugger, my new friend and lifeline. "Where are you guys?" I asked.

"You need to come down here," he said. "We're in Pilsen, we're coming to get you now."

"Do you guys even have your driver's licenses?"

"Fuck off," Dugger said. One of them laughed in the background. "Wait outside the back entrance of the hospital. We'll be there in five minutes."

"Wait," one of the others said. "Give me the phone."

"Hey, it's Chris. Mike, my former roommate, thinks he knows—" Chris's voice stopped. Mumbles turned to raised voices. "Carson said not to say it over the phone. But we found someone who can get us in."

"In?" I asked. "In where?"

CHAPTER TWENTY-FOUR

Here's how it went down: Carson, Chris, and Dugger, none of whom possessed a legal driver's license, screeched around the ER entrance of the University of Chicago Medical Center in a car I'd never seen before. Could have been stolen, probably was stolen, I wasn't gonna ask. Three of us crammed in the backseat. I tried to recall my last shower, or maybe I was smelling someone else. I asked where we were going, who we were meeting, why we were going 80 in a school zone. No one said a word.

"Here," Chris barked.

Carson screeched down a dark street with a broken streetlight. Broken beer bottles carpeted the ground. Welcome to Pilsen.

Carson parked behind what looked like a 1960's era school bus, sans tires, and Chris pointed to me, Carson, and the brick apartment building ahead.

"What. You're going in there?"

"We are," Chris replied.

"You're leaving Dugger here?" Carson asked.

"He speaks Spanish," Chris explained.

At that moment, I didn't need to even turn my head to know that the black van had followed us, presumably the same black van with tinted windows that Carla described as tailing Stavros for the past few weeks.

"Come on," Chris urged as I glanced behind us, eyeing a tall bald guy in the driver's seat.

"What about Dugger?" I asked.

"He can take care of himself."

• ———— • • • ———— •

The building smelled of wet dog and marijuana all the way up the stairs where we stopped in front of a door marked 3. Chris knocked twice, then sent a text. The door opened immediately to a long-haired, blocky guy with a beard.

"Mike?"

The guy blinked back.

Chris explained that he and Mike used to be housemates, and Mike shook his head slowly. "What?" Chris asked in a tone.

"I'm bringing you to a guy. After that, don't mention me, man. And you never come back here. Ever."

"Sorry. What guy?" I asked them both.

Mike unfolded a page where he'd apparently written our coordinates. He took a lighter from his pocket and burned the page while he looked on, me of course wondering if he would inadvertently set the room on fire.

Meanwhile, Dugger was alone in the car and I was the only one worried about him.

Mike lit a cigarette. "These two locations you've given me, they're part of a…well, a place. Sort of. I can't take you there, nor do I know much about it. But he does."

"Your contact?"

"Yeah. Brolly. He's kinda skittish so I'll only take one of you. Meaning I'll point you in the right direction and you're going in alone."

Hard stares.

"You'll have to find your own way out," he added, looking at the floor. He took another drag. "Take it or leave it, that's the best I got. You got a piece?" he said directly to me.

"Of what?"

He shook his head. Had he meant a gun?

"You mean a weapon? No."

"Godspeed, man. Up to you."

"Fuck that, how about leave it?" Chris said, glancing outside.

"I'll go," I blurted suddenly. Of course I should, right? These guys were boys, barely even college age and besides, I found the receipts (or I should say the receipts found me), which led me here. So it had to be me. And that meant some part of me had enough strength to do this. Whatever it was.

CHAPTER TWENTY-FIVE

The dude, Brolly, a tweaker for sure. Unable to sit still or stop moving for more than three seconds at a time, he spoke in a sort of performance art style. Eyes wide, long pauses, wide arm movements and weird cross stepping. Now he was biting his bleeding fingernail stubs. *Riley*, I said telepathically, *where are you?*

"So, Mike," the guy said with a feigned, gray-tooth grin.

I sighed and pulled in air for strength. "Mike seems to think you can explain something to me." I sat now at the edge of my chair, a symbol of my desire to communicate, such as it was.

"What are the addresses?" he asked.

I handed him a Post-It note. GPS locations down to the actual street numbers. The corners of his mouth twisted up, and he peered at me with a devilish grin.

"So, where are they?" I asked.

"I think you mean *what* are they," he corrected.

"Okay." I waited. The guy smelled foul. Brolly grabbed a hoodie, put it on, zipped it, and crouched in front of a bookcase in Mike's apartment. Was he praying? I half expected a genie to arrive in a puff of smoke.

"What are you searching for?" he asked.

"A...building? I'm not sure actually."

He shook his head. "That's what you're looking for. Go deeper. I mean the search. What do you need right now?" His beady eyes fluttered.

"An answer."

"Do you know the question?"

"I guess...what does it all mean?"

"Well, what does *it* look like to you? You're smart, observant, suspicious. That's a good thing."

"It looks like a big setup to me."

"Why?"

"It's just too elaborate and random. All these pieces that don't fit together."

"A broken puzzle," Brolly said.

"I don't know."

"Why the word *setup* though? Setup implies a belief in the existence of an entity behind all the events, but who's doing the setting up, and why? What do they have to gain by what's going on?"

I scrutinized his face—its movements, expressions, ticks, the eyes moving abnormally side to side.

"You think I'm part of the setup," the man said with a smirk.

"Yes."

"What if I am?"

"Jesus. What am I doing here?"

"Dude," he smiled, raising his palms. "I'm not trying to mess with you. You came to me. I'm making sure you're ready for what's on the other side of the door."

"You know that's a bookcase, right?" I asked. "Sure, I'm ready."

Brolly stared me down for a second longer than was comfortable, leaning his neck forward. Then he turned and shoved the bookcase down the wall two feet. Behind it was a wall with a recessed square in the center. He looked back at me. "No cell signal in here."

"In where?" I peered behind him but saw nothing.

He pushed at the center of the square. Then he shoved forward with his head and shoulders, half his body disappearing into the void.

The wall recessed a few inches to a pre-defined position and ended with a thunk. Brolly put his fingers inside the recessed bit and pulled that part of the recessed wall to the left, leaving an opening about two feet wide and four feet high.

"Twilight Zone, okay." I remembered the episode. "The interdimensional portal behind a little girl's bed. That was slick."

"Yeah, well, this one won't be televised."

* — •••• — •

I followed Brolly down a creepy tunnel between brick buildings. It was already dark out. We were definitely outside but it also felt contained. I looked up and saw only more brick, with a faint light. Now my dizziness mixed with slight nausea amid the stench of filth and stagnation.

The buildings were tall and close together which, with the dark sky, made for an excellent horror movie set or at the very least a dark scene in Diagon Alley. But I had no magic wand or special powers. I expected a woman to scream and Jack the Ripper to step out with a blood-soaked scythe. Get a grip, Zak. I wanted to be back with Stavros right now, to ask Riley about the Jane guarding his hospital room, then gather a hundred thousand store receipts and run them through Stavros' spectrometer to see how many were embedded with codes leading to secret addresses to the dystopic ghetto. I wanted to ask Riley, my occasional wise sage, whether my meeting with Brolly was as random as it seemed on the outside, or if we'd stumbled upon some larger scheme. Was the scheme about me, or was I just one of its hapless pawn soldiers?

Brolly, two feet ahead, wore what had at some point been expensive trousers. And I'm no haberdashery but his jacket looked like the same fabric and color. I surmised from this that he had once been legit, his body had been plumper, maybe before he became a crack addict. He stopped at a windowless door on the left.

"Home?" I joked.

Brolly pointed with a trembling hand. "This is your first address." He jerked his head to the right and waited for my reaction. I took a step forward and drummed my knuckles four times.

CHAPTER TWENTY-SIX

A guy, 35-ish, thin, dressed like a concierge, stood there. "How's it going?" he asked and moved aside. "Through here." He waved behind him.

I followed like a suspicious dog, trailed four steps back and not till I got to the middle of a long, empty room did I realize Brolly was no longer behind me.

Shit.

I remembered how dark the woods were in the middle of the night. This was darker. But I heard the thudded steps ahead, clop, clop. I kept walking, either from fear of standing still or lack of a better idea. The footsteps slowed, so I followed suit and stopped...and waited. I saw something gray ahead: the shadow of my concierge walking through a doorway as I approached. Riley, at this moment, felt too far away to reach, as in ever again, and Stavros and David Wade almost seemed like characters I'd dreamt.

I saw it now, an opening with no door, with that damp smell again, like fog, but different. I was standing in an empty warehouse in Chicago's underbelly, a million miles from school. Lifting one foot, I stepped into the nebulous gray glow and, reaching up to touch my face, I noted the miraculous discovery that I was still alive.

CHAPTER TWENTY-SEVEN

An alley, like the one I just came from, and a street twenty steps away. I approached it without looking back, half scared that the opening in front of me was a magic portal and could snap shut on a moment's whim, leaving me stuck, well...wherever I was. It smelled oddly like tar and peanuts. My host, in my fear I'd almost forgotten him, was on the other side of what looked like a normal city street with no traffic. Matter of fact, there wasn't a single car in sight, in broad daylight.

He turned to the right. I followed.

"Watch out!" someone bellowed. I saw only wheels and hair, then noticed the bicycle. I heard a motor behind me, an orange moped, not like the old Vespas but newer with a narrower frame. I trained my eye on the warehouse man on the other side of the street. Could this still be considered Chicago? Every direction had a bicyclist carrying paper-wrapped parcels. I had to have stumbled onto a movie set or something. No pedestrians and no cars implied a sort of nexus of the future and past, but with tar and peanuts. What might have otherwise been an interesting field trip, my elusive host was my only ticket back.

"Rand," he explained, finally.

His name? No handshake. "Want a drink?" He motioned me to a tent on the corner of two streets.

My eyebrows permanently knotted together at this point. Walls made of tarp, bed sheets as a ceiling, dirt floors. How had I been transported to Peru, or Mexico, or World War II Europe?

"Did someone take the building that used to be here?" I followed pavers set precariously atop the dirt floor toward a misplaced, polished, granite counter. A man rose from under it and now I was certain I was at the circus.

No elephants.

"Can I make you a latte?" he said.

I laughed. I couldn't help it. "Suddenly Starbucks?"

The man, blond hair down past his waist, pointed over his head to a large Starbucks sign made of paper. No, made of about forty-five, 8-1/2 x 11 sheets of paper crudely taped together to simulate a sign. Right.

"Latte. Sure," I said, feeling around the back of my pants and not finding my wallet. Wait—it was in my jacket pocket.

Rand, my escort, stepped up. "Hey, my treat."

I was certain my coffee cup would be a) empty, b) filled with dishwater, c) toilet water, or d) cyanide. I nodded at the escort, but now the guy behind the counter had changed to a teenaged girl thin enough to blow over with a sneeze. She was wearing a dirty white apron. She constructed my latte with what looked like shiny, new, official Starbucks coffee brewing equipment, staring at me the whole time with large, terrified eyes.

"It's okay," I said. "I already know you're about to poison me. I'm fine with it, really."

The waif and the hair-guy looked at each other, frozen. Then Step 2: milk frothing.

"We only have whole milk," she explained.

What kind of whole milk? Cow, goat? Breast milk? I heard her Eastern European accent and noticed a slight space between her front teeth. Looking more closely, the hair on the right side of her head looked strange. I knew it was a wig. Why? Forgetting my escort's generous offer to buy me a poisoned coffee, I removed my wallet, with a fiver between my fingers.

The girl's jaw dropped as if I'd removed my pants. "No cash," she said whispering the second word. "BTC."

"Bitcoin?" I said aloud, which caused the waif, the hair guy, and Rand, still standing guard at the door, to swivel and stare. "What, don't say that out loud?"

"Any of those."

Those. I tried to imagine what the girl meant here, holding my expertly-constructed, hand-made, artisan-crafted latte in one hand, her fingers still on a small, black machine.

"So you take any kind of cryptocurrency?" I asked.

"Zcash, Bit, Litecoin and Ethereum," the girl said. "We're not set up for Dash and Ripple yet, and Monero's too unstable right now."

Unless I was an arms dealer, she must mean. I held up my phone. "I have my Bitcoin wallet on here, but I heard there's no connection in..." I looked around. "Wherever we are."

"No internet. But have connection." The girl took my phone, held up the Coinbase app to her machine, waited until a green dot appeared in the center, and flashed once. She handed me the latte, which incidentally tasted exactly like a Starbucks latte.

Rand was back on the street now heading in the same direction, eight steps ahead of me, looking back every few paces. He stayed in the shadows of buildings or tarp overhangs like a vampire avoiding sunlight.

"Rand!" I shouted.

He turned and slowed but kept walking.

"Where are we going?"

"Eighth Street. Keep going."

I was running now. I'd almost caught up when he turned his walk into a slow jog, still ten steps ahead. "Why no internet?" I asked.

Rand stopped, facing me head on. He leaned down to tug my right sleeve to pull me into a shadow against a gray building labeled Bank.

"There's no internet in here," he said.

"Where?"

"Look around you, where we are now."

I sipped the coffee, knowing I needed caffeine right now like a hole in the head. What I needed was water, and rest.

"Where are we? Why is there no internet connection but signal on my phone, and where are you taking me?" And how could this place possibly exist?

"Brolly sent a message that you needed to see someone."

I stared back, waiting.

Rand lowered his head. "Let me put it another way. If you're here, you must not belong there anymore." He made a twirl with his finger. "If you found your way here, you don't belong in your other world. What brought you here?"

"An idea," I admitted, thinking again of my ayahuasca trip, the fairy woman Sunita, and her premonition of my being chased by numbers.

"The only reason people from the other world end up here is if they contact someone on this side without realizing it, or if someone here contacts them."

CHAPTER TWENTY-EIGHT

So I thought about what he said and wondered about the chain of events. I told Rand that someone contacted me, because it felt like the receipt I acquired the night of ayahuasca was not accidental. My gut told me this was true, then so did Stavros and his cadre of geniuses who indirectly led me here. The numbers on the receipts were embedded with messages. I woke up one day on campus, went to class, then found myself in David Wade's bedroom wearing no clothes. I knew in my heart I didn't choose this path or reality. It had somehow chosen me.

Now we were walking again, this time side by side and at a more normal pace. There were still no cars, hardly any sounds, no birds or other animals, an occasional moped, and no foot traffic except us.

"Why would someone from here contact someone on the other side?" I asked, still piecing it together.

"To bring them over."

"What would be the payoff, even if you could get someone to

agree?"

Rand smirked. "Agree? There's no *agree* about it. No one comes voluntarily and no one comes on their own because, you know…how do you explain a place like this…a place that isn't really a place? You come here because you were forced, tricked, blackmailed, or because you lost something you wanna get back. Which is it for you?" he asked.

"Not blackmail. I'm just a miserable student. I don't have anything of consequence. Not even a car."

"Girl? Friends?"

"No, and yes, well…"

"Blackmail isn't about possessions or material wealth. It's about leverage."

I'd heard that word before.

"You have things, in your case maybe people, who mean something to you. That means you might be willing to give up something or pay something to protect them. Is that why you're here?"

I wanted to tell him everything but my instinct said otherwise. "I found an everyday thing, and when I looked closer at it, I discovered it was something else."

Rand nodded, recognizing this description. "Embeds."

"What?"

"Paper, right? Normal paper that turns out to be not normal? Strange properties, hidden information?"

"Hold on!" I stopped walking now. We were out in the open where the alien bounty hunter or Voldemort or some otherworldly villain could cast a spell upon us. I didn't care. At this moment I was closer to the truth of why my life had turned to chaos than ever before. Suddenly it seemed possible that I'd find David Wade or The Janes around the next corner. Rand knew what I was talking about. I was sure of it.

He turned but kept walking, working the power of his advantage over my sudden fear.

"What do you mean by that, not-normal paper?"

"The last one I heard of was someone taking copy paper, you know, like business reams of 8.5 x 11 paper that turned into currency after being exposed to water. Like a sheet's worth of hundred dollar bills, but somehow printed on 24 lb. copy paper."

Still walking, I considered this story, being true to Zak Skinner and searching for the holes. "How would you spend money like that if you cut it to size? If the type of paper's all wrong, you can't spend it, right?"

"You can. People do all the time. You surround the fake money with real money, bury it in a stack. It could go undetected like that for months. Years."

I needed to be seated, certainly not walking, for this kind of discussion. Maybe smoking a cigarette, or weed, drinking a beer, something to help my mind digest it.

"These embeds as you call them, they're like a type of...what..."

"A lure. A category of lures to get people over here, get them involved in the dark net and then they're—"

"The what?" I pressed.

Rand exhaled, obviously tiring of his young novice wizard, but it wasn't my fault if I was clueless. Was it? He spun, waving his hands over his head to denote everywhere. "This...is the dark net."

"You mean TOR, like human trafficking and shit?" Of course I'd heard of the dark net, even before it was on Netflix. But a real place like this? No way. My mind was no longer infirmed by the after-effects of yage, and I'd been born with enough intelligence to distinguish truth from fantasy. But Rand held the only option for getting out of here.

"They're called eepsites or 12P for invisible internet. They mainly run on TOR, the onion router of a 7000 relay underground and unregulated, surveillance-free internet site for free trade. Its US traffic is a $625 billion-dollar cloak economy. It's the dark net network that allowed you to buy your latte with bitcoin from your iPhone. Not the internet, but a different world wide web." Rand started walking again and pointed. "One more block, here."

It all looked the same—brick buildings, tarped commercial entities. I was getting it now. "Starbucks."

Rand smiled. "I saw you notice the sign."

"So, it's official Starbucks equipment, the name, the brand, even the coffee and the milk products are the same"

"Down to the filtered water. Even ice machines."

"And they're bootleg?"

"You could say that. They're official, actual commercial brand materials."

"Stolen? So everything in here is hot? Are you a fence?"

"I'm a liaison. I'm allowed to live in both places."

Allowed. Mental note: come back to that later. "What do you do in the real world?"

Rand stopped again and regarded the question thoughtfully before answering, like he knew his answer could spell the difference between life or death sometime in our future. He turned to face me, squaring off. "I'm a hospital worker."

"Is that supposed to mean something?"

"Does it?" he asked, and I knew I was failing another test. I let the words swim around in my head, the story of stolen Starbucks materials, and my brain churned through it. Someone was acquiring stolen Starbucks materials, setting up a shadow store, selling its products and not turning the money over to the corporation, not paying taxes. Who kept the money? The hairy fellow and his Elvish sister? Why would they live like that, in this place, and how much could they earn in a week or a month here? Because maybe they couldn't live in the other world, the real world. Or were they here running a Suddenly Starbucks because they were positioned for some other kind of commerce that only existed here?

Rand pointed to something ahead. "That's your next stop," he said. "Keep moving."

It was another tarp-office on the bottom floor of another empty office building, jutting out into the street. With no cars, who cares, right? But I wasn't moving. I knew I was close and wasn't letting go of this guy until he gave me what I needed. So I rewound our conversation about ten minutes. "What other kinds of embeds have you encountered?" I asked.

"Paper book jackets, bank withdrawal slips."

"Cash register receipts?"

He nodded. "Anything like that can be embedded with, well…a variety of things."

"Lures," I regurgitated back to him, still not really understanding the concept. "Why me, why now, and—"

"That I don't know. I'm just a bridge from one world to the other."

"Well what ab—"

"Lesson's over for today." His hand went up. "Your next guide's name is Mandy. Welcome to System D."

CHAPTER TWENTY-NINE

I had even more questions and less answers than yesterday, not to mention a new vocabulary and a different guide every thirty minutes. Rand pointed ahead to the only door in sight on a street emptied of cars, people, voices, with an occasional hum of a moped. Tall buildings, some with doors bolted shut, others with the doors removed, not so much as a bottle cap on the ground.

I so craved a cigarette right now, even though I hadn't smoked since high school. My next guide would be someone named Mandy. Okay, not a hugely common name, but could it be *my* Mandy? She'd been lurking around me for two weeks, appearing at the hospital, Stavros' lab, in the hallway as The Janes were dragging me down to the lobby of my building. Coincidence? I didn't believe in the Easter Bunny either.

A hand protruded from one of the open doorways and motioned me in. Not another soul could be seen outside so it had to be directed at me. I walked toward it expecting a headless horseman on the other side. The hand disappeared and the door opened further on my approach. I knew it was her. I was already falling in love with her, I knew it in my body, the way my stomach felt right now looking at her blonde hair up in a messy ponytail, her dark roots and heavy eye makeup. Half of me wanted to grab her and kiss her cinematically, leaning her backward with my arms enveloping her. My other half wanted to scream and demand an explanation for why she of all people could be involved in this dark underworld.

"Hi," she said, just like her 'hi' on the dorm staircase.

"I have nine hundred questions."

She looked behind me and closed the door a few inches, though it was still ajar. "You can't stand outside like that, just hanging out like you would on campus."

"You mean we're not in Kansas anymore?"

Fear covered her eyes today, brows contracted with a slight scowl to her lips.

"What are you doing here?" I asked.

"No. What are *you* doing here?" she hissed back in a snarl.

I relied on my new terminology to articulate this the right way. "I was lured by embeds, in a cash register receipt. There was a code, I found some people on campus to break it for me and it led to some coordinates, one of them in Pilsen. The other one somewhere in... here, well...whatever here is."

She was listening while biting her lip, deciding something.

"Who's Rand and what does he do?"

"You probably know already...if you know about the embeds."

"He said he's a hospital worker on the other side."

"He's a pharmacist at the med school."

I stood back a step, crossed my arms. "He's a smuggler," I said, only realizing it as the words escaped my mouth. "He's smuggling..."

"Keep going, but we don't have much time." Her eyes fixed on the street behind me while she spoke.

"Why not? Who's watching us, or chasing us? A hit squad? There's sure as hell no law enforcement in here."

"Follow me. We've got a half mile to your next contact."

Again, I was following someone, trying to talk to them, desperate for answers and only gathering more and more questions. At least now the view was better. It was still hard to see but it looked like she was wearing sleep pants, sneakers with no socks, and a long t-shirt with a shorter one on top. No jacket. That meant haste. Why had she hastily left her dorm room in my building to come out here today? To help me, or did she have a deeper agenda?

CHAPTER THIRTY

Mandy Pierce, my Guide-of-the-Hour, drew me deeper into the building. I closed the heavy door behind us. Again, like with Brolly, and Rand after him, I was in the middle of an empty warehouse walking in pitch blackness to an opening up ahead, this time with Mandy's hand gripping mine, dragging me forward, almost running. Her palm was sweaty, smooth skin, short half-painted yellow fingernails. On the other side was another tunnel—a dark, narrow walkway like something you'd see in a Basil Rathbone Sherlock Holmes movie, barely wide enough for two people. I wished I'd taken a shower. She stopped halfway through to listen, still holding my hand, then she let go. She crouched against the wall, while I sat on the concrete prioritizing my thoughts. I knew I had but a few minutes to extract some critical information.

I started at the top. "What's System D?"

"A part of the city that's been blocked off and only accessible through these tunnels. There are ten, all leading into different parts of this place. To get out, keep walking until you find a Starbucks tent that has the logo in the form of a flag tied around a metal pole at the very top. You'll recognize it, it's the only one like that. There's a tunnel right across the street. It leads to a spot close to campus. But don't try to come back in here if you get out, because you'll never find it."

"Why not?"

"It changes every day."

"Who changes it?"

"I don't know."

"You said 'if you get out'. What the fuck does that mean?"

No answer.

Okay think Zak, tick tock. "What's with Starbucks?"

"They're T-Centers, for transactions and trading. That's where the exchanges happen."

"And people like Rand and Brolly are, what...couriers?"

"Not Brolly. Rand, yes. You can't ship stuff from here through the post office anymore. They've gotten slick and know about the dark net and have cybercrime and cryptocurrency unit investigators now. So people use couriers lately, for the high dollar stuff."

"High dollar, like equipment?"

She snickered and shook her head. "They're not appliance merchants. Think about it. What do people really want?"

"You said Rand's a pharmacist at the medical school."

She nodded.

"He's smuggling pharmaceuticals? Jesus Christ."

"You're close."

"Street drugs?"

She shook her head and rubbed her eyes. "They're pharmaceuticals, but let's just say they're altered."

"How? They make them in here?"

She looked at her watch.

"How are they altered?"

"They're three times the normal price, for one thing, because you don't need a prescription from a doctor. And most of the time, they lack any active ingredients and are mostly Tylenol and Advil."

"They're small enough where they're easy to conceal certainly."

"Right, and a long shelf life. And it's super easy money for the sliders. All they have to do—"

"What did you say? The what?"

"The pill guys, they manufacture the pills. They pick up shop and move to a different address every few weeks. I've never met any of them."

"How long has this place been here?"

"No idea. Long time I think." She stood. "Time to go. I drop you off on the other side of this tunnel and I don't know what's next. Usually I know who the next guide is but Brolly didn't say this time."

"What's his involvement in this place?"

"You ask a lot of questions," a voice answered up ahead from the dark.

Mandy grabbed my hand, pulling me toward her and away from Brolly, who had his eyes fixed not on me but on her. "I told you to bring him quickly," he said and bent his head down close to Mandy's pretty face.

I imagined what I would do to him if he hurt her, and then checked myself at the thought of violence, remembering suddenly where I was, what I was involved in, and knowing there had to be a slight alteration to my traditional code of conduct when traveling in the dark universe of System D with smugglers and phony coffee baristas.

Brolly's hand squeezed Mandy's shoulder. Her eyelids clamped down bracing for God knows what. Rage vibrated deep in my core watching this, knowing, if I had any hopes of returning to the life I'd known before, I was at his mercy. Brolly, the practiced tactician, caught it, seeing through algorithmic eyes that sensed anything that could be commoditized. My connection to Mandy had just registered on his leverage meter. What would I do to protect her, what might I give up, or pay, or who might I harm or kill to keep her from harm?

Note to self: love = peril.

CHAPTER THIRTY-ONE

"**Take the stairs,**" Brolly instructed, still with one hand on Mandy. He pointed into the darkness. What was it about this place with all the dark buildings? But then, in that moment, I started getting it, understanding what Mandy said about a network but not the internet. If that other network worked as a sort of intranet inside this place but wasn't accessible either to or from the outside world, wouldn't that mean the other system from the outside might not work in here? Like gas and electric, for example. Gas meters for power would need to rely on Smart metering technology in order to report back usage data to utility companies, which meant the utility company would ostensibly be billing somebody, who would then be expected to pay for that service. No one would pay for that service in here, or not with US dollars anyway. So...no lights. Slowly the labyrinth of the scam sank in.

My eyes starting to adjust to the dark, I found the staircase and climbed up a level. No door this time—just an opening, where I heard shuffling. I instinctively stopped moving, wishing now that I'd taken

Mike's advice and brought something with me. Not a gun but maybe a baseball bat, or mace. Something to equalize the playing field.

"Come in," someone said. The voice sounded familiar, low and controlled.

Jane?

Something buzzed in my pocket. I took stock of exactly where I was: second floor of an old building, probably some manufacturing facility by the unfinished, rotted out interior, rusted steel everywhere, and concrete floors. I was still standing on the edge of a stairwell. Hmm. Had I cracked a code? Was there some residual, magical signal in the stairwells that somehow flew under the radar of radar-less TOR? I'd only heard brief fragments of definitions of what Mandy and Rand referred to as the dark net, being a form of the internet that was unregulated, allowing for unregulated, primarily criminal, business transactions. Was this it? Some kind of Matrix with no furniture, no cars, or human conversation?

"There's nothing to fear, Zak," the voice cajoled, attempting to pull me out of the one spot offering a link with the outside world. Could Jane see me from where he stood in the middle of the room? Were his eyes more adjusted to the dark than mine? Was he wearing night-goggles? No, he was too cool for gadgets like that. I didn't need to look at the phone, though. Who else would be contacting me, who else cared about where I was? Riley did, of course it was him. And now I had confirmation that there's a way to make contact in here. Only in the staircases. The stairs are my friends.

Now I proceeded to the middle of the floor, to await my next set of instructions.

CHAPTER THIRTY-TWO

"Where's David Wade?" I began, unsure why I even started with that question, but Wade was where this fucking rabbit hole started so maybe it was a logical place. I was still in the stairwell at that point.

"May I ask what you want with him?" Jane asked.

I was pretty sure this was Original Jane, not one of the Jane-bots. "He was running for his life last I saw him. Maybe I should ask what you want with him."

"Come in, please. I'm unarmed."

"I could use some water."

"What else?"

"How about some fucking answers!" The words shot out of me like from a semi-automatic rifle, the last words half-shouting, half-crying. I came closer, into the center of the room away from the safety of the magic stairwell, hoping there wasn't a Samurai swordsman waiting to decapitate me in one blow.

Jane took a few steps away. Then came a swishing sound. He came back and now a glow from a water cooler lit up the wall. No furniture, no rugs, but a water cooler. Whatever. I took the paper cup he handed me and gulped down the liquid like I'd been walking in the desert all day.

"Help yourself to more if you'd like."

I did and thought about sitting or lying down on the concrete floor, but this was no time for resting. I might have that chance again, to sleep in a bed, with sheets and a pillow in my dorm room with Riley, eating bad pizza watching vintage sci-fi movies, like we always did on Sunday nights.

"Is Wade a slider, or is he a runner like Rand?"

Jane tipped back his head, and I knew he was impressed by my use of new terminology. Sliders, I gathered from Mandy, were the pharmaceutical manufacturers, who manufactured capsules that looked exactly like actual, legitimate commercial drugs, but no words, codes or letters were imprinted on them. I suspected most had either inert or expired constituents. They had to get the size and color exactly right, package them up in actual packaging bottles (stolen no doubt) smuggle them back to Point A, we'll call it, then sell them for three times their normal price. From Rand I'd learned that the US has $650B invested every year in this shadow economy. What else was manufactured here, without taxes, without regulation, without overhead: guns, street drugs?

"He's a runner," Jane confirmed, like it was no sacrifice to feed me one gram of truth on the same plate as twelve ounces of lies. "But not like Rand."

* —— • • • —— •

Jane fumbled with his hands, performing some operation with an object positioned on a shelf that seemed to come out of the concrete wall. Pupils dilating finally, I could identify more detail within the sea of gray. My spine straightened. I caught a glimpse of the object—he was mixing something in a bowl. Jesus, not again, I mused, thinking only of the notebook in my pants, which they would easily detect if I were again incapacitated by one of their bootleg substances.

As much as I needed to hear about Wade, I felt overwhelmed by a desire for lights, for a private men's room stall, or a shear of sunlight to help me read the notebook stuffed down the back of my pants for the past day. Sunita, my ayahuasca fairy, combined with the SmartNotebook technology that I guessed had been developed by

Stavros' girlfriend Carla, could address a lot of my questions. But at what cost? Riley was my confirmation that Point A still existed, but there was no way to check my phone while I was here with Jane. I needed time alone to stand in the stairwell.

"Why are you here?" Jane asked.

There were only two ways I could answer: with another question in order to evade answering, or with a real answer. Fatigue conspired with gravity and pulled at my limbs, my bones toward the floor. Body and brain at dangerous levels of exhaustion, I couldn't even remember food, and Jane's cups of water only increased my hunger.

"I found two sets of coordinates on an embed from a cash receipt, the night you took me to that convenience store, the night of my trip."

His face was deadpan.

I couldn't help but laugh at the irony. "*You* sent me here. You lured me here with your little slips of paper embedded with conspiracy theories and secret codes, knowing who I'd contact for help, knowing the reality of—"

"I didn't know. Not specifically. We never do," he said in a quieter voice. "When you fish, there's a chance you'll catch something based on what bait you use, your equipment, and your technique in how you use that equipment. There are a lot of variables here, Zak. I doubt you can understand that. A lot of unknowns, constant risk, very little reward."

"You mean except for the billions of dollars your army of sliders rake in on expired pharmaceuticals?"

"That's one of our revenue streams, it's true."

This scared me. If he was admitting it to me, here out in the open, where anyone nearby could hear us, he'd obviously planned for me to never leave this place.

"There's a massive market," he went on, "among the sick population who don't have, or can't get insurance, or they have insurance but can't get the specific medicine they need to live free of pain, and I'm not talking Motrin. I mean Inositol for patients in cancer remission. Medicines to help low-income infants around the globe who are born with AIDS or cerebral palsy or blood disorders, and there's not only no insurance but no doctors, no hospitals, no clean water or infrastructure for them. And what about Chicago's homeless population? A large majority of them have untreated illnesses, HIV, dysentery, not to mention mental illnesses which, going untreated for a long per—"

I drew in a deep, quick breath and shook my head to make sure I'd heard it correctly. "Homeless people, you're saying, are the recipients of your counterfeit pharmaceuticals? How on earth would they pay three times retail for those medicines?"

"We employ them. We give them jobs, like the Starbucks you went to earlier today, where they make actual money, and—"

"Well let's be clear," I interrupted, "you don't mean *actual* money as in US currency, do you? No. I suspect you mean crypto, like bit—"

"They're not illegal, so why not?" Jane shook his head.

I laughed. "Well, okay, not illegal because your little Hogwarts Matrix isn't subject to any laws...because there aren't any. You don't have a traffic court here...because there aren't any traffic signals or stop signs...because there aren't any cars. Why? I don't know why!" I rubbed my eyes. "So okay, bitcoin and some other crypto aren't illegal but they're not regulated, so then they're not subject to our laws, not part of the legal system, not part of our democracy, the United States of America. What exactly do you call this other country you're living in? You're off the res."

"You're right," he conceded. "But you're at the very tip of the iceberg."

CHAPTER THIRTY-THREE

"Look, it's obvious I don't know your overall plan or how I fit into it. Just tell me this: Why was I summoned? I mean why me, in particular? Or was I even chosen at all? Was I just some hapless le—"

Jane put up his palm. "You were selected."

"Why?"

"There will be time for that later. For now, I need you to do something for me." He death-stared me, standing about two feet away, his finely manicured hands strategically placed at his sides, as a show of reticence, or perhaps concession. "Your coordinates."

I squinted my eyes, still watching him, trying to understand this strange request. "They led me here. You mean, you don't know where they are?"

"I need the actual coordinates, on the receipt."

I shrugged. "I don't have them."

"Who does?"

I didn't lie, then, because there was no point. I weighed my available options, determined that there really weren't any. "Stravros."

"His students, you mean? Or himself?"

"Don't know, one or the other."

"Can you bring them to me?"

"I can't really imagine why you'd need them, seeing as you're as omnipotent as you obviously are."

Now the arms crossed, and I could see he was wearing another expensive, white suit, the kind you'd expect on the Architect in The Matrix. It's Chicago, for God's sake, I wanted to tell him. "I'm limited by the established parameters of my social structure."

"What the hell does that mean? You *are* the social structure. Don't you have, like, fifteen grown men who jump when you snap your fingers, who kill for you? Buff your fingernails?"

"I don't trust them, Zak."

"Well, I don't trust you so spare me the inner circle speech."

"I need those lures. Get them for me and I'll protect you."

"From what?"

"The villains you can't see."

I tried not to laugh, but nodded. "I'll try."

"Can you find your way out of here?"

I left him and stopped in the stairwell to type an *Am still breathing* text and waited long enough to confirm it was sent. I knew I wouldn't get a response and I didn't care as much about hearing from Riley as I did letting my best friend know that I was still among the living. I knew how he felt about now; I knew he was probably standing guard, pacing, biting his fingernails in the corner of Stavros' hospital room, a dutiful soldier. Watch your back Riley, I told him telepathically.

My eyes on constant alert for blonde hair and ripped jeans, I hadn't seen Mandy yet, but had passed four mopeds going in the opposite direction. I made note, this time, of the riders: all men, late twenties, different races, all wearing helmets. That alone seemed odd. I mean, in a place like this seeing someone take a safety precaution. It was just another enigma. Still heading in the same direction toward where I first entered, I kept my eyes high above each building, looking for a pole with some sort of Starbucks insignia on it. So far only brick buildings; a few had spires; one had a sort of tower but nothing with a pole. I was out of breath and running, I noticed now, no doubt because the sky was beginning to gray. No watch and no phone signal, I guessed it was about five-thirty. As it was November, so it would be completely dark soon. Shit. There was no more time to search for poles because soon I wouldn't be able to see them anyway.

Continuing my pace, I reached my right hand behind me to feel for the notebook, which I knew was there but still needed its firm assurance. Leave it alone, I told myself, though I would have gladly given up pizza for the rest of my life for five minutes with that notebook right now. My eyes squinted to make out the tops of building or tents. Wait, was that…

Mandy.

She was running past me on the opposite side of the street… headed in the opposite direction. Jesus.

"Mandy, wait!" I shouted.

She heard me but only half turned, pointing to the alley she'd told me about earlier today. Then she took off. I could see it now, the alley positioned across the street from the Suddenly-Starbucks now right in front of me. I remembered Mandy's words, standing outside it, weighing the different possibilities that could be awaiting me:

> 1. Rand, who would escort me back to Brolly's bookcase room, or some other undisclosed location in the real world.
> 2. Brolly, who would beat the crap out of me, steal the notebook, my wallet, my phone, etc.
> 3. Jane, who would simply follow me back to Chris, Carson, and Dugger to attempt to repossess the receipts known as lures. I found them; I discovered them; they were never his to begin with. His outlandish creation myth, however, of being the vast force behind the whole operation, lacked credibility considering how desperate he looked asking me for the receipts. He was pleading with me, vulnerable almost, friendless in his tower of control, trying to appeal to my sense of compassion.

Sorry, fresh out.

I had one last thought of buying a pastry at Starbucks, since I hadn't eaten in over a day, but then I took two purposeful steps toward the opening in the bottom floor of a building I didn't recognize. They all looked alike here—and…uh…concrete…my head. I was knocked onto the ground and the right side of my head was cold, footsteps running past me, it sounded like three sets of them running quickly, pounding the concrete in thin-soled shoes. *In Mandy's direction.*

CHAPTER THIRTY-FOUR

Pressing my palms on the ground, I shouldered myself up, then shook my head, hoping to unflatten the right side from being mashed against the concrete. Get up. Find her. Who would be running after Mandy, and why three men? I needed to find a stairwell to check my phone. I made my way to the opening across the street now. Pitch blackness. But my eyes adjusted after a few seconds. I heard nothing, smelled nothing, no birds, cars, cockroaches, because the engineers who apparently built this Matrix hadn't added those features to the program. Two minutes later, I saw a light. I followed it, counting: thirty steps, then thirty more. Was there another opening on the other side like the one I'd come from in Brolly's smoke-filled den? I fumbled my way to a stairwell and climbed to the first landing. This one was higher than the last, I could tell by the echo of my footsteps. I checked my phone. Sure enough, I'd found a loophole in the 'no service' problem and there was signal. Riley had written back the following:

Dean Agnus poised to expel you, pending actual police missing persons report

School…what was that again? A community of some kind, with student peers and teachers who all, in some way, care about your success? I thought of the computer lab, the library, the student union and cafeterias, and they all felt like some distant childhood I had lived long ago. Not any kind of recent life experience. Dean Agnus, now that I recalled, had told me to go find a door. Ironic wasn't it, that this place lacked any real doors but had portals everywhere.

Are you ok? How's Stavros? I wrote to Riley, followed with a quick text to Carson.

Still alive, can't leave yet, soon.

Carson, Chris, or Dugger wouldn't understand my text and would be panicking about now. I pictured them arguing and talking over each other in the back of their ghetto car. But I had more important things to do than manage their adolescent neuroses. I climbed the rusted staircase to the next level, another small, square pad-landing with nothing visible in the darkness except a lot of floor, high ceiling, and a bluish hue out the windows.

Keep going, some inner voice guided me. I swear I felt a sensation on my back, like something vibrating, like the notebook that had been stored there so long I was sure it was now part of my skin.

I reached another level, looked down at the clanky steel pad, and stepped out onto the floor. My eyes started to adjust. I saw the shape of the room now. With the instinct of a hunter, I moved toward the far windows, acting like I was looking for something, but not consciously knowing what it was. I counted my steps—seven from the landing to the far wall, where tall windows were positioned about eighteen inches apart. I didn't look down, though I knew I was three stories up. Instead, I looked up and saw the top of the building across the street.

My eyes caught sight of something on the floor straight across, in a building on the other side of the street. Red and green lights, tiny lights, barely perceptible, flashed on and off in a pattern, like the lights on a router. But they weren't green and orange like in my dorm room. I moved an inch closer to the window, taking care that I wouldn't be seen, crossed my arms, and hunkered down near the wall to peer into that space. I saw movement and instinctively pulled back further into the shadows. Come on, Zak, there's no light in here, you're invisible, just a shadow. And that's exactly what I saw: shadows moving. So that meant there had to be a light source somewhere. How was that light being powered? It was odd that only at that specific moment did I realize it was freezing in this building. My hands were ice. I blew hot air into my palms, still looking, peering, studying the operation, realizing now that they had machines. I couldn't see them, but I heard the hum and my eyes squinted.

Were they the sliders? The drug manufacturers? From what I could imagine, there had to be a hundred different pieces of technology used to produce one bottle of aspirin. I could more likely picture a grocery store the day before Thanksgiving, swarming with crowds, than this controlled environment run by two or three people working in the dark. It was also likely that many parts of the process were now automated. Maybe machines could be programmed to perform parts of the process. But machines ran on electricity. Where was that coming from, how was it routed here…and who was paying for it?

It was late; my new friends would be worried about me. I hadn't eaten, or slept, in way too long. Where was Mandy?

The way it all looked from here, I had two choices: proceed through the building to try to find my way home, or re-enter System D to find Mandy and her pursuers.

CHAPTER THIRTY-FIVE

I started the same way in the new building as I did the last one: the tunnel. I made my way out to the street, looking out for a few minutes before crossing, at mopeds, bicyclists, walkers, or monitors. There had to be a way for someone like Jane to observe visitors to this place—keep an eye on sliders and runners, observe their movements and their loyalties. But how would that work unless there was some kind of surveillance center with cameras and remote viewing equipment positioned through the complex? I needed to find those cameras.

With no visible activity on the street, I crossed over, entered the ground floor opening of the similar, large brick building across the street, and moved close to the center where I knew there would be another staircase. They were all the same so far. I found the first staircase in the same spot as the last building as if one building had been constructed and the rest were cloned. This time, though, no signal. I replicated, waited, still nothing. Wait, the back light on my phone allowed me to see the signal icon and it just moved.

Backlighting. Shit.

If I could see the backlight, maybe someone else could as well. I lowered the brightness, hoping I wouldn't accidentally go blind in this place. I climbed, applying pressure to my footsteps to prevent any sound, as I heard voices upstairs now. Almost at the next level, I crouched low to peer into the space. As I did, my phone vibrated. I pulled it out of my pocket and kept my hand on the face to prevent the light betraying my presence.

Text from Carson: *Can't wait in the hood for you anymore, too dangerous. Will be waiting nearby when you're ready.*

The voices were several levels up. I could tell by the echo. But was I really safe here? Was I being watched? It had been my plan to walk around the complex and look for cameras, but now I'd just seen what looked like an illegal operation, in a city, or a part of the city, that welcomed illegal operations. So far, illegal money in the form of my bitcoin transaction receipt labeled satoshidice@dollydolly.com. Satoshi Dice is a bitcoin game based on small increments of money used as communication devices. I'd seen illegal Starbucks workers, who looked like the unwashed extras from Mad Max Fury Road, using illegal food and beverage equipment, counterfeit commercial signage, not to mention my growing list of escorts—Jane, bearded Mike from Pilsen, Brolly, Rand, Mandy.

I crouched low on a rusty metal stair, low enough to not be seen but able to still hear the vibration of voices above me. I traveled back in my mind to Stavros' basement when I'd first met the protégés, or prodigies. I went over their concocted story about receipts embedded with a Reece cipher, which some old mariner developed to hide GPS coordinates in a series of letters via the Periodic Table. Start there, I thought. But then how do I get from there to here?

Those latitude and longitude coordinates mapped to an address either *in* this place, wherever I was, or near this place. The other mapped to an address in Pilsen, ostensibly at the apartment of Chris' friend Mike. Somehow, I only realized now, the likelihood that Jane and his army of thugs were somehow hip to a World War II cipher was about as likely as me getting to graduate from college. Jane wasn't capable of devising a plan like this. Something didn't add up. Who else was working with him, and who would have put this together? The very thought made my palms sweat, so I pretended for a moment that I wasn't thinking about Stavros and didn't suspect him of anything but being helpful and charitable. After all, he introduced me to smart students who were helping me; he invited me to his home to meet his girlfriend, offered to put us up for the night. No, he was trustworthy. Stavros had proved himself as a friend. So why was my heart warning me otherwise?

Riley, where are you when I need you?

CHAPTER THIRTY-SIX

"**I'm here,**" said someone from the bottom of the stairs. I slapped my hand to my chest thinking it was Riley. But it was a woman's voice. I turned slowly, careful to not make noise. My phone pressed into my leg. Mandy looked strange, hands clasped behind her back like a maître'd on a cruise ship. She wasn't prone to formalities like this. In fact, her style was even more casual, almost irreverent, than other students. I descended two more steps. Something glowed on the top of her head. Something wet. Blood?

"What happened to you? I saw you running. Then I saw—"

Mandy put her finger to her lips, then motioned for me to follow her. "What the hell are you doing here?" she whispered. "This isn't the right tunnel; it's across the street. I told you to look for the—"

"I saw something from the building across the street. There's something going on up there. I saw flashing lights and heard voices."

"Dude, get a grip. And keep your voice down. Are you listening to me? You can't just walk around here at night."

"Why not? Are there hordes of vandals that break into buildings...wait, there aren't any doors so I guess they don't have to break in. Oh...and don't forget there's no furniture, and every building is completely empty, except for the water cooler in Jane's loft that I visited earlier today."

Mandy stopped walking to face me. Her eyes looked puffy. I wanted to take her back to my dorm room, prop her up on my bed, bring her a cup of tea and give her a foot rub. This was the depth of my feelings now. Carnal desires, yes, but something new had taken root in my heart along with it: care.

"You saw Jane?" she asked with surprise.

How did she know about Jane? Shit, the notebook, I'd almost forgotten. It was still stuffed in my pants, safe and undetected. Frustration buzzed in my palms, but I knew I couldn't touch it now.

"What did he say to you?" she insisted.

We were standing by the windows now on the bottom floor of this building, facing the building I'd just come from.

"He needs something from me, though I can't imagine why."

"Your receipts."

So she knew about those too. Well, one big unhappy family.

"Did you give them to him?"

"I don't have them. I told him I'd try to get them, but not sure I can find the guy I gave them to."

"Who?" she asked.

I said nothing, I didn't need to.

"I'm trying to help you, Zak. Why won't you let me?"

What reason had she ever given me to believe her intentions were altruistic?

"What are *you* doing here, and I don't necessarily mean tonight, in this building right now. How do you know about this place? How are you involved in this?"

Those eyes. But no words came. That's alright. I can think of worse things than staring at her all night. But she had some agenda for fetching me here. And, altruistic or not, I knew it had nothing to do with receipts.

CHAPTER THIRTY-SEVEN

It was completely silent in those few moments, me at the bottom of the stairs, Mandy opposite me in pitch blackness with only faint reflections of leftover sunlight bleeding in from the cracks, no more voices upstairs on the upper levels. There was a sort of stagnant peacefulness about this place, whatever it was, invisible segments of our country's economy managed by shadow people with no social security numbers who don't vote and don't even officially exist. I felt lured by my conscience to revert back to my own world, where I was needed, to investigate Stavros and the people I had gotten involved in this mess, to look after Riley, and to continue being a student like I'd planned, or like my parents had planned, for me. But a hunger, almost, to get my questions answered was pulling me deeper into the dark and the thick of this madness, knowing all the while that answering one question just evoked ten new ones.

"I need to ge—"

"We need to get you out of here," Mandy interrupted, touching the hem of my shirtsleeve. I didn't move. "It's not safe here," she explained. "There's a—"

Loud footsteps interrupted us from deeper in the building. A form emerged, a man in a uniform. "You two, come with me please."

"Who the hell are you?" Mandy shot back. Saucy.

"Campus Police," the man said flatly, taking two steps closer to us.

As in…which campus? I surveyed the situation. Mandy and I were about twenty steps from the opening to the street, the staircase to my left.

"Campus?" I whispered to her, to which she quietly replied, "Run," and took off toward the building entrance. I followed and, in so doing, sealed the fate of my even less certain future.

She made a jackrabbit turn to the right down a side street, then another quick left, obvious that she knew where she was going, where we were going. Glad one of us did. The uniformed man lagged now but still in pursuit about half a block behind us, me trailing Mandy by five or six steps. I pushed hard to catch up to her as she paused momentarily to catch her breath. I flung myself against a brick wall and collapsed halfway to get more air in my lungs. My feet hurt, my knees, calves. God please don't let her start running again.

"Where are we going?" I asked, struggling to get words out.

"Here." She pointed to a vague location ahead of us and I had no idea where we were now in relation to our original location near the exit tunnel. But the advantage we had over the Campus Police officer was the dark. We were both dressed in dark clothing, and Mandy's long mane of blonde hair was up in a quasi bun/ponytail that mostly looked dark. We seemed safe for the moment.

"What's going on?"

She sort of laughed, then touched her eyes as if to suppress emotion.

"Okay, I'll ask a different question. Why would Campus Police have any jurisdiction here?" And I was instantly afraid of the answer after I'd said the words. "Are we…on campus?"

Mandy shook her head, still breathing heavily, eyeballing up and down the side street for our pursuer, pacing slowly in a two-foot area in front of me. "Not really, no." But she didn't make eye contact. "It's not what you think it is."

"Really? Quel surprise. Because everything else about this odyssey has gone exactly as planned. Now we're apparently back on the

University of Chicago campus…so is this some—"

She used her eyes to silence me. "It's a code."

"For…"

"Not campus police."

"But he *said* Campus Police."

She shook her head and put her lips up to my ear. "Campus…is short for hippocampus." She pulled away and stared again, seeing if I'd get it. Hippo. Were we on the grounds of the Chicago Zoo and these buildings were hollowed out animal pens? That would explain the smell of peanuts that I'd noticed earlier. Mandy was still staring. Hippocampus. Jesus, I thought. If I remembered my anatomy correctly from high school, was the brain's memory center.

"Oh shit. Are you saying…"

"Uh huh," Mandy confirmed.

"They're gonna wipe my memory, of like, what…this—"

"Everything probably, certainly from today, maybe more than that."

"Can they do that?" I instinctively put my hands over my ears and touched my poor vulnerable head, praying that it didn't get injected with any foreign objects.

"How…how… Tell me how you could be involved in this, with these people. Tell me now," I nearly shouted, not caring suddenly who heard us.

"Let's go," she said with a quick glance at the end of the path, then took off ahead of me. I heard Memory Guy's steps pounding the concrete behind me. Funny, wasn't it, how my feet and calves were no longer the least bit sore and I was running faster than ever. Did he use that retractable ice pick like the X-Files alien bounty hunters, or a syringe to the temple? Mandy and I had gotten to another building now with an opening on the bottom floor on the right side. I knew what to do, still following her. We ran inside, found the bottom staircase, took it up one level, then ran straight into the dark hollow. She ran in pitch darkness and I had to assume she knew the layout and we wouldn't plow into a wall or fall over a balcony or something.

"Here," she said reading my thoughts and grabbing my hand. "Straight ahead there's another exit tunnel."

"On the second floor?"

"The first and third buildings in a block have it on the upper floor, second and fourth buildings it's on the ground floor. You'll memorize it for next time."

I stopped running and no longer heard Memory Man's footsteps. Where was he? Wouldn't he also know the location of the exit tunnels?

"Did you say next time?"

Ahead I saw the opening, exit tunnel or portal that presumably led out of this place, along with lights and the sound of cars. Thank you, Jesus. Mandy was walking behind me and I slowed to hear the answer to my last question. "What did you mean by next time?"

"You're in now. There's no out."

Before I had the chance to comment, a cab slowed on the street. Mandy was on the curb with her hand in the air, her hair suddenly withdrawn from the bun. I've never hailed a taxi in Chicago in less than thirty minutes. Here it was on the curb with a smiling driver.

"We shouldn't be seen together. Can you find a ride...well... wherever you're going next?"

I had so many questions still unanswered, not to mention new ones resulting from the last ten minutes. Time for me was like the cab that suddenly slowed to meet us. This moment had done that, slowed me down so I could catch my breath long enough to fully observe the woman in front of me, eyes tear-stained with creases in her face that weren't there the last time I saw her. Was her strength on the outside with a vulnerability deeper in, or was it the opposite, with a hardness at her core? I couldn't decide that yet. More observation and research was required, and I hoped and prayed I'd have the chance.

I was desperate to ask her about the memory cop, how it worked and if that was even a real threat or just some other wild detail to add to the collection. For some reason the part about never leaving, didn't scare me because I was still having a hard time believing that any of it was real. I watched her slide into the back seat of the cab, her hand still on the edge of the open back door, waiting to see what I'd do next.

"I'm good," I replied finally. "But how will I find you?" I knew how desperate it sounded, and right now I didn't care.

My phone vibrated.

"Now you have my number," she said just before the door slammed shut.

CHAPTER THIRTY-EIGHT

I texted Chris, and before I even hit Send, the white van screeched to a stop in front of me. Seriously, things like this never happened to me. The back door slid open. I jumped in and landed on the floor, my head crammed into the back of a seat.

"Dude, is he breathing?" I heard Dugger say from behind the wheel.

I sat up and pulled my body into the soft bench seat and could have fallen asleep for an entire day. All three of them watched me.

"The road, asshole!" Chris said to Dugger, who swerved away from the curb.

Carson was in back watching me. "You okay?"

"Can we go to Pizza Hut?" I asked in a purposely loud tone. "I'm starving." I leaned over and whispered to Carson, "Let's only talk in the vault, don't say anything here, okay?"

He nodded.

I leaned forward and said the same thing to Chris, and knew

neither of them had any idea what I meant by the vault. I whispered "Stavros" in Chris' ear.

"We call it 'the mill'," he explained. "There's a windmill in the backyard."

In the silence, I looked out the windows at late night Chicago; a couple walking arm in arm, a throng of giggling high-heeled girls spilling out of a bar. I guessed we were probably on Clark Street. Not far now. My exhausted brain and battered body relaxed and drifted, swayed by the jerky movements of the clanky van and Dugger's reckless driving. I pictured my parents, my father's legal career. I hadn't called my mother in several weeks, and I was certain she'd probably called the school guidance counselor by now. Now that I thought about it, maybe Dean Agnus would get his wish after all and I'd be expelled when this was over.

You can never leave here, Mandy had said as matter of factly as telling me the time. The thought occurred to me that maybe there wasn't such a division between campus and *that place*, whatever it was. Maybe it really was on the campus, somehow, like some kind of annexed land parcel used for training or experimentation, or who knows what. I typed a quick text to Riley.

I'm fine, will call soon.

I knew the van was probably bugged, maybe Stavros' house too. But, the way it was constructed, there was no way they could have gotten to his vault in the basement. I thought of calling home, and pulled up my mother's mobile number in my contacts, but turned it off again because, really, what would I say that would sound the least bit coherent? What reason could I give for not calling home in almost a month? More than anything, I knew I couldn't feign happiness or academic pressure, or fake stories about classes I hadn't been to or teachers who'd likely forgotten my name by now. "Skinner, Skinner... right, that tall skinny kid? He came to the first few classes but I thought he'd dropped out" they'd be saying. I picked up my phone to turn it off and saw that Riley was typing a text message. The phone buzzed... from another message coming in. A 509 number I didn't recognize.

DON'T TELL THEM ANYTHING

That's all it said. It would be hard to type in the back of a moving van and all I could think about was who knew where I was right now.

Who are you and why do you care
Save their lives and say nothing

Wtf
Feign an illness, head to the john, slip out back and I'll pick you up
Who are you, "Campus" police?
An interested party
You and your memory probe soldiers can get fucked
Memory wipes are temporary, your friends are in danger. Talk to them and they die. They're just kids.

I looked at each of their faces. They seemed older than their years. Geniuses that the world would exploit one way or another.

Tell me your name or this goes no further, I typed.

Long pause with the three little dots showing someone was typing, no doubt thinking of a pseudonym, or else a string of expletives.

Peders

Riley was still typing the Declaration of Independence.

"Head's up." Dugger drove quickly down Stavros' street, everyone looking at the house for signs of activity. No lights on, no one around, no strange cars parked there. He stopped on the next street, where we tiptoed through people's backyards, jumping fences and trampling rose bushes to get to the back door of Stavros and Carla's house. Carson opened the door a crack and waited, looked back at us, waiting another two seconds, then moved through the doorway. I pulled a chain on a dainty stained-glass lamp on a wooden table then locked the door behind me. For a moment, I stood there gathering my thoughts, then following them to the stairs.

"I'll see you down there, I've got to piss."

I did, quickly, then sat on the lid of the toilet. I could now safely withdraw the notebook from the back of my pants. I don't know how but there was a pen stuck in the middle of it…that I hadn't put there. I wrote "SOS" in the center of a clean page and waited, knowing Carson, Chris, and Dugger were downstairs waiting for me to tell them the most fantastic story of where I'd been for the past twelve hours.

SOS
I'm here, Zak
I don't know who to trust
I think you do
Who are my friends right now?
Whoever has nothing to gain by helping you
Gain, that's subjective
You're wiser than you think. Trust yourself

Mandy?
Does she have something to gain?
She works for them. And the guy on the phone, Peders?
You already know the answer
I don't trust him, but I believe him that they could be in danger
Numbers, patterns of numbers
I smiled, touching the receipts on another page in the notebook.
I have them
Probably not for long. Leave them somewhere, in here

The bathroom was tiny, barely big enough to change your mind, Riley would have said. A toilet, small sink, wall mirror above it, and a small cabinet over the toilet. I opened both doors; creams, jars, lotions, the usual. There was a box of band-aids on the top shelf already had bandages wrapped in paper, so it was perfect. I crammed the receipts in the box and pulled out the band-aids so they'd be easy to retrieve and harder to discover the other odd pieces of paper that didn't belong in a first aid box.

Done
Now go meet your new friend Peders. He'll pick you up

CHAPTER THIRTY-NINE

Luckily the vault was down twenty steps from the main floor of Stavros' estate, so I didn't think the boys would hear the door click shut. My receipts were in the band-aids box in Stavros' half-bathroom, I thought, careful to not say it aloud for fear of some listening device stuck to the inside of my jacket. So far at least, they hadn't probed my brain.

I stepped down the backyard path, jumped the neighbor's fence again, and made a point to stand visibly in the middle of the street. I knew whoever was about to meet me was likely doing so at great risk. For me, what was the risk, really? I mean, how much more chaos was even possible? A fancy silver car rolled up to me. A clean-shaven blond man with an eager face, leaned his head down to make eye contact. Time would tell, but I liked his face so far, more than others. Without ceremony, I opened the door and sat beside him, unsure of where my life was headed next.

"Dane Peders," the driver said with what seemed like a genuine smile. What could he possibly be so happy about? For God's sake his white teeth were giving me a headache. He insisted on shaking my hand, his elbow craned awkwardly up to present his hand in just the right position.

"I guess you already know who I am," I said. "How did you find me? Is everyone tracking me now? Where are we going?"

"A little park near the zoo, we can talk there."

A zoo. After dark. Were locks still on the cages? I don't know why this frightened me. Everything frightened me now. The dark interior of his Mercedes or Bentley, or whatever kinds of cars guys named Dane drove, smelled like mint. "Can't we talk here?"

The man laughed aloud. "This is my car, of course it's bugged." I noticed he hadn't lowered his voice, almost as if he was fine about being surveilled.

"By who?"

"By the people who feel threatened by the things I know."

"Wouldn't they just take you out?" I asked, now suddenly talking like a mobster.

"Noooo, they need me. Right up here." He pointed but all I saw was darkness.

Please God, not another tunnel leading to the underworld. We parked in an empty lot and walked around one building. Sure enough, a park with grass and benches. Peders didn't choose the first one, I think, because it wouldn't give him a vantage point of someone approaching. Wow, I must be learning. Three months ago I never would have considered that tactic. I observed him standing by each bench, then scanning the area. He looked about forty-five, not wafer-thin but agile, high-energy, smiled easily. I took some comfort in the idea of him not being afraid. Then again, he was still shopping for the right bench. "Here," he said and took off his trench. "Take off your jacket."

"Ever heard of winter in Chicago?"

"It's not winter yet. Do it. We leave in five minutes."

"Where?" I demanded, already bored of the tradecraft nonsense.

"A diner," he explained, apparently visible through the buffer of pines behind us. I leaned forward to remove my jacket and realized the notebook showed on the outside of my pants, that I'd forgotten to lay it next to my skin under my shirt when I left Stavros' bathroom. Did he know? Was he the one writing in the notebook?

I leaned back on the bench and crossed my ankles. "Who are you and what do you want?"

The man frowned; then the affable smile returned to a face well practiced in the art of negotiation. I was proving to be less of a pushover than he'd expected—you know, picking me up after a crazy ordeal, barely escaping with my head still intact.

"I've already told you, Dane—"

"Yes, Peders, I remember. Why would my friends be in danger if I told them about—"

Peders' palm went up and he shook his head. "Not here."

"Are there spies in the bushes? I thought you chose the bench that wasn't bugged." I leaned forward and rubbed my temples, the weight of exhaustion crumbling my composure.

"I'm trying to help you...and frankly you need my help." His voice was strained and desperate. So exactly how many people were trying to help me right now? A lot of good it had done me so far. We were sitting about two feet apart on a six-foot, black wooden bench, Peders shivering from the thirty-five-degree wind blowing across the clearing.

"I doubt it. I'm sure you're wanting, or should I say planning, to force me to help you in some way. Just tell me what you want."

"Cooperation," he said, the first straight answer so far.

"In exchange for what?" I asked.

"Protection."

"From?"

"Everyone who wants to kill you, Mr. Skinner."

My spine tingled when he said it, sitting alone in the dark with another stranger.

"From what I understand, there's a growing list."

"Why all the cloak and fucking dagger? I mean why not just threaten to take Riley so I tell you what you want? You know he's really the only person I care about in the world. Other than Mandy Pierce, whom I suspect has already crossed over to the dark side."

"We have him already."

I don't know how I knew he was lying. But *Riley!* Because it was him, I had to assume he was in danger. If they took him, they'd just done it because an hour ago he texted me about Dean Agnus.

"I'll tell you what you want. Just don't hurt him."

"We wouldn't dream of it. He's right where you left him. Follow me."

Peders wrapped his trench tightly around his body against the stiff wind only Chicago was capable of. I followed him through the trees, thoroughly confused by the confession that they had Riley. Did they have him or not? There was no way to text him from here without being seen, as Dane was five steps in front of me. I had to try. I pulled out the phone to prepare a text to Dugger and Riley. Peders stopped. Fuck! Now my hands were freezing and stiff.

"Please, do message your friends. That's fine. But the bloodhounds tracking us will find *them* before your friends find their way to us. It's not you giving me information, Mr. Skinner. It's the other way around."

• —••• —— •

Okay, so yeah: truck stop diner accessible through the back via pointy clumps of pine trees or, when accessed normally, from the freeway. Godawful neon lights everywhere, country music, swaggering men in cowboy boots, and a sea of tractor trailers in the huge lot outside. The size of the place was barely the size of even one truck. Inside at the bar stools sat truck drivers of every conceivable size, shape, age, race condition, elbow-to-elbow with huge plates of yellow and brown food. I followed Peders to a well-lit booth in the middle. Is this really how it went for people like us? Chased victims and paid spies talking about perilous secrets in an open diner surrounded by truckers? I knew the depths of my inexperience and suspected that was the point. Hiding me in plain sight.

A red-haired server set down menus, napkins and forks in quick, bird-like movements. "Coffee?"

"Coke," I replied, though I needed water more than caffeine. "And water," I added. She didn't bat an eye. Peders ordered coffee. I pushed the menu aside and folded my hands in my best receiving-posture.

"Aren't you hungry?" he asked.

"Cheeseburger is fine."

"The menu is eight pages long. Don't you think ordering just a cheeseburger will elicit a hundred questions and decisions—"

I opened the menu and closed it again. "Fine. Cheeseburger #2."

"You're fast," she replied, having overheard me from the next table. Peders ordered chicken potpie. She set down our drinks and I drank the glass of water all at once.

"What are the rules?" I asked him.

He smiled.

"Do we, like, write questions down and pass them back and forth

155

across the table, and do the coffee stains mean something? Or lower my voice only when you say something, like, grenade, or walk to the men's room and only wash my hands but don't take a piss?"

"What do you want to know?"

"How much time do we have?" I asked.

"I should think as long as it takes us to eat. Thirty minutes, unless you save room for cherry pie." Peders liked me, that was obvious, and could be used to my advantage. Now I just needed to determine what he needed from me. My only defense right now was leverage, and I had it but didn't know what it was.

"Where's David Wade?"

"Where you just were."

"Why didn't I see him?"

He laughed now, with his head back. "It's a big place."

"What is?"

"You know the name already." Peders tilted his head.

"System D is one name."

"Indeed," he said. "What do you really want to know?"

"What goes on in there?"

"Any number of things, and it changes, very frequently. Some of them you know already."

"You're, like, a bureaucrat, or campus police? You're too old and smart to be a runner, and you don't seem like a slider to me."

"You've learned some things." He sat back, I could tell deciding whether to be impressed or jealous. "No, I don't make pharmaceuticals. I'm in another sort of, how do I put it, department of the organization."

"So System D's an organization? I thought it was a place. Is it a corporation, like with a CEO and a board?" I was only half joking.

Peders sipped his coffee and blinked slowly. I was asking the wrong questions.

"No, you're asking the right questions," he said.

I nearly spilled Coke all over the table. I'd only thought it, not said it. "How the fuck did you do that?" I was about to stand up and leave.

Peders calmly pointed at me, over and over, tapping the air in front of him.

"What?"

"The notebook in your pants."

I reached around to touch its reassuring presence, still there. "So let me get this straight. The notebook reads my thoughts…and you hear them? Do you know how that sounds?"

The server brought our plates of food. I smelled the aroma of charred beef like I hadn't eaten in a month.

"It's not a corporation," he said when the server left. "No one has the authority to run or oversee any part of it."

"So in the absence of leadership or authority, who are the warring factions vying for power?"

Peders nodded as he started eating. "You're not as young as I thought. As anyone thought."

I used the time to fill the empty cave in my stomach with the greasiest burger I'd ever eaten. Delicious.

"The world might not be what you think it is. And I'm not talking about politics either, or even economics, specifically. Perhaps both, but the point is that the things pundits and analysts and journalists think are making the biggest impact on the global economy and distribution of power aren't exactly correct."

"Rand, one of your runners, gave me this speech yesterday," I commented. "Something about $650B of commerce coming from System D. What I want to know is, your role. What do you do to contribute to this counter-economy or drug cartel or whatever the euphemism of the day is?"

"I don't do anything." Peders wiped his mouth, slowly, sat back, stared, crossed his arms, and then came forward in a conspiratorial move.

I remembered Woodward and Bernstein stringing together the details of the greatest conspiracy of our lifetime in a McDonald's in *All The President's Men*.

"At least not anything to…how shall I say…contribute to it."

"What the hell does that mean?"

He nodded. "I can tell you this: we call ourselves The Valve, and we're sort of a…group within a group."

"Working counter to the interests of sliders?"

He nodded. "Exactly. Sliders are fringe. Anyone can be trained to do anything if they want it bad enough, and if the reward adequately remunerates risk."

"You mean, like, homeless people, indigents?"

"Keep going. Parolees, sex offenders, political outcasts, whistleblowers, shamed corporate embezzlers, immigrant drug runners, arms dealers more than anything these days. Fringe, of every high and low."

"Valve?" I repeated, processing. "You're a bunch of Nobel peace prize winners then? Philanthropists taking down the world economy as a, what, fucking public service? Come on."

"Pretty much."

"I don't believe altruism really exists," I said.

"But you believe in notebooks that write themselves, though, don't you?"

I snapped my fingers in mock protest. "Damn, and I was winning this argument too." I let a tiny, genuine smile creep across my lips, because I knew, not from any scientific or empirical knowledge but from my gut instinct, that Peders was telling the truth, and trying in some way to protect me, maybe to save my life. Not that he didn't need something from me, but Jesus Christ he was the only person telling me anything real about whatever this all was. The server refilled the water, coffee, and Coke.

"I'm an urban planner, a sort of zoning guy with a background in sociology and transportation. I graduated from Columbia Business School and have an MBA from here, University of Chicago."

"Do you guys have like an electronic grid of this place, like a video game console?" I asked, admittedly a little giddy at the prospect of it.

Peders smirked and shook his head. "We'll get there. We have two Harvard economists, two pharmacists, former intelligence officers, a doctor, a chemical pharmacologist, hackers, a mathematician, and lawyers. My partner, Mason, he's one of the lawyers."

"Mathematician?" I asked. "Why?"

"A Number Theorist."

Stavros! Jesus. I sipped the Coke and tried not to react.

"How many are you?" I asked.

"Ten, made up of five different races, men, women, one transgender, aged 25 to 67."

He watched me as he spoke, watching my eyes, waiting to see what I'd piece together on my own as I downed perhaps the largest cheeseburger ever made in America.

"So, obviously—" I wiped my mouth—"you're anarchists working as a sort of, what, opposition arm of the black market? The alt-alt-economy?"

"Very good. Why? What are we rebelling against? What's the most divisive issue facing the White House right now?"

"I'm not political," I lied.

"Healthcare. The population is aging. Fifteen-percent of the US population is over sixty-five, that's forty-eight million people. The cost of pharmaceuticals is downright scandalous. Pharmaceutical sales last year accounted for nearly two-percent of GDP—again, that might not seem like much but that number means $333B and it's growing every day."

I nodded. "So you guys, what, make your own pharma and sell it for three times as much?"

"Wrong."

"Okay, five times as much?"

Peders cleared his throat before speaking. "We give it away. For free."

CHAPTER FORTY

"**What? Why?**" I glared at Peders with disdain. What would he have to gain by conning me?

"Both the US economy and System D's dark economy exclude a whole demographic of consumers—elders. They're left out of the best healthcare because many elders live in poverty, are in poor health because parts naturally wear down on any machine. That means pre-existing conditions, which is a loophole that the ruling, affluent class uses to avoid subsidizing. So what happens? Patient A: seventy-nine-year-old female with osteoporosis and rheumatoid arthritis, and she's legally blind in one eye. She doesn't move easily because of the RA, and her bones are frail, she's visually impaired. A steroid anti-inflammatory like sulfasalazine costs $35 for about a hundred pills if you get it discounted by insurance. If not, double that. Fosamax for osteoporosis is about $150/shot, glasses $450. Good insurance plans cover fifty-percent of her medicine and no reimbursement for her glasses. How would she pay on a fixed income for these meds year-round? Patient B has stage-four lung cancer, eighty years old and no insurance. We're very selective about who we support, so a young, bored, suburban housewife addicted to opioids—no. Elders of every race are unilaterally and systematically marginalized because they're old, sick, and poor. It's atrocious how we as a society and as a government treat them. In fact, we don't treat them at all if we can possibly avoid it.

"So yes, System D does have a group that manufactures illegal meds, often made from inert ingredients or mostly Tylenol, yes they do package these meds to look like real prescription pharmaceuticals and sell them for five times retail, because people will pay almost anything if they don't need a prescription. They're not us and we are not them. We're the shadow. We, The Valve, re-manufacture real meds with real ingredients and deliver them as angel runners to people who desperately need them. We use Big Pharma's science, then steal it, repackage it, and give it away."

"I don't believe you."

"Believe it. If we wanted to, in five years, The Valve could systematically shut down the pharmaceutical industry in a month, and Wall Street would crumble."

"Well, why don't you?" I had to ask.

"We turn our services on and off depending on variables, mainly to avoid detection and publicity. But also to keep monetary and fiscal wheels moving."

"How do you find recipients of your, well…program, or whatever it's called?"

"It's called tagging. Hackers scrape the internet from pharmacies, drug stores, Walmart, Costco, to see what people are buying, when they stop buying, flagging accounts for life-threatening things like cancer and HIV, also flagging children as well as elders, and they track their ages, list of ailments, medical charts. It's a sad thing to see in real time, I'll tell ya."

"What about the sliders though?"

"Great question, especially because you've just seen what they are, some of them, and what they can do. We're hunted. We're underground. But we're also hunting them."

"Where do you get all your equipment, like production equipment?"

"We have people on the inside, and we basically steal as much as we can from them, dismantling their massive empire one bottle or one needle at a time."

I signaled for another Coke from the server and drained my glass, desperate for more caffeine to help my brain process the craziest story I'd ever heard.

"But where did you get all your startup money? There had to be a huge investment at first, by someone, to set up your operation, right? Is that in—" I waved my hands—"wherever I just was yesterday?"

"Let me start with the first question. Some of us, at least half, met each other in an early online community of bitcoin enthusiasts, known back then in 2011 as cypherpunks, based on a book by WikiLeaks founder, Julian Assange. Back then, no one really understood the potential of bitcoin and other cryptocurrencies, and they were cheap as hell to buy. A bitcoin traded back then for like twenty dollars, whereas now one coin costs about ten thousand USD. So, we were very early adopters and collectors of bitcoin, really just as a hobby, and because digital currency was a topic that gave the DOJ migraines. So some of us in this group are what you'd call bitcoin billionaires, and we've used all that money to fund our operations, which is another feature of our economic prominence."

"Meaning what?"

"Economists call it 'cost of capital', signifying the amount of money it takes a company to bring in $1 worth of net sales. Our cost of capital is nothing, which means our operation would be all profit."

"Except you give away your products."

"Yeah." He laughed and put his head down. Peders my new ally.

CHAPTER
FORTY-ONE

My belly was full. Now I needed to see Riley and the boys again to test my grasp on reality. But the hunger in my belly had been replaced with another hunger—sliders. I wanted, no, needed, to see them, see their process, the science performed by alt-Capitalists living underground, under radar, off grid. I told Peders this as we walked back to his car.

"I'll show you," he said, as easily as offering to take me to lunch.

"How do we get back? I only know the way through a wall in a smoky studio in Pilsen."

"There are lots of ways in, not so many that lead out," he replied.

"What about Riley?"

"He's fine. They're all fine. I don't think I have to tell you that the less you talk about what you now know, the safer you and they will be."

Peders drove us to the hospital where I'd left Riley with Stavros, which felt like a week ago by now. He took out a small pad and a fancy pen from his pocket and wrote something, handing it to me. I looked at the paper—empty. "What is this?"

Next came a tiny spray bottle. "It's luminol spray. It makes ink visible only for thirty seconds, so memorize the address when you see it."

I stared at the blank page.

"The tunnels, like the bookcase and the wall you went through, change every day. This is where a tunnel will be tomorrow night. Ten p.m. See ya," he said, and put the car in gear about to take off. I was still in the passenger seat. "Zak, go, now."

"What about all my questions I didn't get to ask? What about Jane and my receipts that he's waiting for me to bring him?"

Peders smirked. "I think you found the perfect spot for them."

• ———— • • • ———— •

And there I was standing outside one of the side entrances to the Uni Med Center, feeling like I could drop to my knees and fall asleep right there in that position. Since the truck stop diner, the wind had died down, but it still carried the same biting chill. I hadn't yet considered how I would get upstairs to the third floor undetected. I could do what Harrison Ford did in *The Fugitive* and steal a lab coat and stethoscope and walk around normally like I owned the place. No way, I thought, even though I'd just had an encounter with an asset. Or was I the asset? I loved all that tradecraft terminology. My options were stairs, an elevator, possibly a freight elevator, if I could find—

"Can I help you, son?" someone said behind me.

I whipped around. Carson. The bastard. "Aren't you funny now."

"Thanks for ditching us."

"Sorry, I just needed to walk a bit."

Carson stepped back to appraise me, Dugger and Chris pulled away to make a circle.

"What?" I demanded.

"Where've you been all night?" Chris spoke this time, the second arm of their three-way interrogation.

"I didn't go anywhere, just stayed in that smelly room. Brolly came in and talked to me about what to expect." They knew I was lying and there was nothing I could do. What Peders said was true; they'd be in danger.

"So you want us to believe that you spent the past six hours hanging out in a smoky den in Pilsen?"

I paused a second too long. I was no good at this shit. "That's right."

All six eyes circled around. Carson, this time, stepped forward and put his hand around my neck. He seemed to pull something off the back of my shirt collar.

"What the fuck are you doing?" I whined and swerved out of his grip.

He held up a tiny silver disc; everyone stared at it and I hung my head.

"That's how you knew where I'd be when I came out of the tunnel?"

"We've been tracking you on a GPS," Chris explained with a peevish stare that told me he didn't appreciate being lied to.

Carson, the saltier one of the group, looked at the ground. Dugger was silent but observing everything.

"You heard everything?"

Chris gave a minimalist nod. "We're out here because I know the van is bugged, somewhere, even though we've taken it apart three times already."

"So that's why the rear bucket seat feels like you're on a boat," I replied, not necessarily intending to lighten the mood but grateful that I had, even in a small way.

"Peders is ex-CIA," Chris said with a sigh.

"He implied as much when we were at the diner," I affirmed.

"He spent a lot of time moving around black sites near Prague in the nineties—"

"Black sites?"

"Locations where highly classified, unauthorized projects take place —could be research, surveillance, interrogation, sort of a broad term that can mean different things in different regions."

"He was conducting these interrogations?" I asked.

"Maybe, or maybe being interrogated himself. We can't tell. Looks like he spent about five years over there, and came back weighing about twenty-five pounds less."

"So he was a political prisoner in a military prison?"

"Not military," Chris explained. "There's really only one question that matters: Do you trust him?"

What choice did I have? I never trusted David Wade, and that instinct turned out to be right. Same for Jane. And Mandy. The thought of her made my chest ache and I was too exhausted to feel pain right now. "Where's Riley?"

"The Mill. He was there waiting for you when you skipped out," Chris said.

Shit. "Can I just, like, go in the van and sleep for a few days?"

CHAPTER FORTY-TWO

Riley sat on the edge of the twin mattress in Stavros' basement where I'd been apparently sleeping. Was it the next day? Had they drugged me? I blinked a few times and leaned on one elbow to grab the mug of coffee he handed me.

"I heard you're a coffee drinker now."

"How could you be here right now? You were in the hospital."

"Just drink."

Two sips, three. Okay there may be hope for me here.

"Stavros is okay. They're sending him home today. Carla's been with him the whole time. I checked in on Granville West; everything's okay there. I saw Mandy. She looked sullen as usual."

"Any sign of Wade?"

"No, I looked." Riley ticked off items on his imaginary status report. "I called your mom, told her a good story."

"Probably had a search warrant out on me."

He smiled.

"This ought to be good." I sat up.

"Your economics teacher was showing signs of being drunk in class, so you used one of your electives and registered for Political Science and you've been on a field trip to Washington D.C. for the past week."

"Omigod, you should get an Academy Award for that. Did she buy it?"

We enjoyed the moment and the brief silence, knowing full well that when they checked the veracity of his story they'd discover it was a lie, like everything else in my life. Even still, it bought me time. "Thank you," I mumbled. "How about you?"

He stood up, raised his palms, shrugged, and moved to lean against the wall. Oh no. I watched his face working through something.

I had to tell him everything. How could I not? "Here's the thing —"

"Mellon's dead."

Nothing came after those words, but I waited to see if maybe it was some kind of sick joke.

"He didn't have food poisoning either like we originally thought," he said. "He was *poisoned*, as in, like, you know, administered…for the purpose of…harm."

Now I was out of bed. "You're telling me that the pizza Mellon ate was the one you ordered for us?" I had my hand, oddly, covering my mouth, unsure if I was trying not to cry or vomit or just to keep my mind from running away with me. "Did you tell them?" I angled my head toward the other room.

"No." Riley slid down the wall and sat on the floor opposite me. "We heard everything, where you went, what you were doing, Brolly, Rand, Jane, Mandy, now Peders. Is there more…more layers of this… this conspiracy? We're all known to them now, all of us, that means our lives are over and our futures, well…"

"I'm the only one who saw anything and there's no way to prove otherwise," I said, trying to calm him down knowing it wouldn't help. I gulped the rest of the coffee. "I'm going back there tonight to see what I almost saw last night. I more than just want to know, I need to know. I've alienated my parents, I've just about been expelled, and I have no future prospects in any direction. The truth is all there is now. And I'll just gently remind you that I never chose any of this."

"I know, it chose you. Any idea why it didn't choose me?"

Riley, bless his tender heart. "Because of your unimpeachable character, of course. I'm shifty and unscrupulous, didn't you know?"

"Hey." Carson motioned us into the main room of Stavros' secret, bulletproof, technologically-advanced hideout.

"Wow so that's like a...bedroom, sort of?" I commented on the tiny, furniture-less room with a twin bed.

"I'd call it a fainting couch," Carson said.

"Seemed fine for you for the past few hours," Chris added. "We could hear you snoring upstairs."

"Quick, what time is it?" Ten o'clock, I remembered from Peders.

"Eight thirty, you're fine."

"How far am I going? Did you find the address?"

"Not yet." Carson held the tiny bottle. "But we tested the contents and it's *luminol*, a chemical, and hydrogen peroxide. But I don't see how it will work unless he wrote the address in blood."

"Or grape juice," Dugger added.

Chris shook his head. "No, the acid in grape juice can detect a message written in baking soda.

"So we don't know if it'll work," I concluded. "Depending on where the address is, we have a little over an hour to figure it out."

"Chris and Dugger are working on that," Carson said. "Check this out." He was on a stool with a small laptop on the edge of the large table. Riley and I peered onto the screen that showed a live map and a moving target.

"Is that a game console?" Riley asked. "Tron?"

"He loves Tron," I explained.

"Who doesn't? This—" Carson pointed to the small, yellow dot moving up the middle—"is Peders." He was smiling.

"How the hell did you do that? Do you know him?" I glanced at the others.

"I heard the door when you left and followed you out there to see what car picked you up, and I put a tracer on the undercarriage."

"Don't those fall off pretty easily?" Riley asked.

"Magnetic. Did Peders say he would meet you at ten tonight?"

"No." I touched the paper Peders gave me. "Just that this address was the location of where the tunnel entrance would be. They change every day."

The three students sat at attention.

"What?" I asked.

"That's the part we haven't figured out yet," Carson said. "The Jane-factor doesn't make any sense."

Chris now. "We were tracking you while you were inside, you know, in the other place, and listening and trying to put some of the pieces together. We thought the variable location entrances were to keep out Jane. But I don't think so."

"So why does he need the coordinates embedded on my receipts?" I cut in.

"Who put them there and why?" Riley added.

"That's the million-dollar question," Dugger said, using his typical economy of words. "We're ready. He had the spray bottle and small, white note paper on the center table. "If it doesn't work the first time, I think we'll have two chances."

"Why wouldn't it?" I asked.

"If Peders used the wrong pen or maybe didn't press hard enough for the ink to seep into the paper fibers." Dugger sprayed twice, saturated most of the page. Carson stood behind him with his laptop ready to record the address into the program he was using to track Peders.

CHAPTER FORTY-THREE

41.8018059

-87.6342512

"You got it?" Chris asked Carson, fingers already entering the corresponding latitude and longitude coordinates.

"Got it. 325 W. 51st Street. Fuller Park."

"Great, another lovely neighborhood." Dugger shook his head.

Chris pointed. "The ink's disappearing. Look, that's way faster than —"

"It's gone," Carson announced.

Something flashed in front of my eyes for one of those split seconds that seemed to last longer than it should. A message only meant for me? "Did...anyone see anything before the ink vanished, by chance?" I asked, checking their faces. They shook their heads. "No one saw it and there were five sets of eyes staring at the same thing? Come on."

"Maybe you have special powers?" Riley whispered.

Carson raised his brows and pointed to something behind me.

"What?"

"The notebook, maybe?" he asked.

"What did you see?" Riley demanded. "Describe it."

"I don't know exactly," I stammered. "Something between the two lines. A dark smudge at first but then right before the ink disappeared it looked like there was writing on it, like a dark spot with white letters over it."

Carson blinked this through his megabrain. "A dark spot? Did it look red?"

I shrugged.

"War ink?" he said to Chris.

"They used a form of disappearing ink the revolutionary war to pass messages, using water and ferrous sulfate," Chris said. "Iron."

"Detectable by what means?" I asked.

Chris smiled. "Heat." He pulled a lighter out of a drawer in Stavros' desk.

"Try not to burn the house down," Carson said.

"How close do I—"

"Give it to me." Carson snatched it from Chris' fingers. He held the flame vertically and positioned the paper next to it. "Do you see it?" He turned his head to see our wide eyes, and pulled his thumb off the lighter.

"There is no way out." I felt the weight of the words fill the basement.

Carson shook his head. "That's what was on the paper?"

I nodded.

"That could be read different ways," Riley commented. "The door…try the door at the top of the stairs."

I felt the fear in his voice at the same time my chest started pounding harder.

"I'll go." Chris moved around the desk and the stairs leading to the main floor of Stavros' home. "It's locked!" he yelled down the stairs.

"Push the button," Carson reminded him.

"I'm pushing it. Someone's…" Chris stopped and descended back down to the main room, his face drained of all color. "Someone's shorted out the power."

"We have power down here, though," I commented.

"The lock on that door has a security panel. There's no code—just a touch pad to lock it. Press once to unlock, twice to lock. Someone could have cut the power just to that door from the console in the front foyer," Carson explained.

Dugger stood at the bottom of the stairs now. "That means whoever did that is…"

"In the house," I realized. "Is there another way out of here? A bathroom?"

Carson shook his head.

"No window in the bedroom either," I recalled.

Chris pushed past me to get to the stairs and crept behind them to open a door. "The boiler room, here, there's a water heater and a window."

"Stay away from it and keep the light off," I bellowed, realizing suddenly that the house had been watched ever since I got back here. We were trapped. I kept my eyes on Riley and watched his chest rise and fall. I looked at him and touched my nose a few times.

"My inhaler? I have one," he replied, still seated on one of the stools at the big center desk, oddly calm for our predicament. Come to think of it, he didn't seem too chapped that I'd gone off the last time, with Peders. I went to him now and searched his eyes. Was this the same Riley, who suffered from claustrophobia, the old lady who panicked at the sound of a raised voice, completely calm at the thought of being trapped?

"I can summon the cops from here," Carson said. "I maintain Stavros' security system."

"Are there cameras outside? Can you see anyone?" I pressed.

"Nothing, and no cars parked nearby either." He and I traded glances, then both headed up the stairs.

"Can you trip the door lock?" I asked quietly.

"Not without resetting the power to the whole house, and the alarm going off," Carson said and waited. "That would attract a lot of neighborhood attention, but it would be quick, almost like a car alarm that someone runs outside to turn off."

"Try it one more time," I said. He pressed the green touch pad once and the door clicked and the pad turned red. I tried the door— locked. "Okay," I nodded. "Do it."

"Let me go ahead of you. I need my other laptop," Carson said.

Riley was still wide-eyed and looking strange, Dugger was pacing, and Chris sat with his head in his hands. "Resetting the system. Get ready. There'll be a complete blackout—"

"Just this house?" Chris asked.

"Yes," Carson said, "for about five seconds and an alarm will sound for that same amount of time. Then the system will reset itself, lights come back on and the upstairs door should be locked only until we press the touchpad."

"I'll be in the boiler room," Chris said. "I wanna look out that window when the motion lights come on."

"Fine. Everyone else stay put. Here we go." Carson hit one key. A second late I heard a series of clicks upstairs and down, and then everything went black. One one thousand, two one thousand, three..."

CHAPTER FORTY-FOUR

My iPhone buzzed in my pocket, a text from Peders. *I'm outside, can take you to Fuller Park.*

Negative, I wrote back. *We've been ambushed and are stuck down here, I need to make sure we can all get out.*

Come now, I'll call in support for the rest of them.

I felt the notebook buzz in my back and I didn't have to read it to know. Divide and conquer, right? Peders wanted to separate us, or at least separate me from them. Why? I didn't know that yet, but I had one second left to put the phone back in my pocket before the lights went on again.

"Should come on…now," Carson announced, followed by another set of clicks, then lights.

"Chris," I said, remembering that he'd left the room to check the water heater window.

I caught a chilly vibe as I shimmied past Riley that I hadn't felt from him before, knowing it could be my imagination. Chris was flat against the wall in the tiny room staring outside. "Anything?"

"No, and the outside flood lights never flashed like they should have. We've done tests a hundred times on this system." He turned toward me. "No cars, or killers, out there anyway," he added under his breath.

I blinked through this information, recalling Carson's idea that someone had cut the power to the door lock from the upstairs foyer. Had someone come for me, or for them?

"Peders is out back." Carson pointed to the yellow dot on his GPS map.

I turned to Riley. "Come with me this time, please. I don't want to do this without you again." It's true, I knew what to say to him and how to say it to get the desired response, and I thought I knew why he was so withdrawn. But my heart didn't totally trust that he was either okay or completely himself right now. I had to find out.

"You don't need me there," he play-argued but I could tell he'd already decided to come.

"You have a way better sense of direction, and we're gonna need it," was my lame-ass argument, knowing full well that in addition to that truth was the fact that he was color blind, afraid of heights and tight spaces.

Carson moved to the small desk against the wall and opened the middle drawer, from which he pulled out two small metal discs. "Bend down," he said and snapped it onto the inside of the back of my shirt collar, and did the same to Riley.

"Trackers, that's good," Riley said. "So you'll know where to retrieve our bodies if we suddenly stop moving."

"It's not safe down here; you guys have to move," I said to Carson, then to Chris and Dugger.

"We have other places," Chris replied with a sly grin.

I had this sinking feeling I would never see them again.

CHAPTER FORTY-FIVE

A red car pulled up to us on the street behind Stavros' house—not Peders' car and not Peders behind the wheel. The car stopped and a driver in a business suit turned toward us extending his hand.

"Do you know him?" Riley asked me.

"No." I called Peders and listened to his phone ringing over and over. What the fuck was this?

The window slid down and the driver leaned toward us. "Problem, gentlemen?"

"Who are you?" I asked in my interrogation voice, strategically stepping back a few inches toward the curb.

Riley watched me and followed suit, folding his arms in defiance. The sky, meanwhile, had clouded over in this thick, gray mass still holding a slight glow of afternoon sun. I felt more annoyed than afraid, reminding myself that all the things my new friend Peders told me could be half-truths or partial lies and I only had my own wit to count on.

"The driver," the man said in a theatrical voice, betraying an Eastern European accent.

"Let me talk to Peders first or we're not getting in."

The driver hung his head in exasperation.

"I don't need you to get there, I have the address of the entrance for tonight." My phone rang just then—Peders. "Where are you?" I demanded.

"Get in the car, Zak."

"Where are you and what's with this song and dance? You told me to meet you at the address you gave me. Why do I need an escort now? We could just as easily call Uber or something."

"Things have changed," Peders replied.

I heard a peculiar sound in the background that I couldn't place.

"In the past few hours? What? The entrance has changed?"

"Let's go back inside," Riley said.

But I started walking away from the red car and the house, toward the main street fifty yards ahead.

"Yes," Peders confirmed finally.

I was still walking, Riley right behind me, every instinct telling me to not get into that car. "If you want to pick us up, come and get us. If not, we'll be at that meeting point in Fuller Park per your prior instructions." I disconnected and knew I'd have to deal with both Riley's questions and the red car tailing us now.

"Is he coming?" Riley asked.

"I don't know," I admitted. "But we're going back to where I came out last night."

Riley stopped walking and turned. "You don't believe Peders' story about the entrances changing every night?"

I shook my head. "It's too much trouble to coordinate all that. If any of what he says is even remotely true, they've got a pretty involved set of operations that go on in there and I doubt they'd have the manpower to maintain that type of logistics. More likely some guard dog Janes to monitor the entry points."

"Can you find your way there again?"

"Hire us an Uber, off-campus," I replied.

CHAPTER
FORTY-SIX

"**Steel Workers Park,**" I announced as we slid into the back seat of an Uber. "Take 41 South and get off at East 87th."

"What are you doing?" Riley asked.

"Carson. You guys get that?" I said into the air while leaning my head to the right near the tracking device in my jacket.

My phone buzzed with a text, from Carson's phone. *Roger that.*

"It's the only thing that makes any sense. There's a lot of empty, unused, abandoned space with no power and huge multi-story buildings."

"Abandoned steel mills?"

"We'll find out. I spent the past two days in a huge industrial park with no visible industry except a couple of makeshift, fake Starbucks. I thought it might have been on the grounds of the university, but why wouldn't the university be using that space? This is the only thing that makes sense, and it's not that far from the U. A few miles south and closer to the Calumet River."

"Is there a party out here or something?" the teenaged Uber driver asked.

"Just scoping it out," I said. "Up here's fine. Drop us off outside the gate."

"Dude…" Riley looked out the window. "You sure about this?"

"Trust me." I got out and headed toward a massive concrete structure that looked lightning-charred.

"You know we're like twenty miles away from Pilsen, right?"

"That wasn't the only place I entered. The second time was in Calumet Heights, which is right here." I pointed.

"Another sketchy neighborhood," Riley commented, following me and zipping his jacket up all the way. "I don't suppose you brought a flashlight with you, or maybe a few police escorts?"

"Try here." I moved through the opening. I'd only been outside for a moment and was already frozen.

"So, you don't know if this is even—"

Car tires screeched. Well, that didn't take them long. I looked back. Our Uber driver had already taken off. A door opened and slammed shut.

"Run!" I took off into the dark with Riley's steps behind me. "I'm pretty sure we're in the right place."

———•——•••——•———

My phone buzzed with a text. Carson. I didn't respond so then it rang.

"Hey can't really talk now," I said out of breath.

"Keep going in that same direction and you'll run right into the building you were in last night. I got the whole layout of the place in front of me."

"How far?" I turned to Riley, who was right behind me. I didn't see anyone tailing us yet.

"Two football fields," Carson replied.

"Shit, we'll be dead by then. Okay."

"You're being tailed but he's walking and he's way behind you."

We slowed to a fast walk, then a slightly slower walk. "Two football fields," I said to Riley.

"I heard. Tell him about Mellon."

"We're on it," Carson said. I put him on speaker. "Melton Federman from Grand Rapids, Michigan."

"Was he poisoned?" Riley asked.

"Oh yeah. *Aconitum napellis* or aconite, an herb also known as devil's helmet or monkshood. It contains several toxic chemicals and as little as two milligrams can be fatal, whether it's absorbed on the skin or ingested as a tincture. Could have been on the box and he touched it, or a tincture used to administer a few drops of it on a slice of the pizza."

I felt sick. I stopped walking feeling like throwing my phone out the window. There weren't any windows in here, which was worth noting even in my present state.

"Either of you could have been the intended target of that attack," Carson said in a more official voice. "I can see where you are, where you're going, and we're hearing everything you're saying. So keep going. We got you."

"Just don't do anything stupid," Riley said.

I resumed our fast pace, still with Carson on speaker phone, still churning through the reality that our next door neighbor was dead, as in no longer living...because of one of us and ultimately because of me. The worst part was, according to Peders, Riley was also in danger. How could anyone want to kill Riley? He was like a Golden Retriever. Me, on the other hand, had seen things I shouldn't have. That meant I was a liability. It also meant I was a threat to Riley's safety. I had to get away from him somehow but I couldn't leave him alone in this place. He'd never agree if I asked him to go back, or even if I escorted him.

"Dude, are you still there? You're close," Carson narrated. "Just keep walking in the same direction and you'll cross a threshold, like a catwalk sort of. Then you'll be in the building you were in before."

"How do we get to the opposite building without being seen?" I asked.

"Let us work on that. No more calls, only texting from now on. Is your phone charged?"

"Yes," Riley answered, "I charged it while you were asleep."

CHAPTER FORTY-SEVEN

The biting cold combined with Riley's lack of conversation was scaring me. Was it wrong to admit that to myself, that I needed comfort and felt afraid every minute of every day now? Was this temporary, or a new normal?

Riley kept up but didn't so much as glance at me. Sure, due to lack of hydration, sleep, food, and an overdose of adrenaline over the past several weeks, it was possible my mind was unraveling. But all I had in my world was what was within an arm's reach right now. An empty concrete building, a phone, an old friend, and three warring factions of killers chasing us because of what I'd discovered. I would have gladly traded a kidney right now to unsee it all.

We'd passed through two more buildings, like Carson predicted—walking along these concrete catwalks up high, exposed, connecting one part of a building to another. There was a third coming up. Riley stopped jogging and halted at the sound of a car door down below. I could barely peer around the corner of the catwalk plank to see below without being detected. It wasn't Peders' car, or not the car he drove the last time, but I recognized his blond hair and trench coat from three stories up.

"Peders," I announced to both Riley and Carson.

"Is he getting out?" Riley looked down there now, holding onto the edge. "He looks…"

"What?"

"Like he's…sleeping."

"Carson, you there? When did that car arrive here? Because there's still someone else here tracking us." My phone buzzed with the text chime.

Affirmative, a second car drove up a few mins ago
Should we go down there?

I knew Riley's inclination was right but there was no way I was going backwards now. I could see the next building just ahead of us on the same path. From our high vantage point, I could see the Starbucks sign haphazardly taped around the metal pole.

"We're almost there," I replied, hoping that would answer his question. The sky was lighter than the night before with an orange stripe on the horizon. "Slow down," I said, realizing we might be more visible tonight. I stopped walking and looked at my phone to make sure I could deploy the video recorder at a second's notice.

Riley stopped, crossed his arms and shivered. "Do we have a plan? Who are we meeting?"

"I don't know yet."

"Peders?"

"I said I don't know," I replied, knowing in my bones what he was about to say.

"Because I think he's dead. Why else would he be not moving?"

"Maybe pausing to look up, looking for us, talking on the phone?" I replied, knowing that none of those were likely to be true. I ran across the next catwalk, waited on the other side and motioned for Riley. "I want to find someone named Mason: Peders' partner."

We started walking again. A staircase now was visible fifty feet ahead and my instinct, or maybe the notebook, guided me to walk past it.

"Why?" Riley asked.

"Corroboration, to see if his story matches what Peders told me about this place. And no, I'm not sure I can trust him if we even find him."

I knocked the floor a few times with my shoe. The echo sounded different in this building. Ah, another staircase. Riley was ahead of me now, a few steps.

"Take this down," I instructed and followed him down two flights to the main floor. I could see out the same wall of windows from the other night. "Don't get too close," I said, knowing we might be visible to someone looking out the windows opposite us across the street. A moped sounded a few blocks away, and someone on a bicycle rode beneath us carrying a brown-wrapped parcel. Riley looked at me for an explanation I couldn't give.

"Slowly," I narrated, pulling him behind me toward the row of windows, staying behind the large pillars in the middle of the room.

"It's completely dark in there." Riley moved an inch closer. "Is there—"

"Maybe," I said, "keep watching."

"Maybe what?"

I sighed. "Maybe it's dark, maybe it's not. I saw lights before, red and green lights going off at odd intervals."

"Like production equipment you're thinking?"

"Yeah."

"How do you know which type?"

Omigod Riley please please shut up, I thought, then hated myself for thinking it.

"Type?"

"Well, you're thinking what you saw was related to…sliders. The black ops pharma, right?"

I blinked back, waiting, keeping my eyes on the other building, still nothing.

"What if it's not them and it's the other group? If there is another group."

I hadn't thought of that.

My phone buzzed with a new text at the exact second a red light started blinking, a single light this time, on—off—on—off—on—off.

"Are you watching?"

"Is this what you saw?" he asked.

Shit, the phone, but I couldn't take my eyes off the lights. I pulled out the phone, pressed the camera icon and slid my thumb to the right for the video option. Lights still blinking, I expanded the view. There was no way to get anything on camera from this distance. "We have to get closer."

I moved in slow motion to the next pillar toward the stairs.

"Wait!"

"Come on."

"Where are we going? There's no way to get over there," Riley argued.

I exited the building on the bottom floor, remembering how Mandy had warned me about staying outside in this place, so I hugged the buildings as I walked. Riley stayed a few feet behind me, no doubt sulking over my non-plan. I couldn't blame him.

I stopped.

"Who's that?" Riley asked of a tall, thin fellow standing in our path facing us.

Rand. What now? Was he a *Campus Police* or a fucking Jane-soldier?

"Hey," he said. "Welcome back." He flashed what seemed like a real smile. "Latte?"

"No."

"Who's this?" He looked at Riley.

"Like you don't know?"

"I'm Pat," Riley said, thank God without the handshake.

"This is Rand."

"Zak said you were a good guy."

"No I didn't."

"Latte?" Rand pointed diagonally across the street, like we didn't have a choice in the matter.

I shook my head. And we stood there like that in a half-circle, weighing, deciding, while the air grew colder and the wind blew harder and I secretly prayed that if things went bad, Riley had his inhaler with him.

"You shouldn't be here," Rand said, matter-of-factly, raising an eyebrow like I should have known this already. "I'm your guide," he added. "Why don't you come with me."

Riley took two steps toward him. What choice did I have now?

CHAPTER FORTY-EIGHT

Rand led us back to Command Central. The Elfish girl popped up from beneath the Suddenly Starbucks counter. I tried hard not to imagine what, or who, she was doing down there. A different tall, lanky fellow ogled her from further back in the tent.

I turned to Riley to explain the situation. "It's real Starbucks coffee, real equipment, no tables, no sugar and, most importantly, no cash."

"No sugar. Interesting. So coffee and pharma are free on your freak-planet?" he said to Rand.

"Coffee's not free, just no cash. Or credit. Only alt-currencies."

Riley listened.

"Allow me to explain something," Rand replied. "If the guards don't know you in here, they'll *wipe* you. You saw them last time you were here," he said to me, "as I understand from the report. The guards know you now. So unless you have a guide, they will not leave you alone."

"Which team are you on again?" Riley asked like he was asking for baseball scores.

Rand's right brow raised, trying not to laugh. "I'm a slider. I move stuff back and forth, a delivery boy, so to speak."

"He's a Pharmacist," I added.

Rand nodded, soberly.

"So if what Peders says is correct, you deliver illegal but real pharma to old people or mental patients…for free. That's your story?"

"Well, nothing's totally free, but they don't pay for the medicine. Not in money," Rand explained.

I ordered a latte and an iced tea because Riley hated coffee, logged into my Breadwallet app , then held up my phone for the girl to scan.

Riley continued his attack on reality. "Let me guess. Blood, plasma, teeth, kidneys, human hair, ovaries?"

Rand's face didn't change. I actually wondered if he might be an artificial life form. Did this place manufacture people too?

"I'm still trying to find out what team you're on. Are you good pharma, bad pharma, regular pharma, or one of the Janes?"

Drinks were ready. I knew Riley liked his tea sweet. "We do have sugar," the girl explained with difficulty. "It's just…different sugar."

"I work wherever I'm needed," Rand said to Riley behind me. "I work for what I'd call real pharma, the U Med Center, and—"

"And you steal meds from them, right?" Riley again. Geez.

"One pill from each bottle that they use for testing and validation only. Testing for, like, measuring exact size, shape, color, coating, and imprints."

I sipped and listened, monitoring the man behind the counter who looked like he might mount the blonde girl right here while we watched.

"Can we see it? See the operation, how it's done?"

I was glad Riley asked; it would have been my next question.

"Sure," Rand said. "It's a forty-minute walk, but we can take peds."

Mopeds? Rand and the creepy Starbucks guy exchanged words in what sounded like Russian, I recognized from one of our floor mates in Granville West. I suspected it was Chechen. Riley and I spoke telepathically as we sipped our drinks, eyes wide and blinking, awaiting whatever arrangement was being made on our behalf.

"Good question," I conceded.

Riley shook his head slowly. I could hear his thoughts.

Rand and Riley were on one moped, me on the other. I followed them at a slow speed down the dark, empty streets of my new apocalyptic hideout, straight ahead with two left turns. The mopeds were left on the street below and we followed Rand up two flights into the same building I'd observed now for the past two nights, confirming that I was on the right track by monitoring the blinking lights.

As we climbed another staircase I heard sounds, muffled talking, faint shuffling of shoes on the concrete floor, and metal clanks of machinery that made sounds at even intervals. Rand turned around to check on us every few seconds, like we might run off or something. It wasn't a knocking sound—more of a clicking or pressing of something against a surface. Rand got to the top of the stairs first. It amazed me how quickly my eyes adjusted to the darkness. Like reading my thoughts (had he?), Rand bent low and clicked on a tiny light, which gave shape and size to the large room. I saw three forms, not sure of the genders, wearing masks, gloves, and gowns. Hence the muffled voices last night.

"Just observing, for tonight," Rand explained to one of the three masked workers.

The worker nodded, then moved to the edge of the room and clicked on two more of the tiny lights.

Well, I didn't need to take a video of the operation since I was being given a proper tour. Riley, still holding his cup of iced tea, moved closer to one of the machines and crouched to get a better look. Rand watched but didn't interfere. I knew enough to not initiate contact with the workers, if they were even capable of speech.

"They're drug imprinting machines," Riley whispered to me, then looked back at Rand, who nodded. "This comes last," he said. "Before distribution, after milling, drying, compression, then coating."

Rand gave a faint, irritated nod, and I wondered when Riley had time to read up on pharmaceutical manufacturing development stages. I headed back down the stairs. Unattended by my System D guard dog, I pulled the night air deep into my lungs. How did they get around the cleanliness issue? These buildings were caked in dust and completely unfinished, with no electricity that I could see.

"You have questions," Rand said on the stairs behind me.

"What about industrial hygiene?" I asked, again proud of myself for knowing the term. "Dirt, dust, lack of ventilation, electricity, what ab—"

"There's electricity," Rand said. "You watched me turn on two lights. It's just controlled lighting."

"How do you bring utilities off the grid?"

Rand's brow raised again, this time with a sly grin. "It's on the grid. Just a…different grid."

"Okay, who pays utility bills in The Matrix?" Riley asked now, brushing past Rand to stand beside me, hands in his pockets. His war stance.

"We do. All of us."

"How? You pay using US dollars and the money's zapped out of your bank accounts?"

"Thousands of US companies now accept bitcoin as a legitimate currency, including some utility companies. We pay using bitcoin and the money's zapped out of our bitcoin wallets. It's perfectly safe, completely legitimate, an—"

"By whose standards?"

I liked hearing sheltered-Riley argue the legitimacy of bitcoin as a reliable currency.

"There are many transactions here that are above board. There are also an equal amount of shady deals, including street drugs and weapons."

"You do that too?"

Rand shook his head. "I'm just a pill guy, strictly pharma."

"How about Wade?" Riley asked.

"And Mandy?" I added.

"I've got to get back." Rand moved toward the mopeds parked to the left of us.

"Who's Mason?" I called out in my practiced, adversarial voice.

Rand stopped mid-stride. Ah. So we at least got points for surprising him. He made a sort of ceremonial turn and breathed deeply, like he was about to divulge spy satellite frequencies. "A shadow. I don't know him, any of those guys. Only that they play by a very different rule book."

The wind howled as it pushed between buildings, down walkways, kicking up dirt at our feet while we all tried to steady ourselves against its force.

"Do you want to be here?" I asked now. His eyes told me no, or maybe that he didn't have a choice.

"Want." Rand repeated my word and lowered his eyes. "What is that? We're an anti-corporation, an anti-corruption stopgap working against a system that uses fear as currency for the purpose of creating dependency and weakness."

"Pharma?" I asked. "You're saying the medicines that they're selling are habit-forming—all of them?"

Rand's eyes were contracted, his eyebrows, forehead, his brain was working through something and the filter that protected Riley and me from knowing what we shouldn't was shutting down. He needed to talk, get it off his chest. We didn't move.

"Habit forming. Funny to hear that phrase. Comfort is habit-forming. The absence of pain is habit-forming. There's a website that tracks pharma payments and gifts to physicians each year. They're growing, they were like $11B in this country last year, so much that there's now regulation and policy enacted to manage it. Why do you think this matters?"

We stood frozen, listening. The wind died down a bit.

"Doctors can't even work," he continued. "The pressure is so severe. They're targeted in elevators, in the men's room, the subway, 24/7 by pharma trolls hiding around corners handing them sports season tickets, fancy pens, Italian leather briefcases filled with samples of often-experimental new drugs that have 'exciting preliminary results' but haven't even passed Stage 2 of clinical trials. You think clinical trial results are regulated? Untouchable? Think again. They're an appetizer on the TOR menu of what you can buy and influence off the grid, without regulation, without IP address tracking, taxes, or accountability. And people die as a result of this every month, every year. I read the clinical trials findings, I see it, I'm disgusted by it to the point that I eat antacid pills ten times a day and I have bleeding ulcers for which I take prescription drugs. It's a full circle and I'm trapped. I'm drowning in it every day of my life."

Rand touched the corners of his eyes. They were wet. Okay, maybe he wasn't artificial then.

"The only thing that keeps me going is knowing that by the work we're doing in here, I'm taking them down one pill at a time, hacking the foundations of their empire by constructing a new supply and thereby building a new demand for that supply. We're capitalists with a simple, elegant, destructive agenda. Wish I could say the same of the others."

"What others?" I asked.

"Their sales pitch is strong," Rand said. "Giving away

pharmaceuticals to cancer patients for free. It sounds like the world in 1950, doesn't it? At a time when gain and money weren't the only thing driving change."

"And by they you mean Peders? And Mason?"

"He won't talk to us," Riley surmised. "Let's get out of here."

"They don't pay," Rand confirmed. "Patients don't pay for the meds we manufacture, and it's true they don't need a prescription to get them."

I recognized the look on his face by the hole I now felt in my stomach. Jesus, what were they doing? "What do they give then?" I asked. "Kidneys? Body parts? Blood? What?"

"Their will. Meaning their estate."

CHAPTER FORTY-NINE

The mopeds wobbled against a heavier wind going back. I kept circling the phrase "the others" through my brain. Had Rand meant Peders and Mason and their consortium of highbrow philanthropists? Now they were delivering meds to cancer patients in exchange for being added to their last will and testament? Rand motored around the side of the tent where the bikes had been parked. The blonde waif stood outside with her bodyguard. Rand parked the one bike. The girl waved him over, then huddled them into the tent. I inched closer to listen, and thought I heard the word "she" but was diverted by Riley pointing to the street behind us and what looked like a Campus Police on a larger, black moped. It stopped well behind Riley. The uniformed person approached me.

"Rand!" I motioned Riley towards me, safety in numbers, right? The crew cut and six feet of him towered over all of us. Rand emerged from the tent and clasped his arms behind his back. A diplomatic touch.

"Yes?" he said. "I'm the Guide. What's the problem?"

The officer shifted his eyes between me and Riley, then an absent glance at the baristas. "The girl, the slider. You know her?"

"Mandy. What about her?"

"She's been requested by CP headquarters for questioning in connection with...a student."

Mellon? Riley looked at me, thinking the same thing. But why Mandy, unless they were questioning everyone on the floor.

"We might be next," Riley lip-synched. He was right, we lived next door to...I still could hardly believe it to say it. Mellon. Dead. Holy fuck.

"I haven't seen her today," Rand said, moving even closer to the officer, obviously unfazed by his stature.

"It's after dark," the man commented, visually scanning us. "It's not safe out here."

"We're conducting legitimate business. Thereafter, I'll escort them out," Rand replied with a 'fuck off' chin-raised stance.

"Unsafe from who?" Riley asked the minute Campus Police got back on his bike.

But I knew the answer already.

Rand pulled us under the protective covering of the Starbucks tent. "The Dream Market," he explained, "Alpha Bay and a few other smaller black market TOR sites transact illegal weapons and drugs, not only that, but predominantly. Sometimes they're shipped to less regulated countries, and sometimes they're shipped here disassembled."

"Also re-assembled here?" I asked.

"Yes, but not directly. Some parts are sewn into the insides of dolls, like stuffed animals."

"Guns inside a—"

Rand shook his head. "Grips, barrels, maybe just ammo—they're disassembled because they're undetectable that way. So only enough that a teddy bear would still feel like the correct weight of a teddy bear with bean bag stuffing. We also use soccer balls."

"Wouldn't that make them like rocks?"

"We load them with gun parts and use a higher concentration of helium to adjust. The weight's all wrong but it's enough to get you through a border check."

Genius. I looked around. "Doesn't really seem like a viable environment for toy manufacturing here."

"Believe me, no toddler will ever play with a bear that comes out of here. They're essentially a transport casing in the event a runner gets stopped en route to a drop. Then, when they reach their destination, the furry casings are removed and discarded. If anyone looked inside a package and saw a bag of teddy bears, it immediately neutralizes drug-running suspicions. Plus we choose our runners carefully."

"Wade, the bastard, looks like a bloody magazine cover," I said. It was true.

"You're right. He's clean cut, smart, fast, smooth talker, reliable," Rand affirmed, and seemed too careful with his words. "The weapons purchased from one of those markets, many of them, arrive here disassembled on container ships through the Port of Chicago."

"Unsafe from who?" Riley pressed.

"Your friends," Rand replied. "The Valve."

"This is not normal," Riley mumbled as we made our way down the long tunnel heading back to the entrance to Steel Workers Park.

Surrounded by concrete, and three flights off the ground, a scuff of a shoe made an echo that sounded three times as loud. My fragmented mind imagined a sniper following us in black clothing wearing night-vision goggles and carrying an automatic weapon. But every time I thought I heard a noise, it went quiet.

Rand was a few steps ahead, apparently on the hook to properly deliver us fully intact back to the real world. He seemed shaken by the encounter with the officer, or maybe from being grilled by our existential questions. We were putting him in danger; I knew that now. Riley was right, certainly. We couldn't return to our dorm, and Stavros' home was no longer safe. Running back to the safety of our parents would be unthinkable. All I could think about was Stavros' equation, which Carla mentioned only in passing and which I hadn't had time to process. My gut told me, somehow, it was the key to everything. My feet ached and I now hated these shoes, I only now realized.

Rand pointed to a shade of light ahead of us. "Follow this out," he said. "Can you get picked up by someone? It's not safe here at night."

Oh, the irony. Riley's terrified face cracked me up. The echo of my laugh bouncing off the cavernous walls and rusted, steel floor to make it ten times as loud.

"Safe. You're funny."

"Be quiet, we're probably being observed even now."

"Are you fucking kidding me?"

Rand stopped, apparently sensing my loss of composure.

"Where *would* we be safe right now?" I asked.

CHAPTER FIFTY

I texted Chris, praying they were parked behind a dumpster somewhere close. *Do you want me to call an Uber?*

No almost there.

Out in the open air again, Riley and I emerged not quite knowing how Rand had slipped back into the shadows, but I couldn't see him anywhere. It was a different opening than where we entered but on the same side of the building, facing a dank pond of rain runoff that flowed into the Calumet River, chain link fencing, rusty scrap metal and a tinge of yellow blinking off the water from the waking horizon. I had no conception of time.

"The car's gone," Riley said, of the car we'd seen earlier from the top floor when I'd been thinking it had been Peders and dreading he'd been dead.

"I see that."

"Are you okay?" he asked.

I tried not to laugh.

"Yeah, great."

He stared. "You know what I mean."

A different, newer, smaller, shinier white van drove toward us. I recognized Chris' aviator glasses in the driver's seat. It pulled up fast and slowed at the last minute. I heard a scuff behind us. Rand stepped out, arms crossed, watching us. He was near the first opening where we'd originally entered.

"Come on." Carson slid open the van's side door.

Riley climbed in, and, as I was about to turn, I saw a shadow in the second opening further down, where we'd exited the building. Squinting, it looked like Peders' trench coat...and a gun held down at his right side.

"Jesus." I looked into the van. "We need to get Rand." I pointed.

"We can't get through; there's a fence," Chris replied.

"Fucking run it down, for God's sake!" I dove into the van headfirst and held onto something under the seat, bracing myself for the van's lurch forward but instead heard a shot fired. Fuck.

"Back up back up back up!" Dugger shouted, ripping the van door closed. As we backed out, I peeked my head just above the dash and saw my ally, Peders, in his unbuttoned trench coat standing over Rand with a gun in his right hand. Rand was on the ground. Peders' right hand was rising up.

CHAPTER FIFTY-ONE

They were like our three surrogate mothers. Chris driving; Carson beside him; and Dugger in the back with us. There was a bag with two chicken sandwiches, fries, two bottles of water, and two large Cokes. Nerves thready, every limb sore, I reached my fingers up to the front seat and sort of grabbed them each by the arm to acknowledge the certainty of their physical presence. It was a gift, that sentiment, on a shiny silver platter reassuring me that the humanity I'd known still existed somewhere. I was okay, Riley okay, our friends okay.

Rand.

I didn't know where we were going. Three bites into my chicken sandwich, my mind shifted to the long, horizontal shape of Rand's body on the ground. Our van screeched away from Steel Workers Park and our latest assailant, Peders.

"So what *was* that, then?" I said aloud, "Peders' cloak and dagger routine at the park, then the diner and telling me all his secrets?"

"Did you guys catch it all?" Riley asked.

Carson turned toward us. "I've been trying to find some transaction history to verify Rand's outrageous story about Peders and Mason."

"An old person's will; is that in the public domain?"

The three of them cracked up. "There's this thing called the internet," Dugger said, "maybe you've heard of it?"

"Hackers."

"It's not our primary occupation," Chris replied. "Anyway we looked and didn't find anything."

"Yet," Carson added. "I doubt they use their real names, if they are getting listed on someone's will. I'll find one."

"And then what?" I recognized the main entrance to campus. "Why are we back here?"

"We have a bunker," Dugger explained.

My head pounded. "You're gonna, what, tell them the truth then?" I asked Carson.

"No, *you* are," Chris answered me this time.

I forced down three sips of Coke. Riley took the cup and sipped. Chris slowed the van to a crawl and rolled us around the back of the music building. It was barely light out, probably not even four am.

"This'll be open now?" I asked.

We got out and I heard a violin playing. Okay, so this was what discipline looked like.

CHAPTER FIFTY-TWO

We walked in a silent procession through a miraculously unlocked side door to Fulton Recital Hall in the Goodspeed Hall compound that housed University of Chicago's Department of Music. Chris led us up one flight of stairs, through a long corridor to an elevator, then down three floors. The elevator chunked at the bottom and the doors opened. It smelled like my grandfather's basement. Another cold, dark building. Riley put a hand on my shoulder, naturally knowing my state of mind even before I did myself.

"I'm okay," I said.

"You didn't eat," he replied.

"Quiet," Carson whispered.

We wound our way through three empty hallways, a carpeted staircase to yet an even lower level that stopped at a door. Chris stuck a single key in the lock and opened it, turning on the lights to reveal a spacious practice room with a grand piano in the center.

"There are no windows in here," Riley observed. "We're below ground. So if it's a practice room it's probably soundproofed."

"They're gonna torture us, see, and no one will hear our screams."

Riley whipped around to face me. "Oh, that's fucking funny."

"So this is your bunker?" I asked.

The three of them seemed to be deciding how much to tell Riley and me about this place, and why Chris had a key to it if none of them were music students. "We know people," Chris replied.

I wasn't sure, still, what we were doing here, other than some debrief huddle in lieu of Stavros' basement. Dugger adjusted the lighting so there was only a spotlight over the piano, and he and Carson took possession of the only pieces of furniture in the room: two long benches.

"They put a hundred thousand dollar Steinway in this room and couldn't put a few chairs?" I said.

"It's a practice room for chamber ensembles. They put their music stands in a circle around the piano and play standing up," Chris explained.

Riley, sprawled on the floor, used his jacket as a pillow. My head still ached. I felt pretty certain that Rand, with whom we'd just spent the past two hours, was now lying dead face-down in a puddle outside the entrance building at Steel Workers Park. Every minute that passed, I felt more urgency. That urgency buzzed in my palms, though I wasn't completely certain what I was supposed to be doing.

"Are you sure that was Peders?" Chris started. "Because it doesn't make sense why he'd need to kill Rand."

"They were on opposite sides," Dugger answered. "Right?" He looked at me now, hoping I would supply the necessary information to assemble a coherent picture of the warring factions operating within one small speck of System D's global enterprise. I just shook my head.

"You guys heard everything, I assume? Through the little device in my jacket?" A snarl came out of my voice that I hadn't quite intended.

"We're trying to help you, dude. Don't turn on us now," Chris argued. I noticed all four of them were clumped together, me sitting opposite. Symbolic, wasn't it?

I rubbed my temples. "I just mean you should have heard everything that was going on in there. And God knows how many other conversations you were monitoring," I said with my brow raised.

"You came to us," Chris shot back.

Carson hadn't said a word yet. Riley sat up straight, poised as the eternal moderator.

"Through Stavros," I corrected him. "And I was led to him by the nose via some mysterious hand-written note. Any idea who wrote that?"

"Mandy...I'll bet," Riley said, and I agreed.

We all sat there, some sprawled across the lavish, red carpet, Dugger and Carson on the benches. It all seemed like a quiet respite, but somehow I didn't believe it. The tension felt thick in the room. I drew in a breath and looked around, surrounded by enemies. My palms were wet and clammy, all eyes on me.

"I don't have any money," I blurted. "In case you were gonna, like, rob me or something."

Chris exhaled and shook his head.

"When did you join their side?" I asked Riley.

"What?" Riley squinted. "What do you mean?"

"Why'd you leave NYU?" Carson this time, with his non sequitur.

"What?" I stared, not sure I'd even heard him correctly.

"Answer the question," Carson demanded. Chris and Dugger stared at the floor. Riley watched my every move.

"I don't—like—why do you—"

"You were a straight A student." Carson's voice was completely calm, devoid of affect. His eyes bored into me. "And in one NYU thermodynamics class, you blew it. Why?"

"How in the hell did you—" I stood and backed away from them.

"Hacker." Dugger pointed to Carson, who stood now opposite me.

OMG, they're gonna jump me, the only friends I have. I backed up a few more inches and came to my knees, assessing the situation quickly, like an operative, like Peders, using all his tradecraft methods to size up the room, the exits (one), potential assailants (four), and the likelihood of escape (none). I stood again, happy suddenly that I was a full two inches taller than Carson.

"It doesn't make any sense, your coming here. Why leave New York at all? You were successful there, your best friend got accepted."

My eyes were watering now, involuntarily, only my eyes, someone else's eyes superimposed on mine. I wiped them. Now my nose was running, and now Riley stood and moved two steps closer to me, symbolically away from the others. My palms were sweating even more and my light jacket was choking me. I wriggled out of it and tossed it on the floor, barely aware of the notebook still stuck in the back of my pants.

"Why'd you leave?" Carson repeated, head down, still in a silky voice. As he said it, I imagined wrapping my hands around his throat. My face was wet now, with somebody else's tears, tears I myself hadn't intended to cry, but yet they were coming from my eyes.

"What the fuck is going on here?" I asked, my voice cracking.

"Why'd you leave?" Carson said in a louder voice now.

I shook my head, fists clenching. "Why...do you...care?"

"Because I think you were running from something, and I think whatever you were running from came here to hunt you down. Because all this chaos, this shit-storm we're all in, started about three weeks ago right after we met you. Why, I've been asking myself. What are you running from? Or who?"

"Tell him," Riley said to me.

It felt like all the blood drained out of my body. In the span of ten seconds, I watched my best friend in the world become a traitor.

"Tell him," he insisted.

The room spun like it had the night I took ayahuasca. I knelt down like I was gonna pray. I felt like praying in this moment, thinking of my mother's face, for some reason. What an odd moment for that image to come to me. Breathing into it, it was my mother's face I saw, but it was all red. I blinked away tears from my eyes again, coming from an empty well without emotion. That's what I'd become, hadn't I? Some kind of automaton chased by killers, by Campus Police, memory police, black market gangsters. Again I thought of my mother's face, her red face, bloody I remembered now, caused by my father's fist. I'd wanted to kill him but only stood behind him holding his arms while my mother writhed on the floor screaming at him.

Now all four of them were circled around me, not standing but kneeling, crouched down, studying me like a zoo animal in an observation cage, Riley next to me. Was he my ally again? Did he change so quickly?

"Tell them or I'm going to," Riley said.

There was no air left in the room, I was sure of it. I stood and walked around fanning myself. "I can't breathe."

"Zak." Riley followed me two steps behind.

"I can't breathe," I said again, between gasps, hoping they were listening.

"Who's chasing you?" Carson asked.

I felt nauseous and put my head between my legs, praying I wouldn't vomit on the expensive carpet, knowing it would seep through onto the carpet pad.

"My father's a judge," I started, not quite knowing where to go next. It was as good a place as any to start. It was true, after all. My eyes kept watering and I didn't have enough sleeve to wipe them. Wasn't that always the case at times like this, cornered, nailed to the exact moment you've been running from and there's one single straw that breaks the poor camel?

"What kind of judge?" Chris asked, confused by it all, though it was obvious Carson's attack was premeditated and he hadn't told the others. "Just tell us what the fuck's going on. *We* can't go home because whoever's chasing you down knows how to find us—"

"They've already found us," Dugger added.

"What happened in New York?" Carson asked. "We want to help you."

"You want to help yourself!" I wailed in a voice that wasn't mine. Whose was it? Whose eyes were these that couldn't stop crying?

"Okay, both, that's fine. Let's start with you," Carson said. "You mentioned your father."

"A judge," Dugger said.

"Federal judge," I said directly to Dugger. "He's a District Court Judge."

"Not anymore," Riley said. We all stared, and he stepped away from me, from all of us.

"What are you doing?" I asked him.

"He's dead!" Riley backed away from me and bent down. My brain struggled to process too much information all at once. "He's dead, Zak, say it!" Riley shrieked, his voice cracking, his face blood red.

My hands shook. I saw an image of my father, just his face, unsmiling like always, sitting at the kitchen table staring out a rainy window, his expression frozen and a thousand miles away.

"You knew, didn't you?" I asked Carson. "If you dug into my fucking GPA, surely you saw the news stories of…of…" My words trailed off and I doubled over in sobs, my face pushed into the soft red carpet. I was so glad at that moment that I hadn't soiled it. It felt comforting against my cheek but reminded me of the red blood on my mother's face after my father beat her.

"Is there a bathroom?" I asked some time later, five seconds, five minutes, I wasn't sure. I stood and quickly slapped my hand to my mouth.

"Right outside the door," one of them said, and in a split second I was doubled over a toilet in a tiny washroom, happy in a way for saving the beautiful carpet and the Steinway from the stench of my sordid past. The only food I'd eaten in two days roiled out, heaving from deep in my belly in ten second waves, and far more material than I'd put in it. God help me.

CHAPTER FIFTY-THREE

Riley stood in the doorway to the practice room, I knew, to prevent me from leaving. I remembered everything now, but I hadn't forgotten anything, just hadn't thought about it, not consciously anyway. Where had they been all this time…these memories? Riley stayed there, watching me flush, wash my face, slurp water from the tap like a mangy dog, because that was his job. I re-entered the practice room, slid against the wall just inside the door, and sat on the floor. And breathed.

"Immanuel Garcia." I said, hoping the truth might settle my stomach. "Immanuel Garcia killed a pregnant woman and her five-year-old son, supposedly in a case of mistaken identity, where he thought it was his own wife and child whom he intended to kill. My father was the federal judge who sentenced him to death. Garcia was executed, a year ago. A few months later, someone anonymously sent my father some evidence in the mail of a video of the murder, from start to finish, like pretty incontrovertible evidence. You've probably figured by now that the assailant was someone else. Could someone get me some water?" I asked.

Riley nodded and left the room.

"How was Garcia convicted then?" Chris asked.

"Circumstantial evidence, along with his fingerprints on the murder weapon, easy access to the victims. They lived in his neighborhood."

Riley knocked on the door. Dugger let him in. I took two sips of ice-cold water from a tiny cup. "Anyway, the video was analyzed by dozens of experts and deemed authentic. My father couldn't live with himself." I shut my eyes. "He...shot himself in our house, and I found him."

I let out a huge sigh and looked around the room, feeling the awkward horror that my baggage caused all of us. "My father beat my mother," now the real tears came, "three times. And I only stopped him twice. I hate him for that."

"You hate yourself for it," Riley added. "And because of that, all this time you've blamed yourself for his death. That's what you're running from. Even now."

"My mother was...I don't know...worried I might do the same thing. Maybe. She thought a change of scenery would be good for me so she told me to apply here, and she paid for Riley to come with me to keep an eye on me."

He nodded. "Good thing she paid me, I never would have come." His face softened.

"I'm very sad to learn of your loss," Carson said with sudden eloquence.

I appreciated his words, the formality of them, the crispness of saying them at the right time, and with what I knew was genuine emotion.

"I don't know what any of this chaos has to do with my father though, if anything."

"Would Immanuel Garcia's family be coming after you?" Carson asked carefully.

I honestly hadn't thought about the possibility before this moment. "My father...died because..." my voice cracked, "of his mistake. He gave his life for Garcia. Isn't that enough? For his family?"

Carson raised a brow. "I don't know if it would be for me. So maybe not."

"Let's not forget about Mellon," Riley said. "He's dead...and are we pretty sure that pizza was meant for us?"

"So now I'm being chased by yet another person, for another reason? First Jane's chasing me because of some fucking code I never wanted to find, which apparently led to some secret world of fake drugs. Then the fake drug dealers, guides, baristas, sliders, memory police, and CIA operatives are chasing me because I've seen...again... what I never wanted to see in the first place!" Now they were real tears, my tears, from my face, my eyes and my broken heart. "Can't I just go back to failing thermodynamics like a normal college kid?"

They all laughed and the heaviness lifted, if only for a moment.

"I need to know about Stavros' equation," I said. "Carla mentioned it in the car a few nights ago and it's been haunting me. Can someone tell me what you know about it?"

"Not much." Chris shrugged.

"Well, we know it exists, and he's been working on it, whatever *it* is, for about twenty years," Dugger added.

"He never told you, any of you?" I asked.

Empty stares.

"Didn't you ever try to find out?" I chuckled. "You're hackers, for God's sake."

Carson shook his head now. "It's not a typical password-protected file." He smiled.

"What?"

"There is no file. It's all in his head. He works stuff out on paper and then shreds it," Carson explained.

"We've seen bits and pieces of it but that's all," Chris added.

"So, like, all this time you thought he was just a regular old math teacher who built himself a bulletproof bunker in his basement capable of withstanding nuclear fallout? What did you think he was doing down here?" I was asking all of them.

"He didn't build it, it's Carla's house. Her grandfather built it," Chris said, and I remembered now her mentioning that.

"Well, Carla told me at the hospital that she thought the car that hit us was related to his equation," I said. "That he'd been working on something for years and he finally solved some problem or equation or proof or something."

The three of them looked at each other, nodded and mumbled. "Right before the night we met you, that same week, actually," Chris said.

"Did he say anything to you about it?" I asked.

"No. He locked his desk drawer with his laptop in it. He's never done that before."

"I have to go find Carla." I got up. "I can't ask for any more help than you've already given me. It's because of you that I'm even still alive, I think, and you're all in danger. I'll check in." I stood slowly, opened the heavy door and moved through yet another threshold.

The door opened behind me. Riley.

"You're doing it again you know," he said, standing in the empty hallway. "When are you gonna stop running?" I watched emotion fill his eyes. "Because until you stop, I can't stop either. And I can't do it anymore."

CHAPTER FIFTY-FOUR

I wanted so badly to hear my mother's voice right now, five a.m. on a Sunday morning. I walked on the dewy grass, cutting across campus to the entrance on 57th Street, no cars, no voices, no black ops or hit men hiding in the bushes. It was just me, the cold air, and the sound of my steps. Knowing Carla was staying in the house next door, supposedly for safety, I'd decided to take the bus to Stavros' neighborhood. I wanted to stand there at the bus stop for the next hour, longing for the empty space and safety of the three-sided plastic shelter, with the hard bench in the center and the simplicity of this moment. My stomach felt neutral, but my headache was worse, no doubt from the sudden dehydration and sickness. I knew I was likely in a state of medical shock. I knew Mellon was undeniably dead, and Rand, well, if he'd been shot, also dead. Who else would have to die before I found out what the hell was happening, and why? I didn't believe the Immanuel Garcia story. Not because it wasn't possible, or because the revenge angle was flimsy. I just didn't feel it in my bones.

And I was more preoccupied with Rand and Mellon right now.

Would Riley and I be interrogated by the real campus police investigating his death? Had Mandy been already? How could she have had anything to do with Mellon? She didn't even know him. Did she? What about David Wade–did he know Mellon? Poor hapless Mellon, Jesus. I didn't even know if I could go back to Granville, even to get a change of clothes. Were they watching me now on a CTA #6 Jackson Park Express bus? After seven stops, I was within a block of my destination, strategically close but far enough to not be noticed. Then again, did the notebook I was carrying have other technology in it, like a GPS tracker? If I sat outside somewhere near the house where Carla and Stavros were staying, would they know where I was? It was worth a try.

Five houses away, four. A huge oak tree stood in front of the third house. It had a flat, grassy spot at the base. I planted myself there and used the light from my phone to see the pages of the notebook I hadn't opened in what felt like a long time. I flipped back a few pages to see what I'd written before, but it was all gone. I remembered the conversation with my drug-induced fairy godmother on the night of my ayahuasca vigil, and a message about being chased by numbers. I also remembered, just now, sitting here on the cold ground, Stavros talking about Carla, how she was a genius who went to MIT at age sixteen and skipped the fifth grade, and had two Ph.Ds. In what, I wondered now. Also that she'd developed technology that led to the invention of the SMART Notebook, which I now assumed was what I had in my hands, though it looked and felt like a real notebook. This must be some kind of prototype, which Mandy Pierce had handed me in the hospital where Stavros was taken. What did Mandy have to do with all of this? My hands buzzed with that question—I'd only asked it in my mind so far. I went through it piece by piece:

David Wade's relation to Mandy: they lived on the same floor of Granville West dorms. So did I, Riley, also Mellon.

But Rand: how did he and Mandy know each other? Wade must have introduced them, and also introduced her to Brolly.

The Janes: if she was even involved with their operation, would have also been an introduction by Wade…or Rand?

Peders, if she had a connection to Peders: could have been accessed by Rand.

Wade had been there in the beginning: our original connection with the fraternity scouts at The Pub at Noyes Hall, where this nightmare had all started. So that meant Wade and Mandy were the common threads connecting everything, all of us. But what about Stavros and the connection to his geek squad? I ran through it again in my mind: sitting in an interrogation room with the real campus police answering questions about the whereabouts of the missing David Wade, when the officer said that someone had given him a note that read "Biology Lab."

I considered who would have led me there. I thought about who would have had an interest in my connecting with Stavros, and how that person could have possibly known that in my drug-induced state of warped consciousness I was *guided* to the notion of secrets embedded onto a cash register receipt. The whole thing was so far outside of ridiculous I was starting to wonder if it might actually be possible. Okay…think Zak. Had someone been watching me ever since the fateful night at Jane's? But how? I'd been all over the campus and Hyde Park. It wasn't plausible. Unless…and at that moment on the moist grass under a tree in the front yard of one of Stavros' neighbors, I felt the Tom Riddle notebook in my hands. Was that how it was done?

Thinking back now, I wasn't always in possession of it. At one point, it was buried beneath t-shirts in my dorm room closet, later stuffed against the wall behind my desk, and then mailed in a padded envelope…that's right, this one here was a different notebook than the first and given to me by Mandy. Were they all embedded with the same technology, and did they all have the same power? Had I ever been without one of these notebooks? Only after I mailed the first one at the Student Union building, and when I got to the hospital later that same day. So that meant whoever had been tracking me had done so since that first night I spent at Janes. Not only would I have to be extremely strategic about what I wrote next in the notebook, but that it might be tracking my…no, *reading* my thoughts even now while I went through the whole litany of madness. Don't go there, I told myself. Whatever's inside my head was innately and exclusively my property, I kept telling myself that. Stavros' voice echoed in my head now, him telling me about Carla and, later, revealing his feelings of inadequacy as a math professor, and that he only really wanted to live and dream inside the space between numbers. *The space between numbers.*

So operating under what was becoming my core belief, I started my experiment, opened the notebook, and pulled a mangled pen from my back pocket.

CHAPTER FIFTY-FIVE

I know who you are.

Nothing appeared on the page.

What, your next-door neighbors don't have reliable enough Wi-Fi to run your scam from there? Or is Stavros with you right now? Does he know who you are, does he know what you are and what you're doing?

You're tired. You need to stop running.

I'm still running, but now I'm running toward you.

You're going in the wrong direction. You were close, there's still time.

For what? I saw what I needed to see in there.

You saw what they wanted you to see.

I saw Peders shoot Rand in the fucking head. Why?

It's a war.

Wasn't Rand on both sides though? Don't you need spies like him?

Different sides, fighting different wars.

So why did Rand have to die? Did I put him in danger?

Yes.

So then I'm responsible for his death, and Mellon's?
Mellon was a distraction for the police, away from you
And you, I think. Right? The police on my trail would inevitably lead them to
System D, and threaten your little empire.

No response came so I moved from the damp spot under the tree to the front steps of the Jenkins home, I deduced from the name on the mailbox, and waited. Obviously, there was a tracking device; she knew where I was. Hell, had she arranged for Stavros' car to be hit herself? Anything was possible now.

The front door to the Jenkins' house opened. I saw the bottom hem of a tan trench coat.

Peders? WTF?

"Where's Carla? Did you kill her, too?"

He motioned with his hand. "Come in." He held open the door.

I half expected to see Mother, Father, and little assorted Jenkins' gagged and hog-tied on the floor by the fireplace. Peders removed his iconic trench and set it carefully over the back of one of the living room chairs, revealing a 1980s-era argyle vest, with a dress shirt and tight-knot tie underneath. Carla and Stavros sat apart from each other on a long sofa. Across from them, someone I didn't recognize was in an armchair.

"This is…"

"Mason?" I interrupted Peders' introduction. The man shook my hand but didn't get up. I took a small side chair and Peders took the other leather chair. "Was there ever a Jenkins family who lived here?"

"In the 1940's, yes," Mason answered in an English accent. Kensington, it sounded like, from my hours spent watching BBC America.

I looked at Stavros, his right arm in a sling. "Are you all right?"

Slight smile. "For the moment."

"So does the notebook write itself just from your neural interface?" I asked Carla. Her face didn't move.

"It's a very simple program. There's no neural interface yet though it's in the testing phase," she explained.

Peders leaned forward and put his elbows on his knees. "Say what you need to say, Zak. That's why we're all here."

"Stavros' equation isn't an equation," I began, not completely certain where I was going with it yet. My father's dead, I thought. I've just relived this tragedy. Nothing can scare me now.

"It's a proof. Isn't it? You told me," I said to Stavros," that all you really cared about was the space between numbers. That means irrational numbers, and I know from your lesson in your lab that day that you're a number theorist solely focused on the properties and possibilities of transcendental numbers. I think you proved that there's a way to successfully sum two transcendental numbers and get a rational number."

I was either a genius or a moron. Each had an equal possibility of likelihood right now. Stavros shifted his position and Carla moved an inch closer to him. Mason and Peders remained still, the practiced operatives, observing, gathering intel from an informed asset, me, who would eventually need to be neutralized.

"I think this proof has some application on the path to correcting the economic problem of bitcoin orphaned or stale blocks." That was the sum total of all I knew about cryptocurrency, that orphaned blocks were the bane of a collector's existence.

No one spoke. Peders had sunk to the back of his chair with his arms crossed. Mason had apparently become made of stone. I made a note to myself that there might be someone else in this house. I was wearing the same jacket with the device in the collar. I prayed they were still listening.

"You're getting warm," Peders conceded, widening his eyes, waiting for my brain to spiral outwards.

"Transcendental and irrational numbers are all about remainders, and so are orphaned bitcoin blocks. They're created when two miners create a block at the same time. Other reasons, not included in the block chain, can cause them, and therefore, if I understand correctly, are not trackable. Maybe that means that a lot of money is unaccounted for...or lost?"

Peders nodded me on.

"So if this equation can...sort of...resolve a transcendental number to a rational number, meaning no remainders, I imagine that could, in theory, save billions of dollars in dark net transactions."

Peders nodded.

"If it can be used in that context, could it also be used in the context of legitimate transactions, like in the stock market?"

"Well done," Peders said now.

"I thought you said you weren't very good at math," Stavros said.

I turned to face him. "What's interesting is that you, also, said that you weren't very good at math. You said you weren't a good math teacher, you weren't disciplined."

I looked at Carla now. "But you have two PhDs and I'm sure *that* takes discipline. So maybe the summing of e and Pi project might have begun with Stavros, maybe it's how the two of you met, but I think *you* solved the proof and *you're* the one using it to make a $650B industry even more profitable."

Finally, she spoke. "You don't know anything about me."

"I think this was your enterprise, once, something you started, maybe in your high-tech basement bunker next/door, and maybe at a time when you could buy a thousand bitcoin for twenty dollars. I think while Stavros has been finding ways to resolve e and Pi to a rational number, you've been concurrently trying to find a way to transact bitcoin commerce without the creation of orphan and stale blocks. You're the real mathematician, right? So what are these blocks? They're loose ends, untraceable, impermanent and, what's worse, a hole where not just money but economic value can leak out. I sat in your kitchen with you. There wasn't a single hair out of place on your head. The contents of your kitchen counter were all arranged in perfect formation, perfect right angles, because you not only love order but you're desperate to control all the chaos in your world. System D and the world of crypto commerce and alternative currencies are chaos, and they're continuing to grow to an unfathomable scale. Right now the value of a single bitcoin is over ten thousand dollars."

"I haven't broken any laws, so none of your theories are of any importance," Carla said.

"That's only because there *are* no laws yet surrounding these types of transactions. Regulation has started, but there's still so much we don't know about this other dimension of trade and international commerce. For the record, I don't really believe the story Rand told me about gun components and teddy bears. System D's not about guns, and the people who operate in that world don't ultimately care about whether there are more guns in the hands of terrorists, or less. It's about allowing chaos to flourish and trusting that it will find its own sense of order, because that's what mathematics and the natural world, and your equation, are teaching us."

Peders clapped slowly, ceremoniously, adding an unwelcome sound to the anxiety that had filled the room, which I had filled with my immutable theories. "Impressive, Mr. Skinner, I have to admit. Not that

217

you're necessarily correct, but you didn't actually think we would let you leave here, did you?"

It didn't matter. I knew Carson, Chris, and Dugger were searching at this very moment for evidence proving there were recipients of Peders' grand plan.

"I'm sure I won't stop what you're doing, so go ahead and kill me if you want to. I know. And just knowing is, for some reason, enough."

CHAPTER FIFTY-SIX

They had me locked in a back bedroom but hadn't thought to take my phone. So, naturally I texted Chris. He told me to call one of them and use my earbuds to hear their conversation, knowing I wouldn't be able to respond.

"Dude, if you can hear us, use your fingernail to tap three times on your phone," Chris instructed from the other end.

I did it, then hid the phone behind my back, and laid on my side on the twin bed to conceal the headphones hanging down from the left side of my head.

"We know where you are. Can you text us who's with you?"

I did, and then asked where they were.

"We're next door back in the basement; the house is clear. And your receipts were removed from the band-aid box in the bathroom by the way," he said.

I'd figured as much. I heard talking in the background, not sure whose voice I was hearing. I was in a boy's bedroom, about twelve, I guessed from the Nerf Blaster and Xbox console. There was a window on the first level but pretty high up, those loud kind of horizontal blinds that I'd never be able to crawl through without being detected, and I was at the very end of a hallway. It was the worst possible situation, and inconvenient since I still had important business to take care of. David Wade owed me some answers, and Mandy, well, not sure how to even quantify what I needed from her right now. Something occurred to me as I looked at the window: I hadn't heard any noise in the house in about thirty minutes...and there was no locking mechanism on the bedroom door. Still, they all likely had guns and I was a liability to their plans so I had to use caution. I texted Chris.

Bedroom window...can you help me?

Are you fkin crazy?

Not sure but I think the house is empty

Stand by, 2 mins

I heard two taps on the window. Separating two of the blinds, I saw Dugger, this time pointing to his phone.

Raise the blinds with the chord very slowly, an inch higher than the window lock.

The chord pulled smoothly. The blinds were actually plastic, not the old metal kind. I raised them as high as I could hoping no one was outside the door in the hallway to see how the light had changed in here. The window wasn't even locked. What the hell kind of gangsters were these people anyway? I could just as easily walk out the front door. But no doubt someone would find me. I opened the window and slid out into Dugger's grip. With a thud onto the back ledge, I climbed down four feet to ground level. Dugger pulled himself back up to close the window and lower the blinds.

"Is anyone still in the house? Could you see in?" I asked him.

"Can't see anyone in the front part of the house. I suspect there's a basement, like next door."

"Why didn't they put me in the basement then, I wonder?"

"They're probably working down there," Dugger said.

I followed him across the backyard, over the thick pyracantha hedge that had pricked me the last time, and in through the back door of Stavros' house. It seemed all wrong, though, us being here in his house, and him and Carla and his team of thugs being next door.

"We think Stavros was never in on this business," Chris said, when I got to the bottom of the stairs.

"You think he's a, what...prisoner? He's still teaching, isn't he? You don't think the university was a part of any of this?"

Chris thought about this and shook his head. "Not willingly anyway. They need Stavros for his research, and the—"

"No, they don't," I argued. "Carla's the one who solved his proof for him; he just provided the question and the framework for it."

"So, they don't need him anymore, you're saying?" Chris asked.

That's right, they didn't need him and would likely be discarding him in the same way that Peders discarded our friend Rand. Was David Wade next? Was Mandy?

"Where's Riley?" I asked, just now realizing he wasn't down here.

"We dropped him off at your dorm," Chris said. "He was summoned by campus security to provide a statement about Mellon, and you have to do the same by tomorrow morning or there'll issue a warrant for your arrest."

"I'll go. Can you drop me off? Anyone?"

"You've got a few stops to make first," Carson answered, with his hands on his keyboard.

CHAPTER FIFTY-SEVEN

So far they'd found three recipients of Peders' pharma scam. Each had willed a portion of their estates to someone named Dane Peders.

"What kind of dumbass would use their real name?" I asked.

Carson, driving this time, nodded at the question. "It's a smart move actually, and a good tradecraft tactic. The more lies you tell, the more lies you have to remember, conceal, and track. He used his real name because the whole arrangement's more legit that way. His name matches his social security card, all his ID, his—"

"Don't you think a guy like Peders has a drawer-full of fake passports and IDs?" I argued. "What am I supposed to be telling these people?"

"The truth. What you saw, what you know, and that their drug angel is disbursing them fake drugs with inert ingredients—"

"How do we know that, though?" I countered. "Rand said Brolly's operation was based on fake pharma, and Peders was apparently manufacturing real medicine and giving it away. So we now know that he's not exactly giving it away, but can we be sure it's fake meds? I'm just thinking about these elderly cancer patients who are gonna lose all hope if we tell them that their meds supply has dried up or, worse, that they weren't real meds in the first place."

"You didn't create this situation," Carson counseled in his calm, powerful voice, somehow seventeen years old going on forty. "You're just exposing it, and you're the only one who can do that because you've seen it with your own eyes."

"And am miraculously still alive," I added.

Victim #1: Richard Whittimore, age 89, diabetic, emphysema, stage III lung cancer. Here's how our conversation went: I introduced myself by name, announced that I was researching fake pharma scams and his name came up as a recipient. I wanted to let him know about my research and how our records show that he willed part of his estate to...

The door closed on me before I even got out the words Dane Peders.

Victim #2: Marie Attridge, age 78, every known, possible medical condition pretty much. This conversation was slightly longer, though still conducted outside her front door, standing awkwardly away from the door so her impaired vision could adequately size me up. Marie didn't actually give Peders any money, nor did she will him any part of her residual estate after she dies. She converted twenty thousand dollars to bitcoin and put that money in a trust, and told her lawyer that he was her nephew. I explained, as clearly as I could, that Peders was a gangster, was delivering her phony medication, and that she'd fallen victim to a fraud. Her response was that the meds he was sending her made her feel wonderful and she had no regrets.

I got back in the van shaking my head. "What the hell's the point of this if they don't care?"

"You may need to see them several times to properly explain it in terms that they'll understand." Chris handed me a printed page. "There are twelve people on this list. Think of it this way, Peders has very likely extorted at least twenty thousand out of all of these people. That should motivate you enough to keep going."

I snatched the page from his hand, folded it, and stuffed it in my back pocket. "Thanks for the side project."

"What's the matter with you?"

"We can't do this. We can't take down an extensive black ops syndicate without more serious resources. At least now we *know* what's going on in there, who's involved, who's benefitting from it. But taking down Peders' enterprise one patient at a time will take too long and only has about a fifty percent chance of success. Those people don't care if it's a scam. They just want their medicine so they can live without pain, or get their symptoms under control. So it might not even work. We need another way in, and we need backup."

Chris sat back in the passenger seat and considered my proposal. "What do you suggest?"

CHAPTER
FIFTY-EIGHT

"You're right outside his door. Why call him?" Chris argued.

Riley smiled; he knew me. "Because it's a civilized thing to do," I replied, giving Wade a chance to put on some clothes, hide a girl under the bed covers; or otherwise prepare himself for The Inquisition.

"Hey," I said when he answered. "It's Zak."

"Hey Z, been a while. Where are you?"

No one had ever called me Z. So far I didn't like it. "I'm outside your door."

I heard snickering, the phone went dead, and the door opened a crack. Wade's hair was sticking up, no shirt, sleep pants. "Wow, the whole family. Come on, pile in." He opened the door wide. "Riley," he said. Riley nodded back, like proper adversaries. "Have a seat." He pointed to the bed opposite his. "My roommate this term was a no show."

"Carson, Chris, Dugger," I said to Wade, waving my hand absently.

"Good morning," he replied and settled back into the other bed, propping pillows against the wall and sitting cross-legged facing us. He studied me in particular, then Riley, then me again. "You don't look well."

"You wouldn't either."

He laughed and shook his head. The way he did that I knew I'd come to the right place. David Wade was a prep school boy who didn't belong in a school like this with normal people. He'd grown up with money, spent time in yacht clubs, private social clubs learning how to execute friendly debating skills, ballroom dancing, and the importance of custom suit jackets, Italian leather shoes. He came from means, had means, and was more self-possessed than anyone I'd ever known, which meant nothing scared him. Or mostly nothing.

"Been busy?" he asked, probably to break the awkward silence.

"Mmm hmm," I nodded.

"Been anywhere interesting lately?"

"A little too interesting," I replied.

"How can I help?" he asked, obviously trained in the art of listening, negotiation, and how to fill up empty silences with delicacy and grace.

"What were you running from the other day?"

"Same as you were, The Janes as you call them," he answered quickly.

"What did they want from you?"

"Same as you. My time, my loyalty, my soul. Or else. It's a pretty good scam. And once you dip a toe in that water, you'll essentially be swimming for the rest of your life."

I was careful with my next question. "How much have you seen… in there?"

"Not much, I'm just a low-level runner. I owe them three trips a week. I got behind on my quota and they thought I was trying to get out. That's when they ran me down the other day."

"I've seen things in there."

"You have a guide?" he asked.

"Brolly the first night, then—"

"Brolly's no guide." He shook his head. "He pimps out the runners is all."

"Rand took me in, twice, and another time with Riley." I paused to watch Wade's eyes. "He's dead."

Wade looked at his mattress. "Shit, I'm sorry to hear that." I believed him.

"Peders shot him," I added.

"Who's Peders?"

My frustration spilled out in a long sigh. "Look, there's a whole other layer to this, maybe more than just one, and we need help."

"To do what?"

It was an honest question, and the boys and Riley stared me down now, challenging me to make the pitch and do it the right way. "You know people, meaning people of influence. We know enough to be a threat to their syndicate."

"They'll kill you. Don't you know what kind of people we're dealing with?"

"I just told you Rand was dead. I watched Dane Peders, an ex-CIA operative who posed as my friend, shoot him in the head. So yeah, I know. We've seen things, talked to people, heard about two warring factions, and we know their weaknesses. We just can't do it alone."

"And we can't go to the cops," Riley said, apparently feeling the need to state the obvious. "I just spent the afternoon being interrogated by campus security about Mellon. If we go to them with this, especially now—"

Wade waved his hand in the air to cut him off. "How would an Assistant District Attorney for Cook County be?"

Perfect.

LISA TOWLES

CHAPTER FIFTY-NINE

We left Wade's room with the promise of a phone call and some future meeting with his trustworthy contact. Regardless of whether that meeting happened or not, I wasn't yet sold on Wade. We parted ways with Carson, Chris, and Dugger with a plan to lay low for a day or so. Then left out the back entrance.

Threads dangled in my brain, threads that would fray if I pulled too hard on them. I felt desperate to see Mandy, just see her, look at her, not interact and feel awkward and try to be cool and fail miserably. I needed to talk to Stavros, outside of the context of Carla and Peders and the ring of corruption. So while Wade was making the connect with his Assistant DA contact, I was determined to immerse back into college life as I'd known it before—class, sports, studying, eating.

"There's a party tonight, here in the other quad. Wanna go?" Riley asked as I made my way back to our dorm room, which was still partially in disarray from being searched by The Janes for the magic notebook still stuck to my back. I pulled it out and this time placed it under my laptop on the desk. Plain sight, right?

"Party?" Riley repeated.

"I'd be happy to just sleep in a bed two nights in a row and eat maybe two meals a day and see how that goes. You go without me."

"Mari's gonna be there," he said.

"Dude, don't even think about —"

"I wouldn't, don't worry. No one will disturb you tonight. I'll be back early."

I swear I spent a full hour wasting water in the shower, washing my hair twice, my body two, maybe three times, my face, ears, every inch of me, scrubbing away the grime from the past week and the residue of my old life, my family story that I wore now like a layer of new skin. I didn't watch TV, no phone, no music, just me lying in the dark in the safety womb of my college dorm bed with the too-thin mattress, a lumpy pillow with the blinds open and a few promising stars twinkling back between layers of roaming clouds. I reveled in the thought of waking up early, looking at my class schedule, planning a normal day, eating breakfast in the dining hall, then coming back to a boring night of studying and catching up on all I'd lost lately. I knew my dreams would be crazy tonight; how could they be anything else? But I hadn't dreamed after all. I had no idea what time I fell asleep. It could've been nine, or one a.m. All I knew was that when I woke, Riley hadn't come back early like he said he would.

He hadn't come back at all.

No reply to any of my friendly "did you get some" texts, nor to the panicky-sounding "wtf are you" messages that followed. I went down the hall to summon Wade, who didn't answer. His bathroom was steamy and he was the only one living on that side of the hall, so I surmised he'd left for an early class. On our side, it used to be three of us—Riley, me, and Mellon. Poor Mellon, still couldn't believe it. The memorial service was tomorrow night. I had only four hours to talk to campus security before they brought the cavalry. That meant breakfast, visit to security, followed by economics at eleven.

But things rarely turn out the way you plan. I got a text from Wade en route to Security that I had an appointment with someone named Lawrence Hammill and could I get myself to 100 Randolph Street. My stomach growled the whole Uber ride there. I felt terribly under-dressed walking through the security checkpoint, and paranoid that I had a knife or scissors or some type of accidental weapon on me. The monitor beeped green. Two security agents let me through to the main lobby of the Office of the Attorney General in Chicago. I wondered why this building wasn't in Springfield, the capital. Who paid for all the beautiful white marble? Riley would love this place. *Riley*, shit. I checked my phone, but no texts back.

"David Wade set up an appointment for me with Lawrence Hammill," I explained to a man in an expensive suit in the reception area. I didn't own a suit, a tie, or even a nice dress shirt come to think of it. What a deadbeat.

"Mr. Skinner?" A woman poked her head out of an office halfway down the hallway on the right. "He's waiting for you."

I wondered if I'd ever have a job in a building like this. As I took in the white, marble pillars and the wood paneled walls, a lanky fellow with a crooked smile sort of stooped to shake my hand. "Law Hammill." He actually shook my hand, like a discernible up and down motion, rigorously for three full revolutions. This was clearly a world I did not know.

"I'm Zak Skinner. I guess you know that." I sat on a brown, leather loveseat and he sat in a hard chair across from me. Three large windows and plants made the small room seem larger.

We exchanged pleasantries, or as many as I was qualified to deliver, and he asked me to explain "my situation." It occurred to me that I should have prepared a sort of speech to capture everything. I'd failed, and now I was stammering, saying a lot of "ums," talking in circles. I think I'd already lost my place.

"So there's like three different levels of scams going on here, and I'm not sure how related they are to each other. The Janes and exploiting college freshmen to blackmail them into doing runs for them into…"

"System D. Yep I got that," he commented.

I could tell he was dying to jump in.

"The main System D operation, as well as the alternative operation run by Peders and Mason, both of which are related to Big Pharma."

Hammill sat back in his chair. "You said you have a list?"

"Yes, of the names that Peders and his operation have scammed through a will entitlement in exchange for meds."

"Do you have it with you?"

I pulled the twice-folded page from my back pocket and opened it.

He nodded, took it from me and nodded again.

"What?" I asked.

"That's the same list I have."

"You guys know about this? I don't...are you—"

"We don't know enough yet to shut it all down because, as you say, it's a vast operation spanning more than just one city. But we've got someone inside." He half-smiled, showing his crooked bottom teeth and how one of his top front teeth pushed against the other. Crooked teeth always made for a trustworthy face.

"Mandy Pierce," I said aloud.

"Well, she's either not very good at her job or you're uncommonly observant," he replied.

"Meaning no disrespect to her, she's definitely not hard to look at," I commented, carefully.

"Agent Pierce is new but so far on track for a very successful career in law enforcement."

Agent Pierce? I was right?

"Ever thought about it?" Hammill asked.

"Sorry?"

"Law enforcement or the legal profession. Ever thought about it as a career?"

"No."

"Right," he said. "You're an engineering major. That's fine too."

"At the moment, anyway."

"If you did decide to make a change, you've got an excellent criminal justice program here, at the university."

"Thanks, good to know. So what about—"

He mentioned something about next steps and agents and teams in place. He asked for my contact number and, while he was talking, my eyes wandered to a picture on the wall, of Law Hammill shaking hands with Dean Agnus, the Dean of Engineering. Something about his career question made me a bit sick, suddenly. I stood slowly, shook his hand, and followed him to the door.

"I'll be in touch," he said, and I paused before walking out.

"My father's a—" I stopped and blinked hard, I had to start acknowledging it. "My father *was* a lawyer, a District Court judge actually. He died last year."

"I know," Hammill said, gently.

"I will think about your question. Thank you."

CHAPTER SIXTY

Eggs, toast, a small cup of OJ, and enough coffee to fill a large soda cup. Eating alone was a taste I hadn't yet acquired. All I could think about was Riley and what the normal, acceptable timeframe was for a one-night stand these days. I had no personal frame of reference, of course. Then again, this would have been date number two for Riley and Mari, so maybe that required extra time together the next morning. I didn't know her last name or where she lived. Just that...wait, she was in Riley's biology class, I remembered now. She sat in front of him and he noticed her hair at first. So, I could find out her last name if I needed to. I tried another text before I walked into the Campus Security building...again. No response.

"Zak Skinner, here to give a statement as requested."

"In regard to what matter?"

"Melton Federman."

I was instructed to have a seat on the same bench that I'd sat on before any of this craziness started, the day I got a note leading me to the Biology Building. A female security officer retrieved me from the front lobby and escorted me to one of their slightly larger interrogation rooms this time.

"Wait here, please." She left, clicked the door too hard. A second later it opened again to the same officer who'd interviewed me before. I counseled myself: no sarcasm, short thoughtful answers, exhibit fear and vulnerability. That part would be easy.

"Mr. Skinner." The officer sighed after the usual preliminary questions. "This time you're being interviewed in the death of a student who lived next door to your room. Three weeks ago it was about the disappearance of a. . .(flipped a page in his notebook) David Wade. That's right. Can you tell me why you're connected to both of these two matters?"

"We all live on the same floor."

The man nodded. "That's reasonable. Was the matter of Mr. Wade ever resolved?"

"Yes, he's fine. I spoke with him last night."

"Oh?" he asked. "What about?"

Shit. Shit shit shit. Be cool, Zak. "Melton, sir, and his memorial service coming up. I was asking if he knew whether any of us would be allowed to go, since we're not family."

"Yes, I see." He looked up. "I believe the service will be open to the public. Now, when did you last see Mr. Federman?"

I honestly couldn't remember, but that's not a credible answer to a security officer, especially in a potential murder investigation. "About two weeks ago, he was coming out of the bathroom as I was going in," and though it was intended to be a lie, it was probably true.

"What time of day?"

"About eight I think. My first classes are at nine."

The man was writing. "How well did you know him?"

"Not well, he seemed pretty shy and kept to himself. I mean, he didn't socialize in the common area where most of us hang out after dinner or while we're studying."

The man kept writing.

"Did you ever have interactions with him outside of school? Community groups, online groups? Did you know him before you came to this school?"

Another even breath. "No, I didn't. I'm not a member of any groups yet."

"What time did you order the pizza on the night of the 27th?" he asked, searching my face, watching my eyes, and not looking like he was ready to write anything.

"I didn't order the pizza, my roommate did."

Pages flipping. "Patrick...Riley?"

I nodded. "Yes, sir."

"I guess I'd like to know how the two pizzas got mixed up." He had wrinkled brows at this point. He leaned forward, pretending to show genuine curiosity and concern, but I knew it wasn't.

"I don't know. I got home from class. Riley had ordered a pizza and he hadn't opened the box yet. I was the one who discovered that it wasn't the kind of pizza we usually get."

His puckered his lips. "How do you know he hadn't opened the pizza box?"

"The sticker was still on," I answered like only a lame ass college student would, who eats nothing but pizza. "This place puts a sticker over the open side, and you break the sticker to open the box for the first time. The box was still sealed when I opened it."

More staring, deciding, deliberating. He wrote something, finally. "Were you aware that Mr. Federer any medical problems?"

"No." I kept it simple.

That wrapped up my brief interrogation. The man escorted me to the front lobby. I was suddenly starving again and dying for coffee. Before I even got to the exit door, I saw the always-welcome sight of Mandy Pierce's blonde-frosted hair. Her dark eyes blinked at me as she barged through the door.

"Hey!" she said with a glamorous lilt. She hugged me, obviously some kind of show for the security officer, though I couldn't imagine why. "Wanna walk me to my next class?"

"Now how could a guy say no to that?" I turned to look at the security dispatcher at the front desk. He waved me out. I seized the opportunity to wrap my arm around Mandy's waist as we walked out. I leaned in as if I was going to kiss her cheek. "What are we doing?" I whispered.

"Dining hall. I need to talk to you."

"I have a class."

"You're gonna miss it."

Gulp. I can't really say why, but the idea of being bossed around by Mandy Pierce made something throb in the center of my body, or at least my pants. I did like I was told and followed her through the cafeteria line where she assembled a King Henry the Eighth-sized platter of eggs, bacon, and four pieces of toast.

"Carbs," I commented, "those are good for you."

"Get a full plate and two Diet Cokes and meet me at the table." She paid for both of us.

I watched her select the table in the dead center of the huge room, right out in the open. "You know what I love about you?" I sat.

She quickly glanced at me, then back at her plate of saturated fat.

"You know I don't trust you, and you don't care."

"No, I don't," she replied.

"I don't know anything about you, your major, what year you're in, where you're from…"

Quick glance again, not even a second long. She was eating like she'd just won Survivor.

"Psych major?"

She slowed down a bit, thank goodness, and took a sip from the soda I'd delivered.

"I have a theory I've been developing over the past few weeks," I said.

"Look, I need to talk to you." She put her hand up sideways.

"I don't even think you go to this school."

A fork filled with eggs and melted cheese froze mid-air.

"Right. So yeah, you started as the girl across the hall who made my heart stop. And I realized…I'd never seen you enter a specific room. You just always ended up on my floor with a basket of laundry, a book bag, most likely props, and I never see you on campus at night. Why is that?"

Her chewing stopped.

"Because you don't have an access card to get into the locked buildings at night." I snapped my fingers. "Because you're not actually a student here."

I watched her take two more long sips to help swallow the ninety pounds of chewed breakfast in her mouth.

"So that means, what…undercover cop investigating the murder of Mellon? No, can't be. You were around before Mellon got iced. Okay, how about ICE agent trawling for Dreamers to ship them back to Mexico or Eastern Europe?"

"Are you done?" she asked.

I shrugged.

"Mellon died of an allergic reaction. It wasn't murder."

"What?"

"No. Not by you or anyone else."

"Why were the cops involved then?"

"It was initially a suspected homicide. A more thorough investigation revealed a different set of details, and a different picture emerged."

"Okay, what do you want to know? You said you needed to talk to me."

"I need to know what you saw in there, like actually saw with your own eyes," she said.

CHAPTER SIXTY-ONE

I took three more bites of egg, to stall, enjoying my momentary power. I breathed deeply and wiped my mouth as if preparing to answer her question. She stopped eating and stared, wide-eyed. I remembered the talk with David Wade's contact.

"You work for Law Hammill. Confirm or deny?"

"Who?"

To someone who hadn't memorized every curve, wrinkle, and expression her face could form, this tactic might have worked. I stood and purposely scraped my chair, wiping my mouth for the third time. "I think we're done here."

"Wait." She leaned back, blinking her eyes, on which she'd applied extra mascara.

I leaned down. "I know you work for Hammill. I know you're undercover, and you've been playing me, all of us, all this time. We both want the same thing. Either we work together with total transparency, or good luck to you." I sat back down.

"We can't collaborate, if that's what you're suggesting. You're not a trained agent."

"I've seen more than you have," I said in a flat voice, knowing I had her there.

"Sliders?" she asked.

I nodded.

"In production?"

"I have an audio tape." I did, though you couldn't make out anything on it but beeps.

"No video?"

I explained that it was too dark to even walk, let alone see anything. "I saw one part of the process, that's all."

"What part? Never mind that. Could you find it again?"

"I could have, were it not for the fact that my guide is dead."

"Rand? When? Are you sure?"

"Oh, I'm sure. I witnessed it. Two nights ago."

"Rand was both a runner and a guide," she said. "I'm just a guide. So I can get us in, if you can get us to the right building."

"Sure, I can find it again...if they're *in* the same building. What about Brolly?"

The dark eyes blinked a few times. "I'll tell him you're doing a run with me."

"Can we actually do one, for real?" I realized only now how hungry I was to learn the truth.

"I have two more this week," she said. "Can you meet me at my place tonight, nine o'clock?"

I noticed Mandy's ridiculous outfit for the first time now, oversized sweat pants, a wrinkled t-shirt, worn out tennis shoes that she slid only the tops of her feet into and I realized her face, her manner, and her confidence were not befitting of a first-year college girl. Were not frivolous or giggly. Was she over twenty? Jesus, was she married?

"Dude, can you be there or not?"

"Yeah, yeah, I'll be there." I got up from the plastic chair and slid my tray in the trash area.

"One more thing I want to make sure you understand. You've been there more than once. If Brolly sees you again, you're in. That means you're one of us, and expected to do runs and it's not optional at that point."

"Jesus. Riley was with me the last time I was there, and he's off the grid today."

She walked with me to deposit our food trays. "He's missing?" she said, softly.

"Well, he went to a party on campus last night. I think he hooked up with someone."

"Is that unusual...for him? I mean, isn't that what college students do?"

"Unusual for him, yeah. But it was with someone he'd been with already once before, someone from his biology class. Mari. I don't know her last name."

Mandy's eyes closed. "I know a runner named Mari. That would be quite a coincidence, wouldn't it?"

I grabbed Mandy's arm and walked her quickly to the hallway. "Jesus, this never stops, does it? What would she want with him?"

"More runners. We get compensated for new recruits, and not a trivial amount either."

"I've got to find him. I can't let anything happen to him."

"It might be too late."

CHAPTER SIXTY-TWO

I could barely even remember my classes today, except actually going to them was somewhat noteworthy. Econ, chemistry, physics, computing environments. By some miracle, I sat through them, reabsorbing myself in classroom etiquette, opening books, feigning interest, careful not to nod or seem too engaged for fear of getting called on to speak. Nothing from Riley. I stopped texting him at around two o'clock. I took an Uber ride to Mandy's apartment on South Morgan just off campus, and wondered the whole ride whether a man might answer her door, or if a man's jacket was hanging in her coat closet. Shoes under her bed?

I stood outside looking at the huge building realizing I didn't have her apartment number. I headed to the front stairs.

"Hey." I heard her voice from a car at the curb. She was in the driver's seat. "Ready?"

"Where are we going?" I asked, suspicious that she was waiting for me outside, dressed like a cat-burglar this time.

"Same place, different entrance."

"How many are there?" I got into what looked like a thirty-year old VW Rabbit. My mother used to have one.

"Need to know basis," she replied, pulling away from the curb.

"Fuck that. Riley's missing! Do you hear me? It's now almost twenty-four hours since I've heard from him. He might be dead for all I know." My voice cracked.

"He's not."

"You know that?"

"Only if he tried to run would they wipe him."

Wipe?

"He's obedient to a fault, he won't run. Or...not immediately anyway. So...you've been watching him too?" My right shoulder rammed into the door. I quickly fastened my seat belt and locked the door.

"Both of you have been under surveillance, yes," she replied.

"For how long, for God's sake?"

"Since you got here," she answered, matter-of-factly.

I felt my palms buzzing with anger. "What the hell for? Why were we of interest in the first place?"

"You, at first. Wade tapped you as a potential."

"So, you set Mari as a plant to keep tabs on me through Riley." Jesus, Riley was in grave danger now because of me. My stomach roiled.

"Right." She confirmed at least that. Her phone rang; she seemed to answer the call by pressing something on her steering wheel. *On a thirty-year old car?* She had a single ear bud in her left ear already, so she'd been expecting the call. Who was calling her?

I feigned disinterest and looked out the window at the landscape gliding past us too quickly. She drove fast. I didn't need to even think about other ways she might be fast, I knew already. Keeping my eyes focused out the right passenger window, I turned my body so my knees were almost touching the glove box. I opened it slightly, reaching in three fingers and pulling out a single piece of paper, folded twice. I wouldn't have time to examine it now so I coughed and reached around to stuff it in my back pocket.

"Both of us, yeah. Ten minutes," was all I heard. Someone we'd be meeting on the other side? Another runner, or were most of them dead now?

She disconnected her call. "Tell me about Peders," she demanded.

"Who was that?" I asked. Quid pro quo.

She remained stone-faced for a moment, deciding. Could she trust me? No of course not; it was a relationship, a whole network based on lack of trust. I didn't care; it wasn't my world.

"Someone I work with," she replied.

I knew that's all I'd be getting out of her, so I said, "Peders is ex-CIA, steeped in 1960's era tradecraft."

"What did he tell you?"

"All kinds of things about System D, about a culture of warring factions and how his faction, called The Valve doesn't deliver fake or inert meds and charge people even more for them like what Rand described. His group apparently delivers real meds and doesn't charge them anything."

I paused to see if she'd turn her head. She smirked instead, probably knowing what was coming.

I told her how his group secures pharma payments, and the list I'd showed to Hammill earlier today. "How's this going down tonight then?"

"I do a pick up, leave through an exit portal. Then we enter again through Steel Workers Park and you take me to where you saw the sliders."

"That's not a plan! What if we're discovered, and what about Riley?" I shot back, fearing now that she had no intention of helping me find him.

We drove in silence back to beautiful downtown Pilsen, replete with dented cars missing back windshields, boarded up homes, the smell of fire-charred wood.

"Here?" I said, aghast, knowing that in one of these abandoned buildings was a long hallway that led to another hallway that together made some kind of tunnel, leading to a world I wanted no part of. Ahh, now I got it—the dark clothing, the thirty-five-year-old car parked haphazardly against the curb, tradecraft. It was some kind of senior community center—originally anyway—now with the windows boarded up, the front door replaced by a piece of sheet metal welded to the trim. I followed Mandy around the right side of the building, down a walkway, jerking my head back every two seconds half expecting a drive-by shooter or a gang. But there was no one, tonight, not even crickets. She lifted a tarp, obviously having been given instruction by someone, and we walked underneath it. We found a flimsy wooden door ajar. She pushed through it and held it for me.

"Don't close it all the way."

I added the tradecraft tips to my mental file cabinet. The senior center was part of one continuous block of brick buildings in downtown Pilsen. By now, we were moving deep into the bowels of the building's basement, down sixteen steps, I counted them, and into the dark. I'd read that Pilsen was called Pilzen and named after a town in West Bohemia and was settled by German and Irish immigrants, near the railroad. This row of buildings could have been a huge mercantile, or a feed store, or a German bakery, or a brewery.

Oddly, the foul smell I'd expected was only a slight musty basement smell, like old concrete. I followed her in this non-place, literally no more than two steps behind her at a purposeful pace heading toward one of System D's portals. I saw something light up ahead—not an artificial light, more like moon glow. And there was no moonlight tonight. As we moved closer and judging by the size of the glow, it seemed like someone's cell phone.

"There's a guard. We might need to go back," Mandy whispered. She moved forward with four more cautious steps.

"Does this lead to the train station?"

"No trains running tonight," a voice said, a voice I recognized but I wasn't sure from where.

Trains? Was that a euphemism?

"Something's wrong," she whispered, turning to me. "One of the plays must have been altered."

"Okay." I pretended to keep up. *Plays?* Where was the glossary that should have come with this fucking place?

"Brolly's the only one who has the credentials to change them."

The hair on my back of my neck pricked up as I recognized gaming terminology. First of all, why was someone blocking our passage, and who was it? Plays altered, credentials, holy shit. Was System D...

"We're going back, quickly." She grabbed my hand with a jog back through the empty, dark space. I don't know why but I just knew that tacky door would somehow be locked. Breathe Zak, just breathe and walk. Breathe and walk. Riley hold on, wherever you are.

CHAPTER SIXTY-THREE

By some miracle, the flimsy door was still ajar. We pushed through it. Careful not to run, she told me, moving at an even pace back out to the car having finished conducting our normal course of business at an abandoned senior center. More ridiculous by the minute.

Wade stood facing us on the other side of the door.

"Christ, you scared me," I said jumping back. "What are you doing here?"

He walked around me and addressed Mandy. "Did you see…"

"There's a guard. Why?"

"Nothing's on today," he said.

On?

"Someone's changed something. The whole terminal's been changed, I suspect."

"We can't talk here, come with us." She eyed the car at the curb.

"Someone tell me what's going on," I insisted.

Wade pointed to the car and we got in, silently, no one seeing us, no one approaching us with guns, asking if we wanted to buy drugs. That alone was odd this time of night, in Pilsen anyway.

"This whole complex. They're called terminals," Wade explained.

"There's more than one?" I asked.

He nodded, sitting in the back seat and checking behind us every few seconds.

Mandy and I sat up front. "They're in cities where postal services and e-commerce is highly regulated to flag and prevent illegal transactions and quasi-legal currencies."

Wade looked at Mandy now, checking her eyes in the rear-view mirror. "But you know all this, right?" he asked her directly.

"Brolly brought me in and, you know, everything with him's need-to-know," she answered in a carefully calculated voice. She was smart, more than I'd originally thought, maybe the smartest of all of us..I was watching her in this moment seize an opportunity, and now knew her singular job here was to broker Law Hammill's proverbial pound of flesh: intel.

"I've got a run today and Zak wanted to see the sliders operation," she told Wade.

"I thought you saw them already, the other night?" Wade asked as a question.

I blinked back. "It was too dark," I answered. "And how would you know that?"

Wade flashed his magazine-cover smile. "Need-to-know, bro'. Where's your pick-up?" he asked Mandy. Then, "Who's your contact today?" he added, expecting, it seemed, her story to be ill-prepared and suspect.

"You mean...Rand?" she said. "I have a med pickup in building two."

"I'll go with you." Wade shifted a quick glance to me.

I looked outside. I hadn't been paying attention to where we were driving. Steel Worker's Park. Not again. All I could picture outside was Rand lying face-down in a puddle and Peders' tacky trench coat tented out by his feet.

We entered the opposite side of the first dark building. Wade led the three of us. Somehow, I felt Riley in here. From my last tour of Wonderland, I knew a staircase would be visible ahead on the right.

Wade halted. "Guards."

Mandy stopped too. "Which guards?"

"I don't—" Wade bent down to see. "I don't recognize him, or the uniform. Maybe from another terminal."

I watched and listened, typing a light speed text with just one character: ? I hoped Riley, wherever he was, might have an opportunity to see it and type a single letter back. We'd done this when we were ten, way before we knew how to type. We devised a language of one-letter codes to identify geographical coordinates and assess well-being.

? = are you okay

0 = yes

1 = I will be

2 = maybe not

3 = SOS

By my ?, he would know that I knew he'd been taken, was in trouble, that his survival (or lack) was part of someone else's agenda, and that I was likely in the vicinity. My phone buzzed back a 2 and my heart relaxed a tiny bit. Better than nothing.

"They're just parked out there," Wade reported. "Two on mopeds but different than ours here." He turned back toward Mandy and me. "We can't go this way. Pull back." We retreated into the dark. As I stepped backward, my right foot touched the edge of something, I knew was the rail of a staircase. My inner voice said *go up*. Without even conscious thought, I did and took two stairs at a time, hearing Wade's and Mandy's voices below. At the top, I continued walking in long steps toward the tunnel in the next building. By their voices, I could tell they didn't know I'd taken off, and I was going twice as fast as them.

In the next tunnel now, I was in Building 2 second floor, knowing Mandy had absolutely no intention of picking up meds from her unnamed source and David Wade didn't give a rat's ass about ensuring the safety of us…or Riley.

Help me find you, I texted.

All he wrote back was: *Coffee*

I knew that meant Suddenly Starbucks.

Order something, tell them you're waiting for your guide

Roger that

So I surmised that I was now in the right building and on the same floor as the drug manufacturers I'd seen before. The room was completely empty of its clunky, beeping, and light-flashing equipment as well as its gowned worker drones. I surveyed the space, I guess making sure nothing of interest had been left—a stray pill, anything to help me prove I saw what we saw before. As I looked down, something reflected the light from my phone. I bent to pick up a plastic card on the floor. Access card maybe. Access to what, though? I knew there had to be another level here or part of the compound the part Peders talked about. *The Valve*. And I knew because I felt it in my chest that I'd just picked up the key. The question was whether they'd moved out quickly and, in haste, someone accidentally dropped the card, if so why did they leave, or was it left here intentionally…for me?

My phone buzzed again. I moved closer to the stairwell. The text from Riley read: *Call me*

I dialed his number. "You're on a staircase?" I asked, because it was the only place to get signal.

"Yeah, but I don't know where." He was out of breath.

"You took off from the Starbucks?"

"Yeah, going further in, I turned right at…well…the first intersection."

"Good, keep going," I replied, glad that I was finally feeling the shape of the complex. "Find the next—"

"I'm here," he said, "second floor staircase."

"Go up one level and follow it in. Just keep going, I'm close."

"Wait. Why is there signal in here?" Riley asked.

"The whole complex is wired," I answered, only piecing it together as I spoke. "Sometimes it's active in the stairwells, sometimes the top floor of buildings. Keep walking."

"Who changes it?" Riley asked.

"Anyone with the right access credentials," I said and felt the white card in my pants pocket.

"I'm about—"

"I see you," I interrupted, catching the glow from his phone. Or… someone's phone.

"Is this you?" he whispered.

"Yes, keep going." I was out of breath now and felt slightly dizzy, but felt a puzzle piece falling into place somewhere deep in my head.

"Where the hell are we?" he asked, now in a regular voice coming up to me.

I put my hand on his shoulder and just stood there, grabbing onto him for minute, happy to see his familiar face. "Hyde Park. Fountain of Time," I replied. Another puzzle piece.

"That's where this all started," he said, "the night of your brilliant idea to socialize at The Pub.

"We need to keep walking," I told him, heading further down the dark tunnel. It felt like we were one story below ground.

Riley was beside me but looking at the curved walls and the shape of some ambient light refracted against the smooth surface. "These must be the secret tunnels I've heard about. Freight, transit, water, cable car. There are six systems of them all underground beneath the city," my encyclopedia-friend recited.

"There's more than six," I replied.

"How do you know?" he asked.

I pulled a sheet of paper out of my back pocket. "Mandy had a map in her glove box." I held it out but there was no time and not enough light to see it. I explained how it was a map of Chicago's six underground secret water spillover tunnels.

"I guess you know about Mari?" I asked, heartbroken for him.

Riley's mouth tightened to a tiny dot. How could he not have been hurt by that? She'd probably been his first. "She's a runner, I guess? Like Mandy?"

"She's an undercover FBI agent. They both are, indirectly reporting to the District Attorney's Office."

"Fuck."

I nodded, soberly.

CHAPTER SIXTY-FOUR

We walked back to Granville from the Fountain of Time, normally a fifteen-minute walk. Tonight it felt like an hour. The air was humid, unusual for Chicago in late fall. One thing I always appreciated about Riley was his ability to tolerate silence, not having to chatter on about nothing to fill it up. Silence was comfortable for him, not the opposite. I knew this was because he was an only child, having spent most of his childhood alone until they moved into our neighborhood. Then we became de facto brothers. We were both only children. That meant we appreciated solitude and companionship as equally beautiful gifts.

A feeling of stasis permeated the next few days, for both Riley and me, waiting it seemed for a shoe to drop from the sky and blow open every half-truth we'd investigated over the past two months of chaos. It went like this: alarm clocks followed by swearing, showers, dining hall, classes, usually skipping lunch, more classes, library to study, back to room to meet and walk to the dining hall together, with barely any substantive talking in between and no phone calls or texts, like we knew the other was fine and that we'd crossed over some kind of invisible threshold into a temporary safety zone. We knew too much, but whoever was watching us likely knew that we'd talked to Hammill and had friends in high places.

Or maybe that just meant that our days (or hours) were numbered.

At some point on the anxiety continuum, I reached the end. It had turned to some apathy, like an emotional train wreck, but I no longer cared how much adrenaline I leached with every breath, how much stress caused my cells to age, and how nothing new or fresh felt even possible now. What used to make my palms sweat now just froze my face colder, and concretized the dull look in my eyes. I was a college freshman again, at the very beginning of all beginnings, and I no longer believed in anything.

Our genius friends sent texts every few hours to monitor our life signs. They said they were continuing to monitor Peders' movements and were now in direct contact with Hammill's team on new developments. Stavros was apparently back to a semi-regular teaching schedule. I'd asked them to confirm Mandy's story about Mellon dying from an allergic reaction instead of poison, and they did. Mellon died from a combination of substances to which he never knew he was deathly allergic. If it hadn't been this pizza, it could have been another.

I still had lingering questions about Carla and how the equation was expected to change the transactional value or global quantity or traceability of cryptocurrencies.

I walked on South Drexel along the west edge of campus. Peders was very likely watching me at this very moment, probably with some kind of sensor in my coat like Chris had installed on me, or a bug in our dorm room in the light fixture. I didn't care anymore that we had no privacy, because I didn't do anything that required it. I did see Wade at the end of the hallway, occasionally stepping barefoot, towel-clad and dripping wet from the bathroom back to his room. He always left early and came home late, no doubt raking in money doing jobs for Brolly or the Janes or...well...was there much difference?

CHAPTER SIXTY-FIVE

Riley and I flew together from O'Hare to JFK the next weekend to see his parents and my mom, and so I could go to my dad's grave. Riley tried to go with me to offer support, and, I suspected, to make sure I didn't skip out. But I went alone, knowing he had to break me open in front of Chris, Dugger, and Carson because I didn't have the strength to acknowledge my father's suicide on my own.

I couldn't help but wonder why I hadn't seen any trackers on our trip. None of the Janes, suits, Peders, or any of our other pursuers. Of course, they knew we were leaving town. Of course, they knew what we knew. We were a walking liability for their enterprise, their web of secrets. And they would always be watching us, waiting for us to make a move. The thought felt like hands around my throat. But they also had to know who I'd talked to, which might explain why they were allowing us to leave.

I'd checked the virtual gravestone on the funeral home's website and knew the location but wanted to look it up anyway, as if seeing my father's name on the website would somehow prepare me better for seeing the actual stone in the ground. *Robert A. Skinner, beloved husband of Cynthia Skinner, beloved father of Zachary Skinner, RIP.* Seeing my name on the epitaph and now on the tall gray stone in front of me opened the part of my heart that clamped tightly closed the day he died…one year ago tomorrow. The cheerful birds chirping in the throng of locust trees nearby somehow comforted me, allowing me to not run from my tears. I let grief strangle me and let it spill out of my eyes, my nose. I felt him watching, touched by how much he had meant to me, so much more than even I'd realized. I didn't stop to wipe my eyes, or blow my nose, or lean my head down, or cover my face. This was real, and the scary thing is that the realness of it felt reassuring, when I considered the web of lies surrounding me.

I didn't know what any of it meant, what I was supposed to be doing at that school, what would become of my future. But at least I could now acknowledge that my father was dead. He'd ended his own life with absolute certainty just like he'd done everything else in his life, to show the world he'd been duped into sending the wrong man to the electric chair. For whatever steps brought him there, Immanuel Garcia was dead, and my dad created the same outcome for himself, to somehow even the scales and make the world a more balanced and understandable place…for me. I could hardly breathe now, the sobs erupting from the pores in my skin. Yes. Release. I release you. I release myself *from you*. All I had to say to my Dad that I never had the chance to say, I would have to somehow right that wrong with the rest of my relationships while I still had the chance. I kissed the stone and held onto it for an extra second.

And as sure as the sky was blue above my head, Riley was leaning against my mother's car in the parking lot.

CHAPTER SIXTY-SIX

"I have something to tell you," he started, with great pain in his face.

"I know you're leaving. Or staying. Well, both, I guess."

We were sitting in my mother's car now, in the parking lot of the cemetery, me in the driver's side.

"How do you always do that?" he asked, almost sorry that I'd taken away his opportunity at a rehearsed speech.

"Chicago's too fast for you. I never understood why you were going in the first place, other than to make sure I didn't jump into Lake Michigan and drown myself."

Silence.

So I kept talking. "Did you apply to go back to NYU? You hate Manhattan."

He nodded. "Cornell," he said, with a smirk.

"It's in Ithaca. Madeline Forester goes there, doesn't she? Ahh, thinking below the waist again," of the first girl who had broken his heart in tenth grade.

"Not just that, but yeah that's a selling point for sure. Ithaca's nice. It's quiet, green, pastoral."

"It's also freezing," I countered. "You hate the cold."

He turned to face me. "Will you be okay there alone?"

I knew I would, but I wanted to fake it a little bit to make him feel like I needed him all this time. I had. "Will you come and visit every month or so, at least for the first few months? We've never lived apart, you know, since we were ten."

"I can change my plans and go next semester, I mean, if you need me to. You know I would, Zak."

Riley, my only friend on the planet. If a man only had one, and it was one like Pat Riley, he was truly blessed.

•———•••—— •

Back at the house I grew up in, my mother handed me a white plastic bag. More clothes. Lord, just what I wanted. I tried to be excited as I opened it.

"It's something that sort of reminded me of you," she said and I knew, at that moment, what my absence in combination with my dad's had done to her soul. I put my arms around her even before looking at the tacky, blue and white polo shirt that I'd never wear in a million years. But she knew I always liked the clothes in the Tommy Hilfiger outlet store that was near our house in the Southside Mall.

"Receipt's in the bag," she said.

My stomach clenched. "What did you say?"

"I know you're picky about clothes. Just in case you want to return it."

CHAPTER SIXTY-SEVEN

Law Hammill had emailed me while I was en route back to O'Hare. I was reading it now as the Airbus taxi'd to my gate.

Hello Zak,

Just touching base about the invitation I extended, when we met a few weeks ago and reiterating our interest in helping you with a career in law enforcement, should you ever decide to move in that direction.

In the meantime, we are acting on the intel you gave us and I wanted to thank you again for approaching us. Please stop by and say hi the next time you're downtown.

Regards,

Law

I felt a sort of satisfaction at reading this, unsure yet if I had any inclinations toward his offer or not, but realizing, now, that as I waited for my luggage in baggage claim of the lower level of O'Hare Airport, my fingers fumbled with the hard white access card that had been at the bottom of my coat pocket ever since I picked it up in the System D terminal. There was a lot left to investigate, and now I had a way in. To where? No telling…

I knew my non-descript black, soft-sided suitcase would have met Peders' approval somehow, and despite all I knew about what he and his men were doing, I couldn't help but like Peders. My bag was one of the first out of the chute. I'd already booked an Uber ride, which was probably circling out front. I pulled the case off the conveyor belt and turned to face the sliding glass doors headed back to campus, alone this time. A smile crept across my lips even before I had a chance to process why. Mandy Pierce stood in the doorway, in a business suit with a skirt, bare legs, heels, her hair neatly combed in a side-ponytail, with tiny gold, stud earrings. Warm energy throbbed in my chest. I approached slowly, squinting to make sure it was her.

"I'm Amanda Pierce," she said. "I'm an agent with the FBI. I think we used to go to school together. Not sure if you remember me…" She too was hiding a wide grin and I could see what she felt for me now. Maybe she had all along.

"You don't really look familiar…" I shook my head, "but I do need a ride. Maybe you can jog my memory."

THE END

Acknowledgments

I would like to express my heartfelt gratitude to the following people whose love, time, care, and support helped me during the development of this book:

To my amazing parents – thank you for your constant love, support, cheerleading, acceptance, and encouragement. Through your example, you have taught me how to dig deep, listen to myself, be gritty in the face of challenge and reach for the stars.

To my sister, my most treasured confidante – you're an amazing talent who brings strength, wit, grit, and grace to everything you do.

To Olivia and Cassidy – thank you for shining your radiant light on my world.

To Gail, Missy, Lee, and Apolonio, my awesome beta readers - thank you for your insightful questions, suggestions, reality checks, and encouragement in helping me to improve this manuscript.

To my wonderful publisher, Lisa Orban, and the supportive Indies United community, you're all so amazing to work with.

To my amazing editors, Jayne Southern and Cindy Davis, from whom I have learned so much. Thank you for pushing me to skill-up, be more concise, and strive for excellence in the clarity and quality of whatever I'm writing.

To my cherished MWA and SinC NorCal writing partners - thank you for your companionship, advice, wisdom, and inspiration. I'm not sure I know how to write without you.

To my dear Karuna Circle – through our deep work together over the past year, I feel like everything is possible now.

To Randy and Jill for your support, encouragement, and promotion expertise.

To Amanda, Aimee, Jodie, and Melissa — thank you for your wisdom and healing.

To Jenny, my special beacon of inspiration this year.

And most of all to Lee, my beloved, whose devotion, understanding, acceptance, wisdom, and tireless humor bring me the greatest happiness of my life.

You are all a part of my family and village,

Thank You

About the Author

Lisa Towles has 7 mystery/thrillers in print. Her 2019 thriller, The Unseen, was a Finalist in the Thriller category of the Best Book Awards by American Book Fest and her 2017 thriller Choke won a 2017 IPPY and a 2018 NYC Big Book Award for Thriller. Lisa's published books include The Unseen, Choke, and the following titles published under her previous name, Lisa Polisar: The Ghost of Mary Prairie, Escape, Blackwater Tango, and Knee Deep. She is an active member and frequent Panelist/Speaker of Mystery Writers of America, Sisters in Crime, and International Thriller Writers. She has an MBA in IT Management and works full-time in the tech industry in the San Francisco Bay Area.

Lisa is also a passionate graphic designer and video creator.

CPSIA information can be obtained
at www.ICGtesting.com
Printed in the USA
FSHW012328290921
85104FS